Tool of war.

PRICE: $20.00 (3798/tfarp)

TOOL
OF
WAR

LITTLE, BROWN AND COMPANY
New York · Boston

BY PAOLO BACIGALUPI

Little, Brown and Company

Hachette Book Group
1290 Avenue of the Americas, New York, NY 10104
Visit us at lb-teens.com

First Edition: October 2017

Little, Brown and Company is a division of Hachette Book Group, Inc.
The Little, Brown name and logo are trademarks of Hachette Book Group, Inc.

The publisher is not responsible for websites (or their content) that are not owned by the publisher.

Library of Congress Cataloging-in-Publication Data
Names: Bacigalupi, Paolo, author.
Title: Tool of war / Paolo Bacigalupi.
Description: First edition. | New York : Little, Brown and Company, 2017. | Companion to: Ship breaker and The Drowned Cities. | Summary: In a future beset with rising seas, corporate government, and constant civil war, a bioengineered half-man/half-beast super-soldier who calls himself Tool breaks his conditioning to overcome his genetically enhanced sense of loyalty to the corporation that created him and seeks revenge against his old masters.
Identifiers: LCCN 2016051846| ISBN 9780316220835 (hardcover) | ISBN 9780316220828 (ebook) | ISBN 9780316364775 (library edition ebook)
Subjects: | CYAC: Genetic engineering—Fiction. | Obedience—Fiction. | Soldiers—Fiction. | Survival—Fiction. | Science fiction.
Classification: LCC PZ7.B132185 To 2017 | DDC [Fic]—dc23
LC record available at https://lccn.loc.gov/2016051846

ISBNs: 978-0-316-22083-5 (hardcover), 978-0-316-22082-8 (ebook)

Printed in the United States of America

LSC-C

10 9 8 7 6 5 4 3 2 1

TOOL
OF
WAR

1

THE DRONE CIRCLED high above the wreckage of war.

A week before, it hadn't been there. A week before, the Drowned Cities hadn't been worth mentioning, let alone worth committing drones to overwatch.

The Drowned Cities: a coastline swamped by rising sea levels and political hatreds, a place of shattered rubble and eternal gunfire. It had been a proud capital, once, and the people who inhabited its marble corridors had dominated much of the world. But now the place was barely remembered on maps, let alone in places where civilized people gathered. The histories it had dominated, the territories it had controlled, all had been lost as its people descended into civil war—and eventually were forgotten.

And yet now a Raptor-class oversight drone circled overhead.

Held aloft by humid thermals, the drone surveyed brackish jungles and eroded coastlines. It circled, wings stretched wide to catch hot Atlantic winds. Its cameras swept across kudzu-tangled swamps and emerald mosquito-infested pools. Its gaze lingered on marbled monuments, spikes and domes and toppled columns, the shattered bones of the city's greatness.

At first, the reports had been dismissed as nothing but war-addled refugee accounts: a monster that led child soldiers to victory after victory; a beast that was immune to bullets, that tore enemies limb from limb. A towering savage creature that demanded an unending tribute of enemy skulls...

No one believed, at first.

But later, blurry satellite photos showed buildings burning and troops on the move, and gave confirmation to even the most outlandish accounts. And so the drone came seeking.

The electronic vulture wheeled, high and lazy, its belly bulging with cameras and heat sensors, laser microphones and radio-intercept equipment.

It photographed historic rubble and barbarous inhabitants. It eavesdropped on bursts of radio communication, parsing the movements of troops, the patterns of explosions. It tracked lines of gunfire, and video-recorded the dismembering of enemy soldiers.

And far away—across the continent—the information the Raptor gathered was received by its masters.

There, a great dirigible floated, majestic above the Pacific Ocean. The name on its side was as grand as the warship itself: ANNAPURNA.

A quarter of the planet lay between the command dirigible and the spying Raptor, and yet the information arrived in an eyeblink, and set off alarms.

"General!"

The analyst pushed back from her control screens, blinking, wiping sweat from her brow. Mercier Corporation's Global Strategic Intelligence Center was hot with computing equipment and the shoulder-to-shoulder press of other analysts, all at their own workstations, all busy with their own operations. The murmur of their work filled the room, along with the labored whir of clean-room fans that fought to cool the place. The *Annapurna* prized efficiency of space and maximum eyes-and-ears over comfort, and so all of them were sweating, and none of them complained.

"General!" the analyst called again.

At first she'd resented the wild-goose chase she'd been assigned—an exercise in busywork, while her fellow intelligence analysts foiled revolutions, wiped out insurgents, and fought off price runs on lithium and cobalt markets. They'd made fun of her task—in the mess hall, in the bunkrooms, in the showers—heckling her for not contributing to the bottom line, reminding her that her quarterly profit bonus would be zero for failing to contribute to company profits.

Privately, she'd agreed glumly with them all.

Until now.

"General Caroa! I think I've got something."

The man who responded was tall, his company blues perfectly pressed. Rows of medals gleamed on his chest, marking a bloody rise through Mercier's military ranks. His blond hair, fading to white, was cropped short, the habit of a lifetime of discipline, but the neatness of his personal appearance was marred by his face—a sloppy stitch-work of pink scar tissue, pocks, and puckered divots where battle surgeons had done their best to keep his pale features intact.

His face, if not tidy, was at least almost whole.

The general leaned over her shoulder. "What have we got?"

The analyst swallowed, unnerved by the man's cold gaze. "It's the augment," she said. "The one you flagged."

"You're sure?"

"It's almost an exact physical match." She brought up the drone's live feed. A bestial face filled the screen. "It has to be the one."

The image was grainy, but considering the distance and angle, their view of the monster was a miracle of technological wizardry. The augment could as well have been photographed from twenty feet away—a monster standing nearly eight feet tall, massively muscled. A combination of dog and human, tiger and hyena DNA. A battle terror, clawed and fanged and brutal.

"So, old friend, we meet again," the general murmured.

One of the creature's eyes was scarred shut. Other old wounds showed on its arms and face, giving the creature the appearance of one who had battled through hell and emerged victorious on the far side.

The analyst said, "I have this much of the design code, also." She pulled up a close image of the augment's ear: rows of numbers, tattooed. "Is this the one you wanted? Does it match?"

The general stared at the screen. His hand, seemingly of its own accord, had reached up to touch his own ravaged face, fingers lingering on a puckered scar line that started at his jaw and ran down his neck. Divots and pocks of missing flesh as if his head had once been trapped in the jaws of a monstrous wild animal.

"Sir?" the analyst pressed eagerly. "This is the target, right?"

The general gave her a sour look. Her uniform tag read JONES, ARIAL. No medals. No experience. Young. Another bright recruit, harvested into the security forces of Mercier, courtesy of the aptitude tests the company offered in its protectorate territories. She was driven, thanks to whatever hellhole she'd climbed out of to join Mercier, but she didn't know true battle. Unlike him. Unlike the creature they studied on the screen. So of course she was eager; she'd never been to war.

"That's the one," General Caroa confirmed. "That's our target."

"He looks like a tough one."

"One of the toughest," Caroa agreed. "What assets do we have?"

Jones checked her status screens. "We can put two Strike Raptors up within twenty minutes," she said. "We can launch from the *Karakoram* in the Atlantic." She was smiling. "Havoc on your order, sir."

"Time to target?"

"Six hours."

"Very good, Jones. Flag me when the Raptors are on station."

2

TOOL'S EARS PRICKED, tracking distant gunfire, the comfortable conversational chatter of the Drowned Cities.

It was a polyglot language, but Tool understood all of its voices. The ratchet exclamations of AK-47s and M-16s. The blunt roar of 12- and 10-gauge shotguns. The authoritative crack of 30-06 hunting rifles, and the snapping of .22s. And of course, over it all, the incoming shriek of 999s, the voice that ended all other combat sentences with booming punctuations.

It was a familiar conversation that flowed back and forth—ask and answer, insult and retort—but over the last few weeks the conversation had changed. Increasingly, the Drowned Cities spoke Tool's language only. The bullet patois of his troops, the battle slang of his pack.

The war roared on, but the voices were merging now, becoming a single harmonious howl of triumph.

Of course, there were other sounds as well, and Tool heard them all. Even in the atrium of his palace, far from the battlefront, he could follow the progress of his war. His large ears were better than a dog's, and were always pricked tall, wide and sensitive, telling him much that human ears could not, much as all his senses gathered more than any human senses could.

He knew where his soldiers stood. He smelled their individuality. He could sense their movements by the way air currents shifted across his fur and skin. In the darkness he could see them, his eyes sharper than a cat's in the blackest night.

These human beings he led were blind and deaf to most things, but still he led them, and tried to fashion them into something useful. He had helped his human children to see, to smell, to listen. He had taught them to yoke their eyes and ears and weapons to one another, so that they fought as Fangs and Claws and Fists. Units. Platoons. Companies. Battalions.

An army.

Through the gap in the cracked dome of his palace, Tool could see the bellies of storm clouds, glowing orange, reflecting fires raging, the Army of God's last desperate attempt to stop his troop's advance by creating a battle line of self-destruction.

Thunder rumbled. Lightning spiked across the clouds. A

hurricane was building, the second in as many weeks, but it wouldn't come soon enough to save the Army of God.

Behind him, Tool heard footsteps hurrying down marble corridors, coming his way. The limp and scrape of the person's uneven gait told him it was Stub. Tool had promoted the boy to command staff because he was hard and sharp and clever, and had been brave enough to storm the barricades on K Street.

Koolkat had led the charge when the Army of God threatened to break through and destroy their then-fragile hope, and had died for it. Beside him, Stub had lost a foot to a mine, and yet had tourniqueted himself, and then still dragged himself forward, rallying his fellows to fight on, even after their commanding officer had died. Ferocious and dedicated and brave.

Yes, it was Stub—he had the right scent, and the right limp—but another scent accompanied the soldier boy—fresh-congealing blood, the iron spike telltale of new carrion.

Stub bore a message.

Tool closed his one good eye and breathed deep, enjoying the scent and the moment—the bite of gunpowder, the growl and swelter of the brewing storm, the rich ozone tang of lightning burning the air. He breathed deep, trying to fix the moment of triumph in his mind.

So many of his memories were fragmented, lost to wars and violence. His history was a kaleidoscopic jumble of images and scents and roiling emotions, scattershot explosions of joy and terror, much of it blocked and inaccessible now. But this time—this one time—he wanted to secure the entirety of the moment permanently in his mind. To taste and smell and hear it. To let it fill him completely, straightening his spine, letting him stand tall. To let it fill his muscles with power.

Triumph.

The palace he stood in was a ruin. Once it had been grand, marble floors, majestic columns, ancient masterful oil paintings, a graceful rotunda. Now he stood under a shattered dome, and could survey the city he warred for, thanks to a bombed-out wall. He could see right out to the ocean where it lapped below, on his very front steps. Rain spattered in and made thin, slippery pools on the floors. Torches guttered in the damp, giving light for the human beings, so that they could see the barest edges of what Tool could see without any aid at all.

A tragic ruin, and a site of triumph.

Stub waited respectfully.

"You have news," Tool said without turning.

"Yes, sir. They're finished. The Army of God...they're done for."

Tool's ears twitched. "Why do I still hear gunfire?"

"Just mop-up," Stub said. "They don't know when they're beat. They're dumb, but they're tenacious."

"You believe them truly defeated?"

The boy laughed shortly. "Well, Perkins and Mitali sent this for you."

Tool turned. Stub lifted the object he was carrying.

General Sachs's severed head stared emptily out at his surroundings, forlorn without his body. The last warlord of the Drowned Cities. The man's expression was frozen somewhere between shock and horror. The green cross of protection that the warlord had painted on his forehead was smudged with blood.

"Ah." Tool took the head and tested its weight in his palm. "It seems his One True God did not save him. Not such a savior prophet after all."

A pity not to be there at the last. To miss the chance to tear the man's heart from his chest and feed upon it. To gain sustenance from his enemy. Even now, the urge was strong in Tool. But killing glory was the privilege of the Claws. He was a general now, sending Fists and Claws and Fangs into battle as he had once been sent, and so he missed out on the adrenaline rush of combat, the hot blood of slaughter spurting joyous between his jaws...

Tool sighed regretfully.

It is not your role to strike the killing blow.

Still, there was this small pleasure—one general looking the other in the eye, accepting surrender.

" 'Against nature,' I think you said of me," Tool mused. " 'An abomination.' " He lifted the head higher, peering into Sachs's horrified dead eyes. " 'The patchwork Frankenstein that would not stand.' And of course, '*Blasphemy.*' "

Tool bared his teeth, pleased. The man had lived in denial until the last, believing himself a child of God, made in God's own image, divinely protected from the likes of Tool. "It seems his One True God favored blasphemy best."

Even now, Tool thought he could see the glimmer of denial in the dead general's eyes. The wailing tantrum at the unfairness of being forced to fight a creature that had been designed to be faster, smarter, and tougher than the poor human warlord who had thought himself blessed.

This simple man hadn't been able to grasp that Tool had been optimized for an ecosystem of slaughter. Tool's gods had been far more interested in modern warfare than this sad man's focus of worship. Such was the way of evolution and competition. One species replaced another in the blink of an eye. One evolved; one died out.

But then, the concept of evolution had never been the general's strong suit, either.

Some species are meant to lose.

A heavy boom shook the air. Tool's 999. The foundation of the palace trembled.

The city fell quiet.

And remained so.

Stub looked up at Tool in surprise. Tool's ears twitched, listening. Nothing. No gunfire. No mortar launches. Tool strained his senses. With the storm coming, the breeze carried an electric sense of anticipation, as if waiting for violence to resume—and yet now, finally, the Drowned Cities were silent.

"It's over," Stub murmured, awed. His voice strengthened. "The Drowned Cities are yours, General."

Tool smiled affectionately at the boy. "They always were."

All around, the youth of Tool's command staff had paused in their tasks, some in midstep. All of them were listening, too, all of them anticipating a new round of violence, and yet all of them hearing only peace.

Peace. In the Drowned Cities.

Tool took a deep breath, savoring the moment, then paused, frowning. Oddly, his troops smelled not of victory, but of fear.

Tool scrutinized Stub. "What is it, soldier?"

The boy hesitated. "What happens now, General?"

Tool blinked.

What happens now?

In an instant, Tool saw the problem. Looking over his command staff—his finest, his sharpest, his elites—it was obvious. Their expressions and scents told the story. Stub, the brave one who had fought even after his leg was destroyed. Sasha, his Fist gauntlet, who frightened even the coldest of new recruits. Alley-O, so apt at chess that Tool had recruited him to the central command. Mog and Mote, the blond twins who ran the Lightning Claws, brave and gutsy, with a flair for improvisation under fire.

These young humans were wise enough to know the difference between calculated risk and wild recklessness, and yet they were still years shy of even two decades. Some of them barely had the fuzz of manhood on their faces. Alley-O was no more than twelve...

They are children.

Drowned Cities warlords had always valued the malleable qualities of youth. Savage loyalty was an affectation of children; their eagerness for clarity of purpose was easily shaped. All the soldiers of the Drowned Cities had been recruited young, brainwashed early, given ideologies and absolute truths that demanded no nuance or perspective. Right and Wrong. Traitors and Patriots. Good and Evil. Invaders and Natives. Honor and Loyalty.

Righteousness.

Blazing righteousness was easily cultivated in the young, and so the young made excellent weapons. Perfect fanatic killing tools, sharpened to the bleeding edge by the simplicity of their worldly understandings.

Obedient to the last.

Tool himself had been designed by military scientists for exactly this sort of slavish loyalty, infused with the DNA of subservient species, lashed to blind obedience by genetic controls and relentless training, and yet in his experience, young humans were far more malleable. More obedient, even, than dogs, really.

And when they were free, they became frightened.

What now?

Tool scowled down at General Sachs's head, still in his hand. What did a sword do when all of its opponents had been beheaded? What use for a gun, when there was no enemy left to shoot in the face? What purpose for a soldier, when there was no war?

Tool handed the bloody trophy back to Stub. "Stack it with the rest."

Stub cradled the head carefully. "And after that?"

Tool wanted to howl in his face, *Make your own way! Build your own world! Your kind constructed me! Why must I construct you?*

But the thought was unkind. They were as they were. They had been trained for obedience, and so had lost their way.

"We will rebuild," Tool said finally.

Soldier boys' faces flooded with relief. Once again, rescued from uncertainty. Their God of War was ready even for this terrifying challenge of Peace.

"Spread the word to the troops. Our new task is to rebuild." Tool's voice strengthened. "The Drowned Cities are mine now. This is my...kingdom. I will make it flourish. *We* will make it flourish. That is now our mission."

Even as he said it, Tool wondered if it could be done.

He could shred flesh with his clawed hands, he could slaughter multitudes with a gun, he could shatter bones to dust with his teeth. With a Fist of augments he could invade a country, emerging on a foreign shore to spread blood and slaughter, and end victorious—but what of a war of peace?

What to make of a war where no one died, and victories were measured by full bellies and warm fires and...

The harvests of farms?

Tool's lips curled back, baring tiger's teeth. He growled in disgust.

Stub retreated hastily. Tool tried to control his expression.

Killing was easy. Any child could become a killer. Sometimes the stupidest were the best, because they understood so little of their danger.

But farming? The patient cultivating of land? The tilling of soil? The planting of seeds? Where were the people who knew these things? Where were the people who knew how to accomplish these patient, quiet things?

They were dead. Or else fled. The smartest of them long gone.

He would require a different sort of command staff entirely. He would need to find a way to bring in trainers. Experts. A Fist of humans who knew how to engineer not death, but life—

Tool's ears pricked up.

The placid silence of the Drowned Cities at peace made way for a new sound. A whistling sound, high overhead.

A terrifying sound, barely remembered...

Familiar.

3

"STRIKE RAPTORS ARE on station, General."

"You have the target?"

"Target locked. Havoc 5s, loaded. Havoc in the tube."

"All tubes, fire at will," the general said.

The analyst glanced over, surprised. "All of them, sir? It's..." She hesitated. "There will be a lot of collateral damage, sir."

"Make sure." The general nodded definitively. "Make absolutely sure."

The analyst nodded and tapped her keyboard. "Yes, sir. Full six-pack, sir." She spoke into her comm. "Munitions control, confirm: Six-pack to strike. General Caroa confirms."

"Six-pack to strike, confirmed. Six-pack Havoc."

"Six, up. Six, armed..." She tapped more keys. "Six-pack in the tubes...Missiles away, sir." She looked up. "Fifteen seconds to Havoc."

The analyst and the general both leaned forward, watching the computer screens.

The monitors were filled with a rainbow of infrared signatures. Muddy reds and blues and purples of heat. Small heat blips for the human troops—oranges and yellows mostly—and a large blot of red where the augment stood.

The analyst watched. There were quite a number of heat signatures. The augment's command staff, most likely. Troops all doing their jobs, not knowing that death was arrowing down upon them.

The Raptor cameras were so precise that she could make out the residue of handprint heat when people leaned on their desks. Footprints appeared and disappeared ghostly as a soldier walked barefoot across the capitol building's ancient marble floor. It all looked so still and calm, from this distance. Silent. Unreal.

The augment was standing close to a couple of other troops—possibly giving orders, perhaps receiving some intelligence—none of them realizing that they were about to be erased from the face of the earth.

"Ten seconds," she murmured.

General Caroa leaned forward, intent. "All right, old friend, let's see you escape this time."

The strike monitor counted down.

"Five...four...three..."

The augment must have sensed danger. It began to move. Heat flooded its body as it threw itself into motion.

They were designed to be preternaturally alert, the analyst thought idly. It was hardly surprising that even now, this war beast made one last attempt at survival. It was the very nature of augments. They were built to fight, even when fighting was futile.

The screen flared.

Red, orange, yellow—

White.

Searing white. Brighter than a thousand suns all burning. More impacts followed, flare after flare as missiles pounded the target.

The heat registers on the oversight drone flickered to black, overwhelmed by the hell unleashed.

"Contact," the analyst announced. "Six-pack, contact."

4

MAHLIA WAS LYING on the deck of the *Raker*, which was odd, because last she remembered, she'd been standing. But now she was lying down.

No. She wasn't lying on the clipper's deck; she was leaning against a cabin wall, next to a porthole. No, she was *lying on* the cabin wall. She wasn't standing up at all. In fact, the whole ship wasn't standing up.

My ship is on its side.

Mahlia stared up at the orange roiling clouds overhead, trying to make sense of that.

The Raker *is on her side. My ship is not standing up.*

Mahlia thought about that some more. The world around her felt surreal and distant, as if she were peering at everything through a very long length of pipe. It was all so far away, even though it was quite close.

And hot.

Viciously hot.

Shards of fire looped and spiraled through the sky, flaming crows, swirling. Burning debris, flying free, bright and chaotic in the winds of conflagration.

One minute she'd been supervising the loading of a canvas-wrapped painting, an Accelerated Age masterwork, worrying about getting it secured in the hold before the hurricane rains got too heavy, and now she was lying on her back, staring up at the throb of fire on the bellies of storm clouds.

She had the feeling that she needed to do something urgent, but her body ached and the back of her head was tender. She reached back to probe the wound, and hissed in pain when metal banged her head.

Fates, she was so confused, she'd forgotten she'd lost her right hand to the Army of God's soldier boys years ago, and replaced it with a prosthetic in the Seascape. Mahlia hesitantly reached back to probe her scalp with her left hand, testing with fingers that actually had feeling.

Big lump, but no open wound, it seemed. No shattered skull, no spongy brain. She checked her fingers. No blood, either.

The *Raker* was coming upright, slowly righting itself. Mahlia started sliding down past the porthole. The deck rushed up to meet her. She braced to catch herself, but her legs crumpled and she fell unceremoniously onto the carbon-spool deck.

The clipper ship came fully upright, bobbing and sloshing, pouring seawaters from its decks.

Mahlia struggled to move her feet, afraid for a moment that she had a spinal injury. *Please, let my legs work.* She concentrated, and felt a flood of relief as one leg moved, then the other. She grasped for the lip of a porthole and hauled herself to her feet, groaning. Puppet body, wooden limbs, missing strings, but she made it up, and staggered to the rail.

"Where the hell is everyone?"

Something big had hit them. *Epic big*, as Van would say. Maybe a stray shell from the 999s? Dropped out of the sky, right onto them? But that didn't make sense. Tool was the only one firing 999s these days, and Tool's soldier boys were too well trained to screw up like this.

Mahlia looked down the length of the ship, taking stock of the *Raker*. Her beautiful ship. Water was still sluicing off the deck where it had been submerged, but otherwise, the clipper ship seemed all right to her eyes.

"Damage?" Mahlia croaked. "Captain Almadi? Ocho?" She spotted Shoebox staggering her way, eyes wide and disoriented. She grabbed his arm and pulled him over.

"You know where Ocho is?" She couldn't hear her own voice, but Shoebox seemed to understand. He nodded and stumbled off. Hopefully to find Ocho.

Ash debris rained down, flaming black flakes of plastic, sharp against the darkness of storm clouds. Mahlia followed the flaming debris across the sky and down to its source.

"The palace." She could hear her voice this time.

Where the palace had been, pillars of black smoke boiled up into the sky. She shaded her eyes against the fires, squinting against the intensity of light and heat. The whole palace had been leveled, along with neighboring buildings. Even the marble stairs that led up to the palace—Mahlia stared, astounded. The stairs appeared to be sagging, running lava...

Melting?

It was like the hell that Deepwater Christians wished on unbelievers. Even the lake in front of the palace was on fire.

How the hell does water catch on fire?

Nearby, someone was screaming, a sound more animal than human. Mahlia's hearing was definitely returning. She could hear the roar of the fires now, and the screams of the burned, and the shouted orders of soldier boys down on the docks. The fires were spreading, engulfing adjacent buildings, burning with an unnatural fury. Rising storm winds fanned the flames higher. A gust of heat and smoke washed over her.

"Damage report?" Mahlia shouted again, coughing, covering her face from the smoke. Ocho staggered up on deck. He had a bloody gash on his forehead, but was still moving. He lurched through the smoke to join her.

"They hit the palace," he shouted in her ear.

"I can see that," Mahlia shouted back. "Who did it?"

"Dunno. Van says something came out of the sky. Whole bunch of fire needles."

"Army of God?"

"Can't be," Ocho said. "Tool was crushing them."

Tool. A new, sick horror filled her guts. He'd been in there. In the palace. She'd been stupid not to see it sooner. Tool had been killed. She was alone in the Drowned Cities again. She had no allies. She was surrounded by soldier boys—

Mahlia gripped the rail, fighting against terror. Memories of lying belly-down in mud, praying to the Fates, to Kali-Mary Mercy, to the Deepwater God and every other religion's god or saint or avatar she could think of that soldier boys wouldn't notice her as they gunned down her fellow castoffs. Memories of slogging through the swamps outside the Drowned Cities, starving and alone. Of catching snakes for food. Of finding villages where every single person had been slaughtered. Soldier boys holding her down, lifting a machete high, chopping off her right hand—

And then she'd found Tool.

Thanks to Tool, she'd escaped the civil wars of the Drowned Cities, and then later returned with the *Raker*, for scavenge. Thanks to him, she'd escaped and made a life for herself.

And now, in an instant, it had all been ripped away.

Ocho was clearly coming to the same realization, rocked

by his own memories from when the Drowned Cities had been chaos, and he'd been a soldier boy for the United Patriot Front. "Fates," Ocho said. "This place is going to fall apart. It's all going back to..."

Hell.

The one person who had dragged the Drowned Cities out of chaos had just been burned to ash. The one person who had protected them and allowed them to trade successfully was gone.

A part of Mahlia wanted to scream at the unfairness of it all—*We were just starting to win*—but the other part of her, the wiser part, the part that had kept her alive through the worst years, knew it didn't matter. She didn't have much time.

"Can we sail?" she asked. "Can we get out of here?"

"I'll check with Almadi. See if she thinks the ship's seaworthy." Ocho started to run for the bridge, then paused and waved up at the thunderous black clouds swirling overhead. "How bad a storm you want to risk?"

Mahlia gave him a bleak smile. "You think Tool's former troops are going to let us keep the *Raker* if we stay?"

Despair flashed briefly on Ocho's face. "Fates. Just once..."

Whatever he'd been about to say, he cut himself off. His expression hardened into a stone mask. "I'll get it done."

He sketched a tired salute at her, glanced one last time at the burning palace, and ran for the ship's bridge. He was a survivor, just like her. Steady. Even when everything was falling apart, he was steady. With him at her back, Mahlia could pretend she had the strength to go on. They could both fool each other into believing that they were strong.

More of the crew were climbing out from belowdecks: former UPF soldiers that Ocho commanded, along with Captain Almadi's sailors. The sailors were already telling the soldier boys what to do, all of them trying to get themselves sorted out and oriented.

Two sailors came up bearing Amzin Lorca, Almadi's second-in-command. He had a shard of something metallic sticking out of his chest, and Mahlia didn't have to look closer to know that he was dead.

Where was Almadi?

Down on the docks, Tool's troops were trying to get a handle on the chaos, small groups of soldiers forming into larger ones. Tool's Fists and Claws and Fangs. Tiny biodiesel skiffs had begun firing their engines and heading across the vast rectangular lake that lay in front of the palace, speeding toward the strike zone, circling through flames and hunting for nonexistent survivors.

The troops still looked coordinated, but once the reality of Tool's death sank in, the fighting for control would start again. All those commanders and troops and factions that Tool had conquered and forced into his army would splinter apart.

And then they'd fight to fill the vacuum that he'd left behind.

Either that, or some clever lieutenant or captain would

decide it was time to get the hell out of the Drowned Cities once and for all, and just take the *Raker* for himself.

Either way, she needed to be far away by then.

The fires continued to spread, fanned by rising storm winds. The palace rubble glowed with an unholy lava heat.

Just hours ago, she'd been right inside there, getting paid by Tool's Supply & Logistics people for shipping down more ammunition, and getting her passes stamped to haul their new cargo out. Paintings. Sculptures. Revolutionary artifacts. Old museum pieces bound for the art markets of the Seascape.

If the day had gone even a little differently, she might have still been inside. She might have been sitting beside Tool as he and his officers plotted their attacks on the Army of God.

By now, she would have been ash and fire and smoke, rising up to meet the war gods that Tool claimed as his own.

Ocho returned with Captain Almadi. The captain was tall and regal and, by the standards of the Drowned Cities, ancient.

Mid-thirties, at least.

When Mahlia and Ocho's soldier boys had first escaped the Drowned Cities with their initial haul of art and historic artifacts, Mahlia had used the proceeds to buy the *Raker*, and then hired Almadi and her crew to run the ship. It was an arrangement that had been profitable for all involved, if occasionally troublesome.

Judging from the woman's expression, Ocho had ruffled her feathers. Mahlia glimpsed another person trailing behind them. The glow of electronic implants, blue and ethereal where ears used to be, marked him as one of Ocho's soldier boys. Van, grinning and irrepressible, despite the chaos around them. Or maybe because of it. The boy had come to war young. It had done odd things to his head.

"You see those things hit?" Van could barely contain himself. "Vicious epic boom boom!" He leaned far over the rail, staring out at the flames. "Fire needles and boom boom, baby!"

Mahlia ignored him. "What's the story with the ship?" she asked Almadi.

Before the captain could reply, Ocho said, "Captain says we won't sink. We're good to go."

Almadi shot him a glare. "No. I said that we've got a lot of damage. And I'm still getting reports."

"She said we won't sink," Ocho said.

"We're not taking water *right now*," Almadi protested. "I didn't say we could sail into a Cat Three and expect to survive!"

"We don't know it'll hit Cat Three," Ocho said.

Almadi glared. "It keeps strengthening. I don't make bets on the weather. It's why I'm still alive. I'm not a reckless child."

"We lost Haze," Ocho said. "He hit his head, cracked it when the blast hit. Bled out. Plus Almadi lost Lorca."

Almadi's expression said that Lorca was an experienced sailor, lost right when she needed him most, and that she didn't give a damn about Haze.

"Anyone else?" Mahlia asked.

"Anyone else?" Almadi goggled. "That's not enough already to give you pause? I haven't even had the chance to take a roll call. It will be quite a while before I know whether we're fit to sail at all, let alone into a storm."

Mahlia had an overwhelming urge to shake the woman. *Don't you see everything's going to fall apart here?* Instead, she shoved her prosthetic up in Almadi's face.

"You see this?" She turned the artificial hand, showing the captain its skeletal mechanical workings, blue-black steel and tiny hissing joints. "When I lost this, I called myself lucky. You see Van?" She pointed to the former soldier boy hanging off the rail, the blue glows of his implants bright in the thickening darkness of the storm. "You see what they did to his ears?"

"You don't know what's going to—"

"I know what happens to people who wait to find out! All those soldiers out there? They were parts of five different militias, at least! You think they love each other? You think they give a damn about each other? They were afraid of Tool. They were loyal to Tool. And now he's gone. And right now about twenty different captains in different parts of Tool's army are all about to start thinking for themselves again. About what they want. About who they trust. About who they still hate. They didn't stop fighting because they were done hating. They stopped because Tool forced them. Now he's gone, and I guarantee every one of them will have a use for this ship. And none of them will have a use for us."

"Nice thing about a hurricane," Van commented, "is that it just wants to kill you. War maggots round here?" He tapped his implants. "They like to take you apart."

Ocho was nodding in vigorous agreement. "If there's any way to sail—any way at all—we gotta take it, Captain."

Almadi looked from the flaming city to the churning black clouds in the sky. She grimaced. "Let me get the rest of the damage reports. I'll see what I can do."

"We don't have much time," Mahlia pressed.

"You hired me to run the ship!" Almadi snapped. "When it came to the sailing, we agreed that I'd make the decisions. You handle trade. I handle the *Raker*!"

Ocho was looking at Mahlia significantly. She knew what he was thinking. He'd pull together a few of the boys, put a gun on Almadi, and solve things the Drowned Cities way...

Mahlia gave him a warning look. *Not yet.*

Ocho shrugged. *If you say so.*

The truth was that the *Raker*'s crew was Almadi's. Mahlia might pay their salaries, but they were loyal to Almadi. There was no way they'd make it through a hurricane with an unwilling crew. Mahlia made her voice soothing.

"I'm sorry about Lorca. Truly sorry. And you're right, you know the ship better than we do. But we know the Drowned Cities, and once the fighting starts again..." She touched her prosthetic hand. "Some things are worse than storms."

"I don't know. I just don't know." Almadi held up her

hand to forestall more protest. "I'll hurry the damage assessment. Then we'll talk." She strode off, shaking her head.

Mahlia grabbed Ocho's arm. "Go with her. If we could even sail up the coast just a little way, maybe find an anchorage that shelters us before the worst of the storm hits... anything to get out of here. Convince her."

Ocho nodded sharply. "On it."

"And see what kind of storm this really is!" she called after.

"Who cares?" Van asked. "Cat One. Cat Two. Three, Four, Five, Six... It's all better than a bullet in the head. If that lady won't sail, I swear I'll cut her own ears off, give her some real Drowned Cities living."

Mahlia gave him a sharp look.

"I'm joking!" Van held up his hands defensively. "Just joking!"

It was only when Van had followed after Ocho and the captain that Mahlia let herself turn back to the burning palace.

The destruction was overwhelming, as if Tool's war god had slammed a huge flaming fist into the palace, making sure that nothing stood tall, and nothing survived. Rubbing it out completely. Lady Kali stomping everything to ruins, except without any Mary Mercy to follow.

It was hard to believe that Tool was gone. She could remember him still, crouching in the jungle after obliterating a pack of coywolv that had attacked her. A savage, half-human monster, jaws dripping blood, his massive fist offering her the fresh, hot heart of a vanquished coywolv, offering alliance and true connection.

Pack, he'd called it. He'd been her pack, and she'd been his. And he'd been stronger than nature.

And now what? Melted. Vaporized. Nothing left at all.

A part of her had an urge to run toward that towering fire. To search for him. To imagine she could save him. She owed him so much...

"Please tell me you ain't thinking about going over there."

Ocho had returned. He was coldly surveying the spreading fires and the frantic, ineffectual rescue efforts.

Mahlia swallowed, forcing down her grief. "No. I won't."

"That's good. 'Cause for a second you looked like the kind of war maggot that gets herself killed for no good reason."

"No. I'm not." She swallowed again. Grief was for later, not now. Tool was dead. He would mock her for failing to think strategically. "Nothing survives that."

"Captain says we can sail," Ocho said.

"You twist her arm?"

"Maybe a little." Ocho shrugged. "We're going to run for a shelter anchorage up the coast. A couple hours' sail, if everything goes right. Should be able to beat the worst of the storm. She thinks."

"Good." Mahlia pushed off from the rail. "We're out of here, then."

"We coming back?"

"What do you think?"

Ocho looked out at the ravaged city. Made a face. "Too bad. It was a good gig."

"Yeah, well"—Mahlia gave him a sour smile—"nothing lasts, right?"

"Guess not."

Mahlia wondered if her own face was as stoic as Ocho's. Two people, making themselves look strong.

A few minutes later the ship's sails began spooling up, motor pulleys squeaking and squealing as cables ran through damaged and misaligned runners. Carbon-nylon sails flapped, billowed wide, then snapped taut, filling with the storm's rising winds.

Overhead, dark clouds roiled. Wind whipped across the deck. Rain began to hammer down, heavy, bloated drops pounding the deck. Out on the waters of the Potomac, the gray waves were pocked with the falling water.

Through the sheeting rain, she could make out Stork and Stick, Gama and Cent, all working to untie the ship. Mahlia shook off her torpor and ran to help. Ropes came free of their cleats.

The *Raker* began to move, heeling with the wind.

The clipper ship was a marvel of human engineering, designed to sail despite rough weather, but still, Mahlia found herself praying, unsure that the damaged ship would be able to survive the coming storm's abuse.

The sleek clipper ship gathered speed. From the docks, soldier boys watched them go. A few pointed, seeming to wonder if perhaps they should stop the departing ship, but no one was giving orders yet. Without guidance, they were lost.

The *Raker* surged forward, her prow cutting gray chop and froth. Her sails billowed full. The ship began to heave as she met rising seas. Mahlia and her crew hurried to batten down the ship, preparing to battle the storm.

So busy were they with their jobs that they failed to notice a bit of wreckage emerge in the ship's wake. The flotsam surfaced, bobbing like a dead log. It snagged onto the ship's hull, trailing behind like tangled kelp, forgotten garbage that the ship would soon shake free.

Except that it began to haul itself upward.

Hand over deliberate hand, it rose from the waters, slow but implacable, dragging itself from the deeps until at last it attached itself below the aft rail, dangling off the clipper ship's stern.

It was a bestial shape, twisted and horrific, that clung there. A creature out of hell, all charred flesh and tattered skin. A reborn monster, sizzling with the heat of its origins, despite the lashing rain.

The ship plunged ahead, fighting through rising waves. The stowaway rode with it, blackened and smoking.

Burning with fury.

5

"To Blood," General Caroa murmured. "To Blood, and history."

And an end to nightmares.

He raised a snifter of cognac and toasted the view outside his stateroom windows.

Six thousand meters below, the wide Pacific spread, a moonlight-sheened blanket. From the height at which he stood, Caroa almost could imagine himself looking out over the rim of an alien planet, mercury quicksilver seas glittering below him—a dark and still undiscovered place.

In many ways it was. Much of the world had fallen back after the end of the Accelerated Age, collapsed under disasters. Droughts and floods. Hurricanes. Epidemics and crop failures. Starvation and refugee wars had ravaged the world, and left many wide expanses open to human re-exploration.

And he had led that charge. For more than three decades, he had forged into new territory, subdued unrest, and brought the governing hand of Mercier to the disorder.

As befitted a man of his rank, his stateroom was large, appointed with the winnings of his campaigns: a carpet memorializing the North African offensive to control the Suez; a dagger carved from whalebone, taken as a trophy after the battles for rights to the Northwest Passage. On one shelf, brandies from the French agricultural war gleamed, just above another shelf full of books printed on real paper, Sun Tzu and Clausewitz and Shakespeare, some of the volumes very old indeed, and all the more luxurious, given the constraints of space and weight on a Narwhal-class dirigible.

The *Annapurna* carried nearly five thousand souls when fully operational. She required a command and engineering crew of five hundred, and carried a marine Fast Attack contingent of two thousand. She possessed drone and launch facilities, logistics, command, and intelligence centers, all of them overseen by Caroa.

From her decks, with her electronic eyes and ears tuned to satellites and troop and fleet communications, the general's influence stretched across a quarter of the planet—the Americas, from pole to pole, wherever Mercier Corporation required.

His first company patch bore the image of snarling augments rampant, and the words:

MERCIER FAST ATTACK

Below the image, the watchwords that had guided his career were stitched in gold.

FERITAS. FIDELITAS.

Ferocity. Fidelity.

Now he touched the patch, and wondered if his nightmares were finally put to rest.

Far below his feet, the black coastline of Mercier's SoCal Protectorate stretched northward. He could make out the campfire-dabbed ruins of old Los Angeles, accented by the bright necklace of Mercier sky towers where they lined the shoreline of the bay.

It had taken a lifetime to climb this high. Almost no rungs existed above him in the company ranks. All that really remained was promotion to the company's Executive Committee, a directorship on the permanent ruling council where Mercier's finest deliberated on company strategy from atop one of the tallest of the Los Angeles sky towers.

Odd that if he ever got another promotion, he would actually have to lose elevation.

Amused by the thought, Caroa went to his desk and checked his status boards one last time for the night.

There were skirmishes in the Arctic that ExCom was concerned about, possibly SinoKor putting pressure on drilling operations, and there was always the problem of piracy in the Northwest Passage, TransSiberia and their Inuit proxy soldiers reaching out to "tax" the wealth of shipping that crossed the poles. Irritating, considering that most of his forces were still deployed south, on the Lithium Plains in the Andes. Moving troops from the bottom of the world to the top, even with Mercier's fleet of dirigibles, would take time. At least the troops were already equipped for cold weather.

He wiped the screen clean. It could all wait. For once, he could relax and enjoy the perks of his profession. He reached for his cognac once again.

The comm pinged.

Annoyed, Caroa called to the room AI. "Who is it?"

His wall screen filled with a familiar face: youthful, eager features. The analyst...Caroa tried to remember her name...

I'm getting old.

Jones. That was it.

Young, eager, pimple-faced Jones. Irritating Jones. Striving Jones. Overachieving Jones. According to her files, she'd scored in the top tenth of a percent in the Mercier Qualification & Service Examination, the dreaded MX. Her extraordinary scores had lifted her out of her previous life and into service with Mercier. Adding to the accomplishment, she'd taken the aptitude tests when she was only sixteen. So, like him, she'd joined the company early, and risen fast.

Maybe it was the hot breath of competition that annoyed him.

I was the smartest one in the room once, too, he thought. *Don't think you're all that.* She might be sharp as a combat knife, but she was contacting him while he was explicitly off duty, and bypassing every chain-of-command protocol to do so.

"This had better be good, Junior Analyst Jones."

He reached for the commlink, intending to give her a tongue lashing, but then paused. This eager little analyst had, after all, tracked down his old, nagging worry. She'd sifted the data and come up with something that others had missed for years.

Still, this temerity couldn't be encouraged. He opened the comm and glared. "Do you not have a watch officer, *Junior* Analyst?"

She choked on her words.

"Do you *like* scrubbing windows at six thousand meters?"

"Sir, I'm sorry, sir." She quailed. "There's...there's... something you need to see."

Caroa paused on the verge of his rant. He wasn't a superstitious man, nor easily frightened. He'd fought on all seven continents and had the scalps to prove it. And yet the young analyst's tone unnerved him.

"What is it?"

"I'm really sorry to bother you off duty, sir..."

"You've already done it," he snapped. "Spit it out."

"I—I just think you should come see this."

"You want me to *come up to you*?"

She stumbled on her words, but put on a brave face. "Yes, sir. You'll want to see this for yourself."

* * *

Five minutes later, Caroa was up on the command deck, heading for the Strategic Intelligence Center, still buttoning his uniform jacket.

Brood and Splinter, two huge augments from the ship's marine detachment, stepped aside at his approach. Dog and wolverine and tiger. Vicious brutes. They loomed watchful as Caroa peered into the identity scanner's camera lens.

He blinked as the familiar blaze of red crossed his iris. The security systems read his eye-print, authenticating his rank and his right to enter the Intelligence Center. The scanner beeped confirmation. Brood and Splinter relaxed. Even though they knew him, still they watched, every time. Unlike humans, they were never lazy, and never lost sight of their duty.

Feritas. Fidelitas.

Bulletproof doors slid aside, letting out a blast of heat, accompanied by the click of keyboards and the low murmur of analysts busy at computers. Caroa wound his way between workstations. Analysts saluted as he passed, a wave of respect that followed him through the room as underlings noted his arrival and then went back to work immediately, all of them relentlessly keeping tabs on the status of Mercier operations.

"Well, Jones, what's so important?"

She'd been conferring with the on-duty strike officer. They both stiffened at his arrival. The analyst looked a bit more uncertain than she'd been on the comm, perhaps finally aware that she'd summoned a global commander in the middle of the night. *Not so brash and smart, now, are you?*

"Well?"

Jones swallowed. "This, sir." She indicated one of her observation workstations. On-screen, a blot of red wavered against a cold blue background. Other blobs, orange, less hot and smaller, were scattered nearby. Human beings.

The image fuzzed and wavered, then came back into focus.

"What am I seeing here?"

"It's... it's a heat signature."

"I can see it's a heat signature. Why are you showing it to me?"

"It's a clipper ship. It's the augment, sir. It's—he's not dead!" the analyst blurted. "He's on that ship!"

"*What?*" Caroa lunged forward, staring at the screen. "That's impossible! We were on target! We hit him!"

"Yes, sir," the strike officer confirmed. "The hit was clean." He, too, seemed troubled.

"We hit the target," Jones said. "But that's the augment. Right there."

"It could be another augment," Caroa argued. "Some privateer. It could be merchant shipping from the Seascape. The trade combines all employ half-men in their forces."

Jones shook her head. "No, sir." She bent over her keyboard and started typing commands. "Raptor One... I'll show you."

Footage spooled rapidly. Images flashing. Flares of light. The infrared display of the hit and aftermath, all of it running backward. Death undone. Damage healing itself. Missiles reversing their flights—

The analyst slowed the recording.

"This is right before the first strike," she said.

There it was again. The familiar last seconds that he had seen previously. People wandering the building. In the corner of the video, a countdown clock ticked down to missile strike. It was all correct. Nothing untoward that the general could make out.

Now the moment of truth, missiles a mere two seconds away. The last, sudden lunge of the augment as it sensed its demise.

The general clenched his teeth as events unfolded. The augment was fast. They were all damnably fast—it was why Mercier used them. And this one was better than most. But they weren't made of magic. No matter how optimized their DNA, augments were still flesh and bone. They still lived.

And they still died.

"There's the first hit," the strike officer announced.

The screen flared with an expanding ball of searing light.

Jones hit pause.

"Second strike is incoming..." She pointed, then fiddled with knobs. "But I reran the footage and filtered against the heat, looking for the coolest objects, you see..." The analyst trailed off, pointed.

There was a ghosted image, still moving.

"What am I looking at?" the general asked. "This is nearly a textbook hit."

The recording inched forward. The creature was starting to heat up, starting to ignite.

"There! You see it! He's hit!" Caroa exclaimed. "Plain as day!"

"Yes, sir," Jones said mournfully. "Second strike happens now."

Another ball of exploding fire and death, overlaying the first, the creature haloed in fire. Around it, others were dying, curling in on themselves and becoming ash.

The third strike hit. All in mere seconds of motion.

One... one and a half seconds...

Two seconds.

"He's dead," the general said firmly. "He's right inside the blast radius."

"I'm not finished, sir," Jones said, sounding aggrieved. Caroa suspected she'd used the same put-upon tone in her training classes, when she showed her instructors how much smarter she was than them. "We lost the sensors on Raptor One. But Raptor Two was still getting good thermals. So I brought it back around."

"Why on earth would you bother?"

Jones and the strike officer both looked guilty. "The winds were good. I wasn't using fuel," she said defensively, but at a glance from the strike officer, she admitted, "We—I wanted to see what a six-pack did. I've never launched that much ordnance at once."

"Her first Havoc drop," the strike officer said, smiling slightly at her eagerness to rubberneck at the destruction she had wrought. Caroa, too, remembered and understood that awed urge to see the power of the gods that he wielded, to view the crater left behind. With a few typed launch codes, the world dissolved in heat and magma and flames. That rush never died. Not even for old men.

Caroa stifled his smile, not wanting to encourage her. He sighed instead. "All right. Show me."

Jones looked relieved. "It took a little while to bring the Raptor around and get a resolve. There's a hurricane coming in, so it took some jockeying, and the intel suite on the Strike Raptors isn't as good, but I got it locked in and—" She stabbed the screen with a finger. "There. Look!"

The screen was still awash with white heat. Slicks of fuel and payload blazed everywhere. The waters of the great rectangular lake that had lain before the ancient capitol building were streaked by hellish rivers of fire. But in the waters, there was a separate blot of red. A spot of independent movement.

The cameras lost the image.

"Storm," the analyst apologized.

The image returned, wobbly, but clear enough. The heat signature was big, and it was moving. Steadily, deliberately. Moving away from the blast.

As the analyst had said, the cameras weren't as good as those on Raptor One. Raptor Two was for killing, not for spying. But the thing was big, and it was moving...and it was *hot.*

"He's on fire," the general murmured.

"Yes, sir, I think so, sir. The augment is still burning, underwater. I think he took a hit from our first strike, might have gotten splash from the second, but then with the rest..."

"We missed."

The figure swam on.

"Why won't it just die?" the strike officer wondered as they all stared at the screen. "It should be dead."

The general scowled. "They were made tough. They're designed to feel little pain, less fear. They're very fine weapons."

"Yes, sir. But...this is unnatural. Even for an augment."

The general ground his teeth. The strike officer had no idea how true his words were. In his youth, Caroa had believed that one could never have too fine a weapon. Now he regretted his early enthusiastic vehemence. Sometimes it was possible to cut yourself on your own sharp knife.

The blip kept going, but its progress was slow. "He's hurt," Caroa said.

"Definitely," Jones agreed. "We hit him with some nasty stuff. HH-119 doesn't come off. It should have already burned through him. I think the long immersion in water is helping him. It's amazing how long he's staying down without oxygen."

"They're designed for amphibious assaults," the general said. "They can stay down for a good twenty minutes like that. Maybe longer."

"I'm surprised we don't just design them with gills," the strike officer said.

"We tried. There were problems mixing air intakes." Caroa scowled. "I can't believe the bastard is still moving."

"He's cooking, though," the strike officer said. "Look at that heat signature. We're watching him cook. Just because he's moving doesn't mean he's not dead. It just takes more time."

"Where is he now?" the general asked.

Jones sped up the camera. The creature began to shoot through the water, hyperfast, sliding across the lake and then...

It disappeared under the shadow of a ship.

"Schooner. Manta-class," Jones said. "Fast little ship. A smuggler, we think. The target hides under her for a while, and then she sets sail..."

The heat blip appeared at the stern of the ship.

"And the son of a bitch hitches a ride," the general finished. He scowled at the heat signature of the creature. Still alive. Still holding on, like a barnacle from hell.

The screen fuzzed and flickered.

"This is the live feed now?" he asked.

"Yes, sir. The storm is starting to cause interference. Looks like it'll only hit Cat Two, Three at most. Still, nasty to sail into."

"Maybe they'll sink," the strike officer offered hopefully.

The general scowled at him. He shut up.

The ship rose and fell violently on the waves. The screen flickered again with storm interference.

"Hit them," the general ordered. "Sink the ship."

"Sir?" Jones and the strike officer turned to him, surprised.

"Hit them," Caroa repeated firmly. "Maybe that augment is already dying on its own, but trust me, we want to be sure. It's too dangerous to be running wild. It's a goddamn Pandora's box. Sink the whole goddamn ship. No one will notice. It's a no-man's-land out there. It's not like we're sinking competitor cargo in the South China Sea. Ships sink all the time out there. Especially in storms. *Hit them.*"

"But, sir!" Jones protested. "We fired the entire payload! We don't have any more missiles in the air. It will take hours to scramble more Raptors. By that time, the hurricane will make flying impossible." The screen fuzzed again. Jones ran her hands over the controls, frowning. Brought the image back. "I'm already having a hard time tracking."

"You mean we're going to *lose them*?"

Jones swallowed, glanced guiltily at the strike officer, who looked similarly forlorn. "Yes, sir."

"Fates preserve us."

Fear slid fingers up the general's spine: old horror, old memories, rising. He ran his hand under his collar, trying to get a breath. The Strategic Intelligence Center suddenly felt too hot. He fought the feeling of rising claustrophobia, trying to focus on the task at hand.

This is my fault. I rushed it. I should have kept a reserve. Stupid, stupid, stupid—

He realized his hand was up at the scars on his face, his fingers plucking at the memory of his wounds—

With a growl, Caroa jerked his hand away from the ravaged flesh that even cell knitters had failed to fully heal.

It's not the same. This time I have the upper hand.

He focused on the video feed of the clipper ship as it sailed deeper into the storm. "Find it," he said. "Find that ship. Get its registration. Pull everything you have for its movements."

"It's a smuggler, sir. I don't think they record where they go."

"Use your head, Analyst! Show me you aren't just a clever test taker. Smugglers smuggle! They have to resupply somewhere. They have to sell whatever it is that they've pulled out of that hellhole of a city. Scour the Eastern Seaboard. Manhattan Orleans. The Seascape. Mississippi Metro. The Gulf. The Islands. Check London registries, if you have to!"

He stared at the infrared signature of the half-man, still clinging to the ship's stern. A huddled blot of heat, lashed by rain and winds.

Maybe it will die on its own, a hopeful voice whispered, but the general suppressed the thought. Wishes were for victims. Those sad souls who prayed to Kali-Mary Mercy that their seawalls wouldn't break. Fools who begged the Fates to keep a hurricane from turning Cat Six. Deepwater Christians who prayed to God to wash away their sins.

Wishes weren't for soldiers.

Soldiers faced reality, or else they died.

"That ship is going somewhere," Caroa said. "Find out where. We'll burn them on the other side of the storm."

6

Tool clung to the clipper ship as it climbed another mountainous wave face and then raced down its back. Rain hammered down, malevolent. Foaming waters clawed at Tool as the ship sank into a trough. He fought to hang on.

All of his skin was burned, and yet he felt little pain. He was dangerously wounded, his nerves seared dead, and the burn of the missile strikes was still burrowing inward. Even now, heat rose from his skin, his scarred flesh smoking.

He smelled like a coywolv that his soldier boys had once roasted over a campfire, when they'd first begun to retake the Drowned Cities. They were all gone now, he realized. Everyone who had sat around that early campfire. Stub and Sasha. Alley-O. Mog and Mote. All the rest. He could still remember Stub igniting, the boy enveloped in flames even as Tool turned and ran.

Human meat turned to ash, without even a chance to scream.

My pack.

The ship climbed another towering wave. Tool struggled to maintain his grip. He could feel himself weakening, and wondered if he cared. His kingdom destroyed before it could be properly begun. His soldier boys...

They had not been kin, but they had been pack. And now they were all dead in the blink of an eye, become the prey of another, more advanced, predator.

Tool's lips curled. Sharp teeth gleamed as lightning slashed the clouds.

I am not prey.

A memory. A mantra. His truest nature. Something to howl at the gods who rained down fire and sought to wipe him out.

I am not prey.

No human could have survived the missile strike. Only such as he, designed to withstand the perfect crucible of war. He was meant to survive. Meant to live on after other, weaker creatures died.

Or perhaps he was deluding himself. Perhaps he was already dead, and didn't realize. At a certain temperature, all meat cooked. It took time for the deeply burned to die. He had memories of this, he realized. Memories of fire raining down from above. Members of his pack, roasted and dead, but still moving for a few hours longer, not comprehending that they were already gone.

I have been burned before.

The memory was there, a shadow play of jumbled images: augments like himself, igniting, screaming rage as they were transformed into pillars of fire—

A wave of salt water crashed over Tool, dragging him back to the present. Another wave struck the ship abeam, and water rushed across the canted deck. Tool fought to hang on.

The captain of the vessel seemed hell-bent to sail into the storm, but the ship was clearly in trouble. Another mountainous wave came rushing up from behind. As it crashed down, Tool's fingers slipped. He lashed out with one hand, barely hooking the last rung of the rail. Foaming waters swallowed him completely.

Amazingly, the ship righted itself and clawed forward once again. Tool surfaced, spitting water. Squinting into the lashing rain, he could see the ship's crew now up on deck, struggling with ropes, trying to raise more sail. He guessed that their automatic pulleys had failed, so now they were trying to save themselves by hand.

These storms are your creations. You made them. Now you struggle to survive.

It gave him a certain dark satisfaction to see humans floundering so. It was ever the way of them. Diving always into danger without thought, always optimistic that they might win out. And so they died.

Another wave crashed over the ship. Tethers snapped. Struggling crew members blasted across the deck and disappeared into the frothing sea, their screams lost in the roar of the winds.

There was nothing for it. These puny humans would never survive if he didn't reveal himself.

Tool hauled himself over the rail, stifling a howl as shrapnel from the explosions spiked and speared under his skin. He had been burned and flayed and perforated, but still, if there was pain, not all of him was cooked. Where there was pain, there was life. Pain was his ally, assurance that his heart still beat, his claws could still tear, his jaws still crush.

Tool dragged himself forward, clinging to the rail as waters swirled about his waist. A human went skidding past. Tool snagged him by the wrist.

"*Hold fast!*" Tool roared. The crewman nodded, terrified, clutching to him.

Young. Just a boy. Someone with missing ears and an old triple-hash brand on his cheek. Barely into manhood, and now about to drown. Tool dragged the boy back aboard, and the child reattached his survival line.

The boy pointed across the deck and shouted something. His words were lost, but his meaning was clear. Another of the crew was struggling with the mainmast, still unable to raise the sail. Without it, they would founder.

Tool gathered himself and leaped. He hit the mast and barely managed to grab hold before the next wave crashed into them. The sailor struggling with the mast lines looked up, eyes wide. *Familiar.*

"Mahlia!"

Before she could respond, another wave crashed over them. Tool grabbed her before she could be swept away. They both clung to the mast.

Blackness squeezed Tool's vision, but he held grimly on. He was losing strength. The ocean continued to batter him, uncaring that he was using his last reserves. He could feel his strength bleeding away.

The ocean is vast, and we are frail.

Darkness pressed his vision and pain receded. He was dying after all. They had finally succeeded in killing him. Tool bared his teeth, hating that his enemies had beaten him.

Summoning the last of his strength, he grabbed the jammed pulley mechanism. The ropes were hopelessly tangled in it. With a heave, he tore it free and smashed it against the mast. Once. Twice.

Metal shattered.

Tool seized the rope in his teeth and ripped it loose. Fighting unconsciousness, he hauled at the rope.

Slowly, the sail rose.

He yanked again and it rose higher, billowing in the gale. At last, the sail filled. The ship surged forward. Tool swayed, fighting titan winds. Their only hope was forward motion. To cut through the waves, to race ahead of them. And yet now he couldn't pull any more. Could barely hold the rope against the power of the hurricane. He fell to his knees.

Mahlia was beside him, shouting something he couldn't hear. He wrapped the rope around his fist, knotting it there, and collapsed against the mast, still holding the rope, staring up at the sail, leaning back, making it fill. He felt the ship gathering momentum.

Around him, he was aware of people swarming. Humans, frail humans. Humans like ants, frantically working, struggling futilely. He felt ropes being looped around him, binding him to the mast. He heard Mahlia, shouting whip-crack commands, but the meaning of her words disappeared into the howl of the storm.

Darkness crushed his vision.

7

TOOL SMELLED THE scents of his Claw, all squeezed inside the sweltering hold of the attack boat. Wet fur, gun oil, ocean salt, iron blood, rotting fish, burning plastics. They were packed together like so many sweat-matted sardines in the pitch-darkness. The air was heavy and close. He could taste his Claw's bloody breath in the darkness, all of them inhaling one another's air.

Feritas. Fidelitas.

The carbon-fiber hull vibrated with the power of the attack boat's engines as they rocketed for shore. It thumped and banged, slamming over waves. The din inside the hold was like construction hammers, relentless. Tool's Claw all swayed back and forth, shaken by the jerks and shudders of the boat. No one complained. Speed was everything. Speed, radar deflection, and luck.

The shudder of an explosion penetrated the hull noise of the attack boat.

Ears pricked up. Mastiff-like muzzles sniffed the air, questioning. Perhaps a near miss. Perhaps a missile hit. Perhaps out in the ocean, all around them, their packmates were dying, fragments of blood and bone mixed indiscriminately with the shards of a sister boat's hull in their wake.

Another explosion rumbled.

Perhaps all the others were dead already, and they were the last.

Perhaps they would never make the shore.

Their attack boat rushed on, slamming over the waves, a reckless torpedo bearing its payload to the coast.

An explosion hit close. The boat slewed and shuddered. Some of the Claw fell. The iron spike of fresh-spilled blood misted the air, but no one complained. The boat accelerated again and the hammering of ocean waves resumed. Growls of approval rose from the Claw. They would not die on the water. They would reach the shore. They would battle.

A light went on. Red, flashing.

Red. Red. Red.

The Claw readied themselves, struggling to move, packed together as they all were. They checked weapons and one another's gear. Front buckles. Equipment straps. Back slaps of confirmation. Thumbs up. Fangs bared.

Red. Red. Red.

Green.

The rear of the drop boat opened. A whirlwind of tropic sea air seized them.

Go go go go go go.

They piled out. Five seconds, all out, hitting water at eighty knots. Tumbling, sinking, orienting. Now swimming strong for the shore while all around artillery hammered at the surface and did little to stop their swimming advance.

They came surging out of the surf, running hard, foam and waves tearing around their legs. Bullets shrieked past their ears. Attack boats flamed on the beach where they had blasted up onto land and exploded by remote control against shore fortifications, ripping hellholes for Tool and his Claw to pour through.

Tool roared and charged up the black muddy shore. Claw brothers and sisters by his side, all of them baying with killing lust.

Humans awaited. Soft, slow, inadequate humans.

Tool had a machete in one hand, a gun in the other. Explosive rounds spat from his gun's muzzle and humans died screaming, blown to pieces. Tool dropped into the defensive trenches, smelling and hearing his Claw all around him, not needing to see them, not needing to speak, he knew them all so well. His machete hewed through the trench, a scythe, harvesting. People collapsed before his advance, bloody stalks of wheat.

A howl of triumph burst from him, joining the symphonic roar of Claw and Fist and Pack. Platoon and Company. All of them baying triumph and offering sacrifice to their leaders.

The God of War had children.

And yet now, dreaming, Tool knew what he had not known then. It had been too easy. The true slaughter was only beginning, and counterattack was imminent. As he joined his fellows in blood-drenched celebration of dream and memory, Tool simultaneously grieved his Claw, so many of whom would have their hearts ripped out to feed the Tiger Guard of Kolkata.

And yet even this grief was not as painful as knowing that eventually his own gods would rain fire down upon him.

8

MAHLIA CROUCHED BESIDE Tool, trying to staunch blood flow from dozens of shrapnel wounds. The augment's back was a mass of blisters and sticky char.

"Damn, our boy's a mess," Ocho said.

"Straight-up carnage," Van agreed. "You sure you're actually doctoring him?"

"He's better than when I started," Mahlia retorted as she examined another blackened hole where white-hot shrapnel had burrowed deep.

"I'm just saying he's carnage is all." Van hopped over a runnel of blood that was trickling across the deck. "I didn't even know dog-faces had this much blood in them."

Tool's hulking form glistened red in the sun. Even now, after all the stitching and staunching that she'd done, new blood was still pooling around him. Bright ruby jewels. There were dozens of pocks and wounds, still unstitched. Some of his flesh was so seared it was impossible to find the shrapnel wounds that hid beneath the mass of char and peeling meat. Flies buzzed close, feasting, getting caught in sticky clots where Tool's nearly supernatural blood was trying to heal itself.

The *Raker* was anchored in a small cove, bobbing easy on bright blue seas while Captain Almadi assessed storm damage in exhaustive detail. After the fiasco with the auto-sails, Almadi was adamant that they wouldn't put to sea again until she was satisfied, and Mahlia, despite a desperate urge to get Tool to real medical facilities, was inclined to agree. Their near sinking had robbed her of her appetite for risk.

Mahlia wiped her brow with her forearm and straightened. A hornet circled, buzzing, bright yellow-black and vicious, attracted by the feast of meat that Tool proffered. Another buzzed her ear.

"Get these away," she said, waving ineffectually at the insects. "We don't need them clotting in his wounds."

"Not sure how we can stop them," Ocho said.

"Is he even alive?" Van asked. "He smells like bacon."

"He's alive. Trust me," Mahlia said. "He's been hurt worse than this before."

"You think?"

"Just get me more of the StimGrowth packs."

"We're out. You used them already," Van said.

Mahlia whirled. "*All* of them?"

"Don't blame me!" Van raised his hands defensively. "You were sticking needles in him like he was a pincushion. Don't take much for a monster like that to drain us dry. A hundred cc's is like a drop in the bucket for him. I had to sneak past Almadi, like, five times, just to get you all that."

"What do we still have?"

"Maybe four more liters of cell knitters, then we're out of those, too. That beast sucks up medicine like a sponge."

"Go get the cell knitters."

"You sure? He might die anyway. Then it's a waste of good medicine."

"He's not going to die," Mahlia snapped.

"He smells like bacon."

"Just go get the cell knitters," Ocho intervened. "We wouldn't have survived the storm if it wasn't for him."

"We wouldn't have had to run in the first place if he hadn't gotten his ass bombed."

"Van..."

"I'm just sayin'."

Ocho gave him a warning look.

Van held up his hands. "I'm going. I'm going."

The soldier boy ducked down the hatch, but his voice floated back up. "Just sayin' someone wanted his ass dead, and we almost got killed, too. Not sure how we owe him anything, after that."

Mahlia shook her head tiredly. "'Just sayin'.'"

"Don't hate the messenger," Ocho said. "Most of the

crew agrees. We wouldn't have been in that storm at all if someone hadn't dropped those missiles." He squatted beside her and lowered his voice. "And we might still need some meds, too, you know? We got other people hurt in that storm. Chum and Shoebox, we just got them splinted. And there's no telling what else we'll run into before we get to port. Almadi ain't going to like us using every bit of her medicine."

"It's *my* medicine." Mahlia glared at him. "I'm the owner. Not Almadi."

"I'm—"

"'Just sayin''?"

"Come on, Mahlia. It ain't like that."

Mahlia scowled, wishing she could actually be mad at Ocho, but he was only voicing worries that she, too, was fighting to keep at bay. That was the truly infuriating thing about Ocho: The former soldier boy was so damn grounded. He saw things, and called them like they were, and never backed down from what he saw as true. Given that he'd lived amongst sociopathic killers for a good part of his life, that pretty much made him a saint. For sure, it was why the other soldier boys followed him. They all trusted him to see the big picture, and keep them alive, not to lie to them, or himself.

Ocho didn't have any illusions.

But right now she didn't need someone who was grounded. She needed someone who was crazy enough to believe anything was possible.

"Just help me, all right?" She gestured with her prosthetic hand. "I can't stitch with this."

Ocho held her gaze a moment longer, then nodded and took the thread from her metallic fingers. He examined the half-man's ruined flesh, flicked off a flake of black crackling skin.

"He's cooked."

"Would you cut it out with that? He's wounded," Mahlia said. "He'll heal. He always heals." Her voice cracked. "You can't kill him. Trust me. He's been worse off than this. I've seen it."

"Hey. I seen him heal, too," Ocho said. "But this is a whole different kind of hurt. Some kind of crazy swank high-tech missiles. I ain't never seen something like that before. Even the Chinese peacekeepers didn't use this tech when they were in the Drowned Cities."

"That's because they were actually trying to fix things, not burn everything down."

"And these people just wanted to burn things down. That don't worry you?"

"It's the kind of war he was designed for," Mahlia said tightly. "He'll survive."

"Maybe. But we're definitely not designed for it. That's what I'm saying."

Mahlia wanted to retort, but if she was honest, she was frightened, too. She'd never seen war done that way.

Blink, and the world burned.

"Just help me sew," she said, avoiding Ocho's gaze. "I

got the shrapnel out. My prosthetic is crap for delicate work."

"If those people track him or us..."

Mahlia glared but Ocho didn't flinch. Gold-flecked green eyes regarded her, unblinking, unafraid. "Sometimes dying's okay," he said. "Sometimes keeping something alive just means you're making it hurt more."

She wished she could fire him.

You need him, a voice in her head reminded her. She needed him to lead the soldier boys. To provide the muscle. The guns. The defense.

You need him to keep you steady, the unwelcome voice murmured. *He's steady, when you just want to burn everything down.*

But that was the problem. Ocho was steady, because he'd seen too much. He'd seen his soldier boys shot and stabbed and strangled. Seen them blown to pieces. Seen them smashed to jelly by falling buildings. He'd seen people's insides on their outsides. Torn up, ripped out, shattered...

Death wasn't a tragedy to Ocho; it was just something that happened.

Sometimes keeping something alive isn't kindness.

Tool's one good eye cracked open. One yellow bestial eye, filled with rage.

"I. Am. Not. *Meat*," he growled.

"Tool!" Mahlia threw her arms around him, overwhelmed with relief. "I knew you'd make it!"

But the effort of speaking seemed to have exhausted

him. His mastiff-like head settled again, and then his whole huge body seemed to collapse in on itself. Breath rushed out. For a second Mahlia thought he really was dead, but then Tool breathed again. A slow, steady, deep rhythm of breathing. A monster, slumbering. Resting at last.

"You see?" Mahlia jostled Ocho. "I told you he'd make it!"

Before Ocho could reply, Van returned, crashing down beside them with an armload of medical bags. They sloshed as they landed on the blood-wet deck, jiggling and gleaming in the sun like just-caught jellyfish.

"What? What'd I miss?"

"He talked!" Mahlia grabbed one of the bags and started stringing up IV tubing. "He's going to make it."

"Not being meat and actually being alive." Ocho shook his head. "That's still a ways apart."

But despite the doubts he voiced, he took the cell-knitter sac from Mahlia's fumbling prosthetic hand and expertly pricked it with IV tubing, then strung the growth fluid high.

Helping her.

Giving her the hand she didn't have.

9

Jones pushed away from her workstation, rubbing bleary eyes. She'd been hunting for days and still had no clue where the ship was bound. She'd been over the Raptor footage again and again, but none of it had given her a glimpse of the ship's name or registration. Wrong angles, too dark. The harbor hadn't been her focus when she'd been running the oversight drone, and so now she just had a few fragmentary images of the ship and its contingent of sailors.

To top it off, she was exhausted. Ever since the Raptor strike, she hadn't been sleeping well. She kept seeing the moments before her missiles had hit. The people, all walking around, not knowing they were about to die.

When she'd first persuaded Tory to let her take the Raptor back to look again at her handiwork, it had felt like a game. She'd run plenty of sims. But then she'd gotten all the live footage of the aftermath. The bodies outside the main strike zone, twisting and burning. Others, running to their aid, trying to get to dying friends...

It's not my job to worry about collateral damage. My job is to drop Havoc where the general wants it.

But a lot of the people on the infrared cameras had been small. Children, probably. Child soldiers, recruited early. By all accounts, vicious, feral, violent creatures—and yet, she could still see their heat signatures when she closed her eyes. She could still see how their footprints had warmed marble floors, and left ghostly afterimages as they moved through the shattered capitol building.

And then she'd erased them.

One white-hot wave of Havoc, and they were all gone.

How many had she burned to ash, with the push of a button?

She'd never killed anyone before. She'd been schooled in the use of Mercier's standard-issue Mez Cannon pistols and rifles when she'd gone through basic combat training, but she'd never been in with the ground troops. Never shot anyone for real. And now, with the push of a button, she'd wiped out more people than some Fast Attack platoons killed in a year—

"Old man got you working late?"

Jones startled. Tory had come up behind her.

Jones rubbed her eyes. "I need coffee."

"Pretty sure you need sleep."

"Well, the old man doesn't sleep, so I don't, either." *And I don't want to dream about the Raptor strike anymore.*

"Yeah, but he's the old man," Tory said. "You're just a baby. Babies need their sleep."

Jones gave him a dirty look. "I'm not much younger than you." She climbed stiffly out of her chair and headed for coffee. Tory trailed after her.

"You kidding? First time you came on watch, I wondered if they'd started stocking diapers in the commissary. How many years ahead were you when you took the merit exam?"

Jones ignored him. She selected espresso from the machine, three shots, then poured it into a cup of coffee.

"That'll stunt your growth," Tory said. Jones shot him another dark look. Tory grinned, undeterred. "Still can't find your ship, huh?" He pulled his own coffee from the machine and leaned against the counter beside her.

"Caroa's going to kill me if I don't find it," Jones said.

"What's this all about, anyway? I've got half the drones in the North Atlantic out on a wild-goose chase because your ship search is getting a priority tag. What's so important?"

"I could tell you, but then I'd have to kill you."

"Clichés, Jones? I would've expected an analyst who got perfect thousands on the MX to have something interesting to say. New, at least."

"How'd you get my test scores?"

Tory smirked. Jones hunted for sugar. Didn't find any.

"You have no idea, do you?" Tory goaded. "The general's got our baby analyst on a wild-goose chase and she doesn't even know why."

"It makes no sense!" Jones exploded. "And it's not just all the Raptor time. You know how many missiles we dropped on that augment? That was a hell of a lot of Havoc."

"Well, since it survived, guess we needed more."

"But *why*?"

"Look, Jones. You work here long enough, you get used to not knowing certain things. Just follow orders, keep your diaper clean, and you'll keep on rising. It's that simple." He smirked again. "Well, as long as you find that augment."

"Thanks for the pep talk, Strike Officer Jackass."

"It's what I do. Because I care." He checked the time. "Oops. Gotta run. There's a bunch of Houston swamp fighters got a meeting of their own with a Havoc drop. Suckers keep trying to board our floating refineries."

He clapped her on the back and headed off.

"Tory?" She snagged his arm. He paused and returned, and she lowered her voice. "Do the Havoc drops ever bother you?"

"Bother me?" His brows knitted. "Why? You worried about the cost? It's way more efficient to hit these guys with a couple Havocs than get down on the ground with them."

"I was more thinking about the collateral damage."

"Well, it's not like anyone down there is a shareholder." He was studying her with an expression that Jones would have taken for concern, if she wasn't so certain that he was about to make fun of her naïveté again.

But to her surprise, he didn't crack a joke. Instead, he spoke almost kindly. "Do yourself a favor, Jones. Get some sleep. Collateral isn't on you. Caroa authorized it. He wanted a six-pack, you gave him a six-pack. You were textbook. Got it?"

Jones nodded slowly. "Got it."

"Good!" He punched her shoulder, smiling again. "Now, if I were you, I'd spend less time worrying about what's on the ground when you drop Havoc, and more time worrying about where that augment went—if you want to keep your career, that is."

"It would help if I knew why he wanted it dead."

"Not your pay grade, Jones. Just get the job done, and quit whining about what's not your business."

Jones scowled and sipped her bitter coffee as Tory sauntered off, whistling. He wasn't bothered. He was off to drop more Havoc. He'd burn the world down, and sleep like a baby.

Just do your job.

Mercier hadn't recruited Arial Madalena Luiza Jones to be a pain in the ass. They'd recruited her because she'd nailed the MX.

So let it go.

But still, it bothered her. She'd always been curious about things, always been obsessed with questions, and when her mind caught on something, it was hard to make it let go.

She mulled, considering the augment. One routine pattern match, and suddenly Caroa had been all up in her business, making her re-task drones and ordering their North Atlantic assets closer to the coast in case he wanted strike capability.

She'd asked the general which company they were up against, and who was directing the augment's activities, but Caroa had rebuffed her, saying it wasn't relevant.

Her best guess was that the augment had been working for some company that wanted to corner the Drowned Cities' scrap and recycling market. Lawson & Carlson, or someone. But that, too, made no sense. A single augment's activities in one of the world's countless irrelevant hellholes was trivial in comparison with the kinds of operations Caroa normally oversaw. The man tasked thousands of augments to go to battle, to conquer territory, to put down rebellions, and to take over deepwater seaports. Caroa organized military monopolies of the sea trade over the melted North Pole; he didn't waste his time with one augment in one backwater scavenge zone.

Except, now he did.

So now Jones, instead of worrying about whether Mercier was about to lose control of their lithium mines in Peru, was worrying about whether some tin-can smuggler ship from the back ass of the beyond had survived a hurricane.

Frowning, Jones returned to her desk. She sipped her

coffee/espresso combo, made a face at the bitterness, and keyed open her research files.

Lists of ships scrolled past, Manta-class clippers that had docked in dozens of ports around the Atlantic, from Reykjavik to Rio de Janeiro. Even the nearest ports boasted hundreds of likely ships. Jersey Orleans. Seascape Boston. Mississippi Metro. Miami Reef. Or maybe they'd gone farther. London, or Lagos. With a Manta-class, the entire world was within reach. They might be headed for Island Shanghai for all she knew.

She studied the few image captures she did have of the docks. Fuzzy, distant pictures. She hadn't had the Raptors aimed at the clipper ship during her surveillance, so there was really only one good series of stills, pulled from about ten seconds of a Raptor panning shot.

Jones clicked through the images again, unconsciously leaning close to peer at the screen, even though it didn't make the grainy pictures clearer.

Soldier boys, wearing the colors of the augment's troops, carrying some kind of oddly shaped cargo up the gangplank. A dark-haired, dark-skinned young woman looked like she was supervising. Her facial features looked East Asian, but not straight Chinese or Japanese, more African. Chinese and Drowned Cities mixed, maybe? Maybe a castoff orphan of the Chinese peacekeepers, from when China had tried to restore order in the place?

It looked as if the girl was in charge of the cargo, even

though she didn't look much older than Jones. But then, all the people down in the Drowned Cities were young. The old ones had been shot dead years ago. This one looked pretty chewed up. Jones tried refining the image. The girl had scars on one cheek that looked like an old militia insignia. Jones called up her research files.

UPF. That was it. Triple hash, burned into her cheek. Just like a bunch of the others on the ship. United Patriot Front was what it had been called. Jones went through the images again, frowning. The girl had some kind of prosthetic hand, too. Skeletal blue-black metal. High-end, considering the girl clearly wasn't with any of the major trade combines. If she'd been working with Mercier, sure. Lawson & Carlson, or Patel Global... but for an indie smuggler to have that kind of prosthetic?

Jones stared hard at the pixelated images of the mechanical hand. Blew out her breath, frustrated. If the Raptor's cameras had been focused on the girl directly, Jones might have been able to pull a specific design, maybe even a serial number from the prosthetic, then ID the girl and maybe finally the ship... But no.

"Okay," she murmured, studying the one-handed girl. "So what's your business in the Drowned Cities?"

She called up more research screens. The major exports from the Drowned Cities were all raw materials that came from scavenging the city's orleans. Iron. Marble. Scrap. The civil war that had raged along that part of the coast had kept it from producing anything agricultural. Same for manufacturing. And the only things the Drowned Cities really bought were more bullets, sometimes meds. That was the trade: scrap for bullets, bullets for scrap.

So, a gunrunner.

If they were bringing in weapons, it would mean Havana or London most likely, possibly Qingdao. Jones went back through the Raptor images again, this time examining the cargo the soldier boys were loading. Boxes. Crates. Something large and flat. A rectangular shape that sort of reminded her of a large mirror her mother had had...

Jones stared at the package wrapped in burlap and canvas and everyone gathered around it. From their postures, they looked... almost worried about whatever it was, like it was delicate.

Guns or meds were what they'd be bringing down to the Drowned Cities.

So what were the smugglers taking in payment? The Drowned Cities had no cash, and a Manta-class was too small to make scrap worthwhile.

Jones stared at the flat rectangle.

"Art!" she exclaimed.

The analysts around her all startled in surprise at her outburst.

"What the hell, Jones?"

"Keep it down!"

Jones waved a distracted apology at her peers. "It's art," she muttered to herself. "They're exporting art." She had the same electrified feeling she'd gotten when she'd sat for the MX. Knowing answers as soon as she read the questions. Knowing she was right. Knowing that she was creating a future for herself, that she wouldn't cut lumber for life. That she would rise. She could practically see her old teacher, Mrs. Silva, nodding approvingly as she worked. Encouraging her to think more deeply, to be relentless. To never doubt, no matter what her mother said.

Art. It made perfect sense. It was light, it was compact, and it was wildly valuable. Even a small clipper's hold was more than sufficient to ship guns and bullets in, and haul art out.

Humming to herself, Jones started running searches, pulling on the thread of possibility, seeing how far it would take her. A few minutes later, she placed a call to Caroa.

"I know who they are," she said, smiling as Caroa came on-screen. "I know where to look for them."

"Yes?"

"Their clipper ship is Manta-class. I matched her lines. There are plenty of those, but not so many that would want to run to the Drowned Cities. Those ships are fast, but holds are small. You need to move things that are light and valuable. You're not going to haul out a couple hundred tons of copper wire from the Drowned Cities. That's for the Beluga-class ships. Or dirigibles. Yetis, right? Big old lumberers—"

"Get on with it, Junior Analyst."

"Right. Sorry."

She shared one of the surveillance images across the

comm. “I think they’re hauling art, sir. Old imperial memorabilia. There’s all those wrecked museums down there, right? And the capital used to be there, so it’s loaded with loot. I think we’re looking at a painting here. Wrapped up in canvas, obviously, but I think that’s a painting they’re loading.”

She switched over to an auction catalog and sent across more images to the general. Caroa’s brow wrinkled as he examined her finds: paintings; old war items; ancient crumbling texts, written in black fountain pen.

“Go on.”

“I looked for arrival and departure patterns that sync with global art markets, and you see this one ship, the *Raker*, showing up every couple months in Seascape Boston.”

“Why the Seascape?”

“It’s the closest link to the Drowned Cities for the major auction houses. Christie’s. Excavation House. Malinda Lo. Davis & Ink. The Seascape has got a huge deepwater port, and no orleans to get tangled up in, so it dominates polar trade. Plus there’s wealth there. You’ve got Patel Global building clippers there. All kinds of commodity shipping, too, with their interior continent mag-lev links. And then there’s banking and finance. Ever since Manhattan went orleans last century, there’s a lot of money sloshing around up there. With direct links to China over the pole, it’s ideal if you’re in the antiquities business.”

She ran her hand over another screen, pulled up a

display of shipping names, and mirrored it to the general's terminal. "Here..." She highlighted the shipping lists of the Seascape. "The *Raker* shows up right on time for the pre- and post-hurricane-season auctions. And sure enough, when you check the auction catalogs, that's when you suddenly see a lot of First Civil War rifles. You see Pre-Division American flags. Old paintings. Warhols and Pollocks. Memorabilia from the nineteen-hundreds space program. It goes on and on."

"So you think they're bound for the Seascape now."

"Well, it matches the pattern. It's their last chance to catch the Chinese tourist traffic before winter makes polar sailing really miserable."

The general was quiet for a long moment. "Good work."

Jones felt a flood of relief. After the miss of the augment, it was always possible that her superior would decide to blame her for failure. Demote her to work on some Antarctic gold exploration outpost. *Or back to the Amazon—*

"Set Strike Raptors on overwatch."

"Strike Raptors?" Jones tried to master her expression.

"Is there a problem?" Caroa asked.

People, turning to ash. People, curling up and dying.

"I...Sir, it's the Seascape. We have trade agreements there. They have mutual defense pacts. Patel Global. Kinshasa Nano. GE. Beijing has embassies and port agreements there. There's a lot of potential for blowback." Caroa's eyes had widened with surprise. Jones rushed ahead. "We could do a Strike Claw, though. Have our augments wear the livery of Patel Global, or one of the financial factions there. We could use Fast Attack augments from the *Kilimanjaro*. It would be clean."

For a long moment, Caroa was quiet. Jones held her breath. When he finally spoke, his voice was soft.

"Jones..."

"Sir?"

"I'm sure you think you're being clever."

Jones couldn't help wincing at his tone. "Yes, sir?"

"The next time you're feeling clever, Analyst, I want you to put your hand over your mouth and stifle that cleverness. I want you to smother your mouth like you'd smother an unwanted baby in the orleans. Your job is not to give me geography lessons, and your job certainly isn't to tell me what tactical options are at my disposal. The very last thing we want is for *any* augments to get near our target. Is that understood? No. Augments."

"But, sir—"

"No augments, I said! Absolutely no augments!"

Jones froze in the face of the general's fury. *Fates. He's going to send me down.*

"Yes, sir," she said, nodding vigorously. "No augments."

"Good. Better." Caroa visibly controlled himself. "I want that ship burned to the waterline. I don't care if you hit it in international waters, or if you hit it in the heart of the Seascape, but I want you to find that clipper and sink it before it has a chance to off-load the target. Do you understand?"

"Yes, sir."

Caroa switched off, leaving Jones staring at the blank screen. Tory glanced over from his own workstation. "He can assign you to work as a trial subject for Ebola IV, you know."

Jones shook her head mutely.

"Jones?"

"I just screwed up, didn't I?"

"Oh, I don't know. He must like you for some reason. I've seen him send people to Antarctica for less."

When she'd been assigned to the *Annapurna*, she'd been so sure that it was the beginning of a glorious future. A sharp uniform. Profitable responsibilities. The potential for fast promotion.

And now this.

It was just like when she'd been young. Her mother had used to slap her for saying things out loud that wiser people left unsaid. Again and again, she'd made this mistake. A problem of discipline and character, her mother said. More than once she'd broken the silent agreements that kept her mother's fragile world functioning, and that had kept them eating. Arial wasn't to talk about how stupid someone was, or how Supervisor Marco looked at the wood pulp girls. It didn't matter if Arial was right. If you made trouble, trouble came back hard on you.

"He wants to bomb a city," she said.

"So? We do it all the time."

"It's a real city, though. The Seascape? It's not just some orleans."

"Yeah, well, it's the job. If you want the nice salary and the promotions, you do the job."

Jones avoided meeting Tory's eyes.

"What's going on in that pointy head of yours, Jones?"

I don't want to drop any more Havoc.

"Who's above Caroa?"

"ExCom." Tory gave her a look. "Please tell me you're not going to try to go over Caroa's head to the Executive Committee. The insubordination—"

"He wants to drop a six-pack on a trading partner city."

"And?"

"We have treaties with them! They're allies with China! It's crazy!"

Tory shrugged. "I dunno. I dropped Havoc on Prague, once. I think they were an ally of somebody or other. Paris, too, come to think of it."

"I don't know why I'm even talking to you."

"Because I'm looking out for you, Jones, and I'm telling you that you're swimming in some dark waters, and you don't have any idea how many sharks are all around you. Do your job. Don't piss off Caroa. Soldier up." He lowered his voice. "Cover your ass."

"Yeah..."

She wanted to explain her true reasons, but something about Tory's expression made her stop. Anything she said would just put her in a worse position.

"Raptors on overwatch," she said grimly. "Yes, sir."

"I knew my baby analyst was a learner," Tory said. "Little

learning machine. First time I saw you, I knew you were a learning machine." His words were light, but his expression was serious. "Young ones gotta learn fast, or they get dumped back where they came from, right, Analyst? They get dumped back in some hot-as-hell rain forest pulp mill, and everyone forgets how sharp they were on some exam. Right?"

Jones made herself nod. "Yes, sir."

"That's what I thought."

Tory watched her for a minute longer. Jones, painfully aware of his gaze, pulled up the Raptor task panels and started setting overwatch duties.

Maybe I can catch them outside the territorial limit, she told herself. *Then it's a freebie. Drop Havoc, and move on.*

But on the heels of that thought, another followed, the question of what she'd do if the ship made it to the Seascape. If the ship made it safely, would she still drop Havoc? Would she make more bodies? Would she turn the world to ash?

She could hear her mother's voice, mocking and scornful.

You gonna make more trouble, daughter? Gonna show us how smart you are again? Brag about how great you're gonna be, where you're gonna go? Pretend the rules don't mean nothing to you? You gonna make trouble again? That what you're gonna do?

Jones went grimly to work.

No, Mama. I'm going to survive.

10

CLAWED FEET AND hands scrabbled over Tool in the darkness, stomping and shoving him down deeper into the bone pit as his brethren all fought to climb out.

Struggling bodies surged and writhed, snarling and snapping, clawing at one another and at the steep sides of the pit. Fighting blind. Dragging one another down. Bitter warfare in the darkness, everyone desperate to escape. Fighting to be first. Desperate not to be last, desperate to escape before the pit was filled in.

Tool fought. He clawed and bit and tore, proving himself worthy. This was the law of the bone pits, and he had learned it well. From his first days, as a wriggling and mewling pup, he had been taught the lesson of his worth. Only the most savage survived. He had grown to strength with bloody hunks of meat raining down from the trainers above, but never enough, never enough for all. The weak became weaker, and soon fed the strong. But Tool learned quickly and fed well, preparing himself for the day when he would show himself worthy.

And now, clawing out of the pit, into the light of the sun. First of his kind. First from his pit. Birthed out of darkness and into the light. Out of the bone pit, and into the waiting arms of General Caroa, who welcomed him, and named him...

Blood.

Worthy. Judged worthy of standing beside a great general. Found worthy of fighting on Caroa's behalf.

Tool stood tall in the light. Covered with the blood of his lessers, he turned his face to the fabled sun.

11

THE *RAKER* SAILED north under clear skies, gull-white sails billowed taut. Just two days after the storm, the blue waters of the Atlantic glittered under bright sunshine, calm and inviting. On the *Raker*'s deck, Tool still lay limp, an inhuman mound of scorched flesh, but Mahlia had no time to attend him. Now, Mahlia was only aware of her own sweat, and Ocho, circling her.

The sweat soaked her shorts and tank top, and dragged against her movements. It dripped in her eyes, stinging and blurring her vision. It slicked her palm, making her knife slippery in her grasp.

Ocho continued to circle, looking for her to falter.

Sweat bathed him as well, but he never seemed tired. Fates, the former soldier boy wasn't even out of breath. He moved easy with the pitching deck, always sure-footed, a snake looking to strike.

Mahlia knew she couldn't get inside his guard. She'd already tried too many times, and failed every time. He was too good.

Ocho gripped his knife in his right hand. It moved, back and forth, hypnotic and sinuous. She knew he was trying to make her focus on the blade, instead of watching how his feet moved, how his body shifted. He was trying to trick her into watching where the knife was instead of where it would—

Be!

He came in fast. Mahlia stepped into the attack, knowing it would be close, but he'd miss her guts, and now he'd have to deal with her own blade. The pitching of the deck worked in her favor as she brought her left hand around, slicing the air, forcing him to scramble toward the safety of her right side. They banged against each other, a messy brawl. He grabbed for her wrist, ready to grapple—

Snick.

The knife hidden in her prosthetic hand shot out and she rammed it up under his jaw. Ocho froze. Her blade pressed deep against his neck, tenting the flesh. A thin line of blood trickled where the razor edge nicked skin.

Ocho's hands went up in surrender. He broke into a grin. "That's how you do it, war maggot! Just like that!"

Mahlia clenched her muscles and the concealed blade in her prosthetic hand disappeared as quickly as it had appeared.

Snick.

They both relaxed and drew apart, Ocho nodding satisfaction. "Yeah, it's good," he said. "You're getting good with it. Practically ambidextrous. I like that. Two-handed terror."

Mahlia wiped the sweat off her brow. "My lucky left," she said.

"And now with that new hand, you got a tricky-sticky right. With a little more training, we could almost put you in the ring fights up in Salt Dock. Put some money on you. Stork would second you. First blood would be easy."

Mahlia shook her head and sank to the deck, still panting. "I'll settle for winning outside the ring."

Ocho plopped down beside her. His muscular brown shoulders gleamed with sweat and his tank was soaked. He drank from a bottle of desalinated seawater and passed it to her. "Good work. Seriously."

Mahlia took the bottle with her prosthetic hand and drank, then passed it back. Ocho was right. She was getting better with the hand—and with the knife. When Ocho had suggested that she get a weapon installed in the hand, she'd thought it was stupid. Some kind of weird affectation, like she was supposed to be some warrior princess out of the burning lands of Rajasthan, like the Bollywood shows that they pulled in over the satellite.

"It will look crazy," she'd protested at the time.

"Nobody will be able to see it," Ocho had said. "And for sure, no one will laugh after you stick them."

"Doctor Mahfouz used to say that if you had a weapon, it just meant you'd use it, instead of finding a better way."

"Look where he ended up."

That had decided her. Mahfouz had ended up dead. He'd lived in a fantasy world where people were all supposed to see the humanity in each other. And so he'd died. In Mahlia's experience, people were more like animals. Sometimes you could tame one. Even a vicious one. But sometimes, you just needed to put a body down.

She flexed her prosthetic again. The blade *snick*ed out and popped back in. She moved all the fingers, making a fist. It was almost as good as a real hand. Almost as if the Army of God had never cut it off in the first place. She briefly wished that she'd been able to afford one that had feeling, too.

"Big difference a few days make," Ocho said, interrupting her thoughts.

Mahlia followed his gaze to the ocean beyond, a vista of benevolence completely at odds with the hurricane they'd survived.

"Kind of nice not having a storm trying to kill us," she agreed.

Off the port side of the *Raker*, skim fish were jumping, flying high. Probably feeding on a jellyfish swarm. In the far distance, a pod of whales breached. She'd seen them earlier in the day as well, pacing the *Raker*. All the life of the ocean seemed to be rejoicing after the storm.

A shout from the forward decks echoed up. Mahlia turned, shading her eyes. Some of Ocho's soldier boys were working on the ropes and winches, bantering back and forth with Captain Almadi's sailors. Their voices sparkled, as bright as the sunshine on the rippling ocean. Mahlia spied Van, small and kinetic. Stork, too, tall and black, solemn and intense. Muscular Ramos, alongside pale and ever-sunburned Severn, of Almadi's crew. All four of them working under Captain Almadi's supervision.

"Almost looks like they're a crew," Ocho said, mirroring Mahlia's own thoughts. "Another year or two, and old Almadi will have our boys housebroken."

Captain Almadi had been determinedly teaching the former militia fighters the sailor's trade, and now, with the high spirits that survival on the ocean had brought out, Ocho's boys were doing their work with surprising obedience.

"It almost looks like..." She trailed off.

"They're kids," Ocho said. "Take the scars away, scrape off their UPF brands, and you'd think they'd never killed anyone."

"Yeah."

They'd all been part of the United Patriot Front at one point. They'd hunted her. They'd killed people she'd cared about. They'd been just as barbaric as the Army of God, who had hacked off her right hand. Just as vicious. Just as cruel.

And now here they were, laughing. Van had just dumped a bucket of water over Severn's head, and was bolting away. A kid, who'd also used to poke a gun in people's faces.

Her gaze traced across the deck to the huge lump of burned and bloody flesh that was Tool. Thanks to him, she was alive. If, long ago, some fortune-teller had waved her Fates Eye over Mahlia's head and told her that this was her future, she would have told the woman she was sliding high. There was no way a castoff of the Chinese peacekeepers could rise to lead these animals. Time was, these feral boys would have eaten her alive, and now, instead, they wagged their tails when they saw her. She should have been dead, and instead she had a clipper ship of her own, and a crew of half-tamed killers, and it was all because of Tool.

Ocho was watching her, solemn. "Thinking about our big not-meat friend?"

Mahlia laughed uncomfortably. "You reading my mind?"

"Just been around you awhile, I guess."

However much he dismissed his powers of observation, Ocho's gold-flecked green eyes were watchful in ways that the other soldier boys' weren't. At first, she'd thought he was just smarter than most people, but later, as she spent more time with him, she'd realized that it wasn't just his intelligence that had kept him and his followers alive—it was those eyes, careful and attentive, seeing things that were right in front of everyone else's face, too. Most people saw things. Ocho actually looked.

"I wouldn't be sitting here if it wasn't for Tool," Mahlia said.

"None of us, probably." Ocho shrugged. "Before he showed up, UPF were losing bad. Colonel Stern kept saying we could beat the Army of God, but we didn't stand a chance. We were getting exterminated."

"And then Tool showed up."

"You and Tool." Ocho nodded solemnly. "Changed the game, top to bottom."

"Tool was winning, wasn't he? In the Drowned Cities, there at the end. He was winning."

"No, he won." Ocho's gaze went to the slumped half-man. "No doubt on that. He won."

Mahlia tried to read Ocho's expression, the way he seemed to read everyone else, but there was little to glean from his external features. He was good at locking whatever he was thinking deep inside. All you got was the outside. Those sharp glitter-green eyes and that lean brown face with its triple-hash burn scar.

He would have been handsome without the UPF scar, she thought. She'd seen people in Seascape Boston with not a scar on them. Perfect faces, unmarred by fear or pain. Unconsciously, she reached up to touch her own brand. She'd had Tool burn it onto her cheek, and she still winced at the memory of the pain that she'd endured so she could sneak into UPF territory.

"It was quiet," Ocho said. "You notice how quiet it got?"

"What? The Drowned Cities?"

"Right at the end. No fighting at all. Not a single gunshot. Never realized how used to it I was, until it was gone." He nodded down at Tool's hulking slumped form. "If he'd showed up sooner, I might have never had to soldier at all. Might have still been fishing with my uncles. Might have never been grabbed up by UPF at all."

"At least we got out."

"Thanks to our big not-meat friend." Ocho was quiet for a minute. "Almadi's pissed about him."

Mahlia turned her gaze to the captain, who was busy supervising her sailors and Ocho's soldier boys. "She's always unhappy about something."

"I dunno..." Ocho chewed his lip. "I think she'd push old Tool overboard, if she could."

"Seriously?"

"It's what I'd do. He's weak now. Best time to do it. Hit him fast, make it happen. 'Oh well, what can we do? He's in the drink.'" Ocho nodded thoughtfully. "Yeah. That's how I'd do it."

"Almadi knows where her money comes from." Mahlia squeezed the muscles of her right arm. The six-inch blade shot out of her prosthetic, appearing as if by magic, black murder glinting in sunshine. "If she doesn't see it our way, we'll *make* her see it our way."

"Can't keep watch on her all the time. Not her, and all her crew. We lost a lot more than she did in the storm. You notice we're outnumbered now?"

"We just need a little time. Until Tool wakes up."

"That's a big if—" Ocho's words were broken off by a shout from below. Sailors and soldier boys were gathering around Tool, who seemed to be moving.

Mahlia punched his shoulder triumphantly. "You should trust me more."

"I always trust you."

The way Ocho said it made Mahlia pause. She wanted to ask him what he meant, but more people were clustering around Tool, and Ocho was nodding toward the gathering.

"Better get there before Almadi."

By the time Mahlia made it down to the main deck, Tool was standing. Leaning heavily against the mainmast, looking surprisingly weak, but still, standing. He gazed upward, seemingly mesmerized by the sunshine. Van was already there, circling like a yappy, overexcited puppy trying to provoke a much bigger, meaner creature. Others stood at a more respectful—or at least safer—distance, staring in awe at Tool's wrecked mass.

"How'd you heal so fast?" Van was asking. He prodded at Tool's flesh, fearless. "You don't even smell cooked now."

Typical Van, playing it up in front of Almadi's sailors and the other soldier boys. Mahlia half expected Tool to smash the earless boy flat, but for the moment the augment was ignoring him.

"Check it out!" Van said as Mahlia arrived. "You gotta see this!"

He ran his hands over the ruined musculature of the half-man. "He's, like, practically healed already!" His fingers dug into blackened skin. A great sheet of Tool's back flesh peeled off like sticky, charred leather, revealing raw, bloody, gleaming red muscles.

Everyone winced and stepped back, expecting an explosion from the half-man.

"Well, he's mostly healed." Van made a face and dropped the fatty char to the deck, then caught everyone else's appalled expressions. "What?" he protested. "Sometimes when you peel it off, you find new skin." He patted one of Tool's massive biceps. "Anyway, he doesn't care. He doesn't feel any of it. Do you, big guy?"

He started picking at Tool's flesh again. True to Van's words, Tool didn't seem to notice the picking and peeling, but continued to stare up at the sun.

Mahlia pushed between the soldier boys and touched Tool gently on the arm. "You shouldn't be up."

"I am healed enough," Tool rumbled, but his words were almost immediately belied as he sagged against the mainmast.

"Help me!" Mahlia tried to catch him. Soldier boys and sailors rushed in to join her, but he slumped to the deck without grace, too heavy for them to hold upright. Tool's breath wheezed out as he collapsed, but even as he thudded down to the deck, he remained fixated on the sky above.

"What is it?" Mahlia asked, shading her eyes against the glare. "What do you see up there?"

"I seek my gods," Tool said.

"Your gods?" Van squinted up at the sky. "There ain't no gods up there."

"You can't find your gods in the heavens?" Tool asked.

"Ain't religious, actually," Van said. "My people were Buddhists. Bunch of crap about compassion." He shrugged. "Didn't work out too good for them."

Tool didn't reply. Mahlia noticed that a grayish membrane had slid over his one good eye, apparently blocking the glare of the sun.

Van went back to picking at Tool's charred skin. "Anyway, there's no gods living up in the sky," he said. "Not even Deepwater Christians think that anymore."

"And yet my gods live in the sky, of a certainty," Tool said, "and they rain fire down upon me when I displease them."

A ripple of exclamation ran through the gathered sailors and soldier boys, and everyone looked skyward. Ocho caught Mahlia's eye and gave a subtle jerk of the head, indicating Almadi. The captain's expression of alarm was rapidly turning to fury.

Mahlia crouched down beside Tool and lowered her voice. "Are you saying whoever torched the Drowned Cities could hit us here?"

"A single ship in open waters? Clear skies?" Tool nodded. "We present an easy target." He seemed unconcerned that his words sent more angry mutters running through the crew.

Van was less subtle. "Oh, hell no!" he said, shaking his head. "I knew we shoulda dumped you overboard."

"Shut up, Van." Mahlia raised her voice and glared at the rest of the muttering crew. "No one's dumping anyone overboard."

"But we're sitting ducks!" Van said. "You heard him."

The crew was alternating between fearful glances up at the sky and glares at Tool. Mahlia couldn't help scanning the sky herself. The wide blue expanse, previously bright and optimistic, suddenly felt deadly.

"Well," Captain Almadi said dourly. "I never thought I'd hate a clear day so much."

Tool laughed. "Clear or cloudy makes no difference, Captain. If my gods wish to slay me, fire will rain down regardless."

The murmurs of discontent increased. Soldiers and sailors united, for once:

"How the hell do we fight missiles?"

"We seriously keeping that thing on board?"

"We don't even get a vote?"

Ocho was looking at Mahlia significantly. Almadi was boiling. And Tool was surveying the crew with a sardonic expression, as if he'd baited everyone on purpose.

He's testing us, Mahlia realized. *Trying to see who is a threat.*

He was barely conscious and functioning, and yet still he was evaluating his tactical situation, identifying his enemies. Mahlia glared at Tool, trying to make him read her warning. The last thing she needed was more unrest in the crew. Tool gazed back, blandly unapologetic.

It was his nature.

He saved you, she reminded herself. *He helped you, when no one else would or could.*

"They can't—" Mahlia cleared her throat. "Those people can't think you're still alive, though. I mean, we all saw the strikes. The palace *melted.* We all thought you were dead, too. They can't still be looking for you."

"Who knows what gods think?"

But he must have empathized somehow with her worried expression, for his ears twitched and then he smiled slightly, showing rows of sharp teeth. "No, Mahlia. I do not think they will attack again. They rained their fire, and will now feel satisfied. Strike officers will report to operations officers, and thence to generals, and reports will find their way up to their Executive Committee, and they will congratulate themselves on a job well done. I am not a danger to you. Not now." He stared up at the sky. "But it is certain that my gods still hate me."

"Gods didn't attack you," Captain Almadi said. "Those missiles were high-tech military. That was people."

"People." Tool growled, disgusted. He began lapping at the wounds on his shoulder, his long animal tongue rasping across burned flesh.

"Don't do that!" Mahlia said. "You'll rip the scabs off."

Tool bared his teeth and growled. "You have your ways. I have mine."

Mahlia backed off. In his damaged state, Tool looked both more human, and also less. All the frustrations and vulnerabilities of a sick patient, but with the behaviors of his other genetics leaking through. This manlike creature that hungered for battle and always survived, and yet that now lapped at his wounds like a beaten dog.

Mahlia sat down beside the monster. "Clear everyone out," she said to Almadi.

For a moment, she thought the captain would rebel, but then the woman clapped her hands with crisp authority. "You heard her! Break's over, sailors! You've all had your excitement. Back to work."

When the crew had dispersed to their tasks, the captain rejoined Mahlia and Ocho. "So," she asked. "Who was it?" She squatted down in front of Tool, her expression hard. "Who wants you dead?"

Tool gave her a sardonic glance. "Who does not?"

"I'm serious, half-man. If my crew is threatened, I need to know what I'm up against."

Tool went back to licking his wounds. "My old gods worry that I am now more godlike than they."

Almadi laughed sharply. "Still with the gods?"

"You doubt?" Tool's ears quirked. "So. Call them not gods, but humans. *People*, as you say. Small, weak, jealous, insecure, fearful *people*. People who thought themselves clever. People who toyed with strands of DNA, and did their work too well." Tool bared his fangs. "Humans dislike weapons that think for themselves. It unnerves them."

"But why go to so much effort to kill you?" Mahlia asked.

"I believe I ate my general."

There was a stunned silence all around.

"*Ate* him?" Van popped up behind Almadi. "Like, chewed him up? Like, for *lunch*?"

Almadi startled. "What are you doing here? You're supposed to be helping Ramos clean up the clinic." She gave him a pointed look. "The clinic you tore apart looking for meds for this"—she scowled at Tool—"patient."

"Get back to work, Van," Ocho said tiredly.

"I just wanted to know how much he ate," Van said.

"I believe I ate his heart. I'm certain I ate his head." But even as Tool said so, his bestial face showed doubt. "My memories of the time are...muddied. But I do remember the feel of the man's head between my jaws. The taste of his blood..." A growl of contentment thrummed. "I must have eaten him. I would not have let him go, once I had him between my teeth. Perhaps I ate him all."

"Fates." Almadi was shaking her head.

"A human skull, it crackles like balsa wood—"

"Fine," Mahlia interrupted. "We get it. You ate your general."

"I thought augments were always loyal to their...to their..." Ocho hesitated.

"*Masters?*" Tool goaded.

"Owners," Almadi said firmly, glaring. "You are supposed to be loyal to your owners. All augments are loyal to their owners. Unto death."

Tool smiled. "I believe this surprised my general as well."

"Still seems like a lot of trouble to go after one rogue soldier," Ocho said.

"Indeed." Tool frowned. "I thought Mercier had given up."

"*Mercier?*" Almadi almost shouted. "That's who—"

"Owned me?" Tool gave Almadi a dark look.

Ocho whistled. "Well, that explains the firepower."

"You ever think of pissing off someone smaller?" Van asked. "Like China, maybe?"

"Get back to work, Van," Mahlia said. But of course, the boy ignored her, squatting down as if he belonged.

"None of us choose our gods," Tool said. "Mercier created me."

"They're the ones who're gonna fry your ass, too," Van said.

"It seems so. By taking command of the Drowned Cities, I set myself above human beings..." Tool trailed off, looking wistful.

Mahlia watched his expressions shift. The Drowned Cities had been hell for the people who lived and warred within it, but for Tool, it had been his ideal home. The sort of place a creature like him belonged.

Tool was staring down at his huge clawed hands, flexing them thoughtfully. "Once again, I am alone."

Mahlia had never seen the half-man look so defeated. It wasn't the bleeding wounds, or the charred flesh, or his melted pelt, or the vicious scars that closed one eye. It was the droop of his ears. The sag in his shoulders.

"You can have another pack. Another place," Mahlia said finally. "We can help you find a place. Someplace Mercier won't go."

Tool laughed shortly. "No. It is over. My gods are everywhere and they cannot be fought. I must hide. I will find a place where humans are few, and augments fewer. They only allowed me to survive because they thought me lost. In my hubris, I forgot myself. I must disappear, and never become worth noticing again. It's the only way."

"What about crewing with us?" Mahlia asked.

Captain Almadi sucked in her breath, but Mahlia rushed on. "We can give you cover. You can say you're"—she hesitated—"you can say you're ours. You wouldn't stand out, then. You'd just be another augment, employed by a ship. No one would notice you."

"Crewing decisions are mine," Almadi objected. "That was our deal. I run the ship. You run the trading. We agreed that I would have absolute command of the ship."

"So call him cargo," Mahlia shot back. "*I* decide cargo. That was our deal, too."

"Your captain is right to be concerned," Tool said. "Anyone who is close to me is in terrible danger."

"At least stay with us until you're healed. You don't have to decide before then. And after that, wherever you want to go, we can take you. We can at least do that. The *Raker* can take you anywhere in the world."

For a moment, she thought Tool would refuse this offer, too, but then the augment cocked his head. "Where are you bound?"

"The Seascape," Captain Almadi said flatly. "For the fall auctions."

"But you can stay on with us after that," Mahlia pressed, giving Almadi a hard look. "None of us would even be alive if it weren't for you." She looked to Ocho for backup. "None of us."

Ocho pursed his lips, and for a second Mahlia thought he would side with Almadi, but then he said, "Mahlia's right. As long as you want, you stay with us."

Almadi looked pissed, but she didn't protest anymore, seeing herself outvoted.

Tool regarded Mahlia thoughtfully. "Every time I think that humanity is a waste, it seems one of you..." He trailed off. Shrugged. "The Seascape is a good destination. There are wealthy companies there who employ my kind for labor and security. No one will question if I belong to one or another. And there, they will have the supplies I need to complete my healing."

"It's settled, then," Mahlia said. "You're with us." She gave Almadi another warning look. "For as long as you want, you travel with us."

"Yeah!" Van laughed. "One big, happy family!"

"I wouldn't go that far," Almadi muttered.

12

"HOW WOULD I go about finding out about a specific augment?" Jones asked.

Tory glanced over from his workstation. "Sticking your nose where it doesn't belong, Junior Analyst?"

"Hypothetically."

Tory gave her a hard look. For a moment she thought he was about to ream her out, but instead he stood abruptly. "I think we need an intervention." He motioned for her to follow him. "Come on. Stretch your legs."

She glanced around the intelligence section, where the rest of the analysts were focused on their own tasks.

"Now, Jones."

Reluctantly, she followed him out. Bulletproof doors slid aside. Monstrous Fast Attack augments loomed over them, watching as they exited. Brood and Splinter. They were both almost as large as the one she was hunting, but really all augments were terrifying when you stood close to them. Too large. Too many big, sharp teeth. It set off all the ancient alarm bells of the human species to see those creatures looking at you like you were a snack.

Tory didn't seem bothered by them at all, though. "Hey, guys. Just out for a sec." He pointed her down the corridor. "Let's walk."

At first, she thought he was taking her toward the mess hall, but he skipped an elevator and kept walking. They passed navigation units. Barracks sections. More Fast Attack augments standing guard. Engineering techs. Flight squad personnel.

"Where are we going?"

"Here's the deal, Jones. I like you, okay? You've got all that youthful energy and gumption, and that's kind of funny to watch. I like seeing you work circles around analysts twice your age. That's good giggles." He paused, glanced around, and tugged her into a corridor recess. On a wall, the symbols for a weapons locker glowed orange, listing rifles, pistols, grenades, body armor...

Tory looked down the hall one last time. Jones realized they were in a section of corridor without surveillance cameras.

Tory lowered his voice. "If you piss off Caroa, he can drop you anywhere he wants. He doesn't have to put you in an escape pod before he dumps your ass." He made a motion with his hand, an arc of fall, downward, downward. *"Pssseeeeeeeewwwwww. Splat!"* He clapped his hands together and rubbed them, pancake flat, for emphasis. "Stepping into open air at six thousand meters gives a junior analyst a lot of time to think about chain of command. All that way down."

"I was just curious," she protested.

"I think we're both a little too smart to believe that." He gave her a penetrating glare. "It's not your job to be curious."

"Come on, Tory. I'm just trying to figure out who owns it. Caroa won't say who we're up against. Every time I ask, he shuts me down."

"Maybe you should take the hint! Why can't you just follow orders?"

"If I followed orders, we would have sent the Strike Raptors back to *Karakoram*, and never known you missed the target."

"I didn't miss!"

"Okay, so aren't you a little curious about how our augmented friend survived all that Havoc, then?"

"It was just dumb luck. It's like smashing ants. Sometimes one gets away."

"Maybe. Or maybe our augmented friend has more going for him than just some tiger and dog DNA."

"Like what? Asbestos skin? Come on, Junior. Be serious."

"I am serious. I've been looking into some stuff. It doesn't add up. It's... it's weird."

Tory checked his watch. "Look. I don't have time for this. I've got a Havoc drop in twenty minutes on the Trans-Cal water pipeline. And then I've got another in Caracas, right after. You've got work to do, too. Real work," he said pointedly.

"Come on, Tory, you've had them zeroed-in for the last hour. You could burn them to slag in your sleep. I just want to figure out this augment. You have to be at least a little curious."

"Blood and rust." He peered out into the corridor. "What have you got?"

Jones hid her triumph as she pulled out her tablet and started calling up the oversight images of the augment from her drones.

"You've got this on your tablet? Out here?"

"I didn't want it logged. You're the one who's on me about not pissing off the brass anymore." She caught his expression. "Don't worry. I crypto'd it."

"Fates, Jones." He shook his head. "Your career..."

"Just take a look at this, will you?"

He glanced down the corridor again. "Fine. But make it quick."

In contrast to her hunt for the *Raker*, the images she pulled up now were good, aimed right at the target, sharp and clear, thanks to Raptor One's superior intelligence suite.

She'd spent hours tracking the augment, following him by heat inside the old capitol building where he had kept his headquarters, snapping pictures and capturing steady video of him when he was outside, down by the huge rectangular lake that had spread before the capitol building, before the Havoc drop had melted everything down to slag.

"Pretty place," Tory commented.

"If you like warlords and murder." She arranged the images. "It was a civil war, until our augmented friend showed up. Local reports say he started consolidating power a couple years ago, right after the United Patriot Front collapsed."

"Who?"

"Low-rent warlord faction. There were maybe a dozen different militias, all fighting over control of the city and the scrap recycling there. UPF. Army of God. Tulane Company. Taylor's Wolves. Freedom Militia. Minutemen. And then our big, hairy friend showed up, and he wiped them *all* out."

"So he's military."

"Definitely. Perfect tactical and strategic planning. But here's the thing." She swiped through the old footage. "It took a while to catch him in daylight, and from the right angle. And then stitching the pictures together..."

She stopped the footage. Zoomed in on the augment's head. Zoomed in tighter still. "There." She pointed at one of the augment's doglike ears. "Check it out." She handed over the tablet. "What do you think of that?"

A long string of numbers was tattooed into the monster's

skin, bending around the fold of the ear, barely visible through the thick fur:

228xn+228-NX__F3'/___2'

"I think it's a GeneDev ID," she said. " '228' is a platform, but it looks wrong to me. I've never seen a '228xn' prefix, and then have '228' repeat that way. Have you?"

"Huh." Tory frowned. "That is weird."

"Caroa saw that, and as soon as he did, he ordered *Karakoram* across the Atlantic and had me tasking Raptors ready. That's all he needed to see. He stopped asking questions about the augment, about how it operated, all the other stuff; he stopped caring as soon as he saw that number. So? Have you ever seen '228xn'?"

"Do you have the whole number?"

"Pieces and parts. The fur covered up some things." Jones fiddled with the footage, pulling up more and more images. Pinched them together. "This is everything I can get."

228xn+228-NX__F3'/___2'(C8_6C5__
U0111___Y__29_9_4___MC/MC__8xn

"It's GeneDev, all right." He frowned. "But yeah. It's weird. '228' is standard for augments, especially military ones. They mostly get built off a common genetic platform, so you get consistent results when you fertilize in vitro."

"I know about 228," she said impatiently. "What about the rest?"

"You want my help or not? The rest is the genetic branching. If you look it up you can find what 'F3' is. I think it's something from the tiger's tooth-and-jaw structure. But just looking at it, I see some feline, probably tiger, some missing stuff, and a bunch of different canine parts. I think 'U0111'... maybe it's something from badgers or grizzly bears?"

"So it's a vicious badass. I knew that already."

"Okay, fine." He gave her an annoyed look. "And then you have the breeding facility, 'Y' could be fragmented off 'KY,' for Kyoto. They've got a ton of breeding vat labs there. You'd have to look that up and see if there's another match. But..."

"But it's weird looking, right?"

"Yeah, that extra '228xn.' And it looks like it might be a suffix, too. See the '8xn' at the tail end?"

"Maybe that's why it survived our hit. '228xn' equals asbestos skin."

"Hah. Maybe. New tech for sure." He frowned at the stitched-together images of the tattoo. "Oh." He handed the tablet back hurriedly, almost as if he'd been burned. "Oh, wow."

"What?"

"Did you not look at that? 'MC/MC'?"

"I self-taught basic genetics. I don't know everything, Tory. That's why I was asking you."

"That's not the genes, Jones. That's the patent holder and purchaser."

"So that's our enemy?"

He yanked her close and whispered fiercely. "That's *us*, Jones. 'MC' is Mercier Corporation. That's our own augment that we dumped a six-pack of Havoc on. We bombed our own damn asset."

"Why would we bomb our own augment?"

Tory made an exasperated face. "I hate to break it to you, Jones, but when you get to a certain level in the company, it's not all happy-family rah-rah-rah. Finance, Trade, Viceroys. R&D. Markets. Joint Forces. Commodities. They've all got their own interests on the ExCom. Sometimes families have fights, you get me?"

Tory kept talking, but Jones was staring at the augment's design tag again. Kyoto was a possibility. There were a bunch of gene-tech facilities there, and she might be able to trace the augment back to its crèche—

"Jones!" Tory waved a hand in front of her face.

"What? I'm listening."

"Some things are above our pay grade. The less we know, the less trouble we're in if we get called up in front of a Loyalty Board. Your performance is always being logged. This is bad mojo. Drop it. Forget it. Do what Caroa tells you to, and don't stand out on this one. You get me?"

"Yeah. You're right." She theatrically shut down the images of the half-man on her tablet, folded it, and shoved it into her pocket. "It's not worth getting demoted."

"Now you're understanding." Tory looked relieved. He checked his watch. "Look, I gotta go drop some party favors on California."

"Party favors..." Jones's mind flashed back to her own Havoc drop—all the infrared people standing there, not knowing they were about to become ash. She forced a smile. "Good luck with the drop."

"Don't need it," Tory smirked. "Cali militia doesn't have asbestos skin."

As Tory departed to drop missiles on terrorist militants, Jones considered her options. Despite what she'd told Tory, she had no intention of letting it go. She pulled out her tablet and called up the GeneDev number again.

228xn.

She'd start with Kyoto. Trace Caroa's movements, see if there was an overlap with any gene-tech facilities. She didn't have access to his files, but she could call up plenty of surveillance data from that city. Mercier had security agreements there. And she could pull all of Caroa's expense reports, from back in the day. See if anything matched there—

An alert interrupted her thoughts, an alarm notification from an overwatch Raptor. Jones read the information sourly. Things were moving faster than she wanted them to.

Showtime.

13

"I SMELL THE shore," Tool said.

"I guess your sense of smell isn't damaged," Mahlia replied as she peeled away a blood-clotted bandage and examined the matted, sticky wounds beneath.

Tool's ears twitched. "No. My senses are intact, even if my flesh is"—he prodded at the flaking meat of a bicep—"weak."

With assistance, Tool could now hobble about, depending upon three or four soldier boys to support his bulk. If he clutched the rails and masts, he could move slowly on his own.

But looking at his ruined body, Mahlia wondered if he would ever truly heal again. She'd seen Tool survive bullets and shrapnel and teeth and machetes, but this damage was something worse. The missiles had done terrible things to his flesh with their heat and chemicals.

Tool seemed to catch the direction of her thoughts. "The medical advances of the Seascape will help me," he assured her. He jerked his chin in the direction of Mahlia's mechanical prosthetic. "They gave you a hand, did they not?"

"You can't replace your whole body."

"I will heal."

"Have you thought any more about staying on with us? On the *Raker*?"

"Your captain has suddenly become amenable to my presence?"

A voice echoed from the high mast above, saving Mahlia from responding.

"Seawalls, ho!" A second later Van came clambering down the mast, reckless and nimble. He crashed down beside Mahlia and Tool, panting. "Not much longer now! You can see the arcologies, too!"

Tool quirked one melted eyebrow at Mahlia, his expression amused. "Go, see your promised land."

With an apologetic smile, Mahlia got up and went to the rail, joining Van and Ocho and Shoebox and the few sailors who didn't have tasks. Every time she saw the Seascape, she couldn't help but feel a rising excitement.

The Seascape was different from any place she'd ever known. No fallen-down, crumbling buildings. No swamped streets where ocean had swallowed city. Instead, the Seascape gleamed, its proud arcology towers jutting high above the city-state's massive seawall breaks. Bioengineered nut trees sprouted from balconies, and fruit vines tumbled down over multistory terraces, interspersed by the buildings' glittering solar skins.

Mahlia leaned against the rail and breathed deeply. Now she could smell what Tool had scented long before. Citrus wafting from the city, along with the perfume of jasmine flowers. Fish and salt and ocean, too, of a certainty, but also those lemon and orange vines that everyone seemed to have, all designed to survive northern winters.

She remembered her first time in the Seascape, plucking oranges and strawberries from the vines on a quiet brick street in the ancient high neighborhoods of the city. Luxuries, free to anyone who cared to take them.

Luxury. That was the Seascape.

The *Raker*'s bells rang. The crew called out confirmations and orders. Ropes rattled and squealed through the ship's jury-rigged, misaligned pulleys. Captain Almadi was lining up with the buoys that marked deepwater passage through the hurricane breaks and into the Seascape itself.

Another warning bell sounded and the ship's booms swept across the deck. The *Raker* came about, sleek and nimble, far to port of a huge Orca-class trimaran with a Patel Global logo.

Mahlia watched the massive clipper make her own maneuvers. The ship sprouted an array of rigid-wing sails angled to catch the breezes, all electronically aligned by computer, sensors finding the optimum angles for maximum wind efficiency.

The *Raker* pitched and rolled as the larger ship's wake struck them. In comparison with the *Raker*, the Orca-class was both larger and much more technically advanced—more crew, more cargo, and more profit. It was the kind of ship that reminded Mahlia that even though she owned the *Raker*, she was still a very small fish swimming amongst huge sharks.

The *Raker* fell in behind the Orca. Patel Global was more of a trade cooperative, in comparison with the militarized protectorates that Mercier ran, but at root they were nearly the same—companies with almost unlimited resources that could reach anywhere in the world.

Ahead, Seascape Boston's seawalls loomed: piles of bricks, slabs of asphalt from old roads and overpasses, massive concrete columns bristling with rusting iron rebar, all of it covered now with barnacles and draped in seaweed spackled with anemones.

"What do you think of Kanodia's legacy?"

Mahlia startled. Tool slumped hard against the rail, breathing heavily, having managed the short walk from the mast.

"He planned," she said. "He saw everything coming, and he planned."

"A very good general," Tool agreed.

"He wasn't no general," Van objected. "He was, like, some kind of school guy."

"A professor of biology," Tool said.

"*A professssssor*," Van mimicked.

Mahlia shot him a warning look. According to Seascape legend, Anurag Kanodia had been more interested in scientific research at one of the Seascape's ancient universities than in the practical activities of the world. His family had a tradition in trading and finance, but he had always been driven by learning, rather than profit.

But then one day, the marine biologist had abruptly quit his academic life. He abandoned a treatise on the adaptations of corals to acidifying oceans, shut down his research, and then, as legend told it, he had walked out into the city, carrying a piece of chalk.

A piece of chalk in one hand, and an altimeter in the other.

According to the stories the Seascapers told, he'd circled through the city, marking a contour line with his chalk—a line many meters higher than most estimates of sea level rise.

The seas are coming, he said when anyone asked him why he was marking chalk on buildings.

People took it as self-aggrandizing performance art, and laughed. Then they scrubbed the silly man's scribblings off their homes and offices. But when people washed off the chalk, he returned with paint, graffiti-spraying sea level promises in fuchsia and chartreuse, blaze orange and neon blue—gaudy colors, too rude to ignore. Colors that refused to wash away.

He was soon arrested for vandalism. Bailed out by a wealthy sister, he returned to his midnight graffiti raids.

Marking and re-marking his city with the stubborn line. He was arrested again, and fined.

Then arrested again.

And again.

Defiantly unapologetic each time, he was finally jailed for a year. At his sentencing, he laughed at the judge. "People don't mind that the sea will swallow their homes, but woe to the man who paints their future for them," he said.

When he was eventually released from jail, his vandalism took a new form. If people only understood business, then business it would be. Kanodia had the blood of merchants in his veins and so now, with the help of his sister's connections, he went about gathering investors, buying as much as he could of the city that stood above his old painted lines.

Eventually, he and a few major corporate partners purchased nearly all the real estate above the line. They collected rents, made steady money, and waited patiently for the inevitable Category Six hurricane that research told him must eventually arrive.

In the aftermath of Hurricane Upsilon, which destroyed much of lower Boston, Kanodia turned his investments to the devastation below the line, buying up the wreckage, and harvesting from it. He was an old man by then, but daughters and sons continued the project. The seawalls were the result. Rising high across the mouth of an anticipated bay, they were comprised of every bit of wrecked architecture that had lain below the storm surge line.

"He didn't pretend things would get better," Mahlia

said. "He made things better, because he saw how things were."

"Indeed. A rare talent," Tool said. "Very few choose to have it."

The *Raker* slipped in behind the first seawall break. It made its tack cleanly and sliced down the sea-lane between the first and second wave break. Seagulls roosted upon the anemone-clad ruins, pecking at crabs and seaweed that draped the shattered rubble of the ancient buildings. Seals sunned themselves on concrete slabs. Children fished all along the line and picked in the cracks for mussels that had attached themselves to the piled debris.

A girl waved at Mahlia as the *Raker* passed. Mahlia lifted her metal hand in turn.

"They live soft lives, here," Tool observed.

Part of Mahlia felt jealous that they had it so easy, but another part found herself glad that somewhere, someone had grown up fishing and watching pretty ships sail by, instead of cowering from soldier boys in a jungle.

The *Raker* reached the final buoy and tacked again, came out beyond the third break. Before them, the Seascape lay revealed: calm and blue, dotted with the glittering, floating arcology islands of the wealthiest trading companies and combines.

Mahlia could make out the flags of corporate headquarters flying atop the floating islands in the center of the bay: Patel Global, GE, Lawson & Carlson... She wondered if Mercier was somewhere in the Seascape as well, keeping a corporate embassy here, even if they didn't own territory the way these other firms did.

Along one edge of the bay, the dry-dock construction platforms of Patel Global bristled with cranes and swarmed with armies of workers as they laid the bones of huge hydrofoil trimarans. At the deepest edge of the bay, shipping and container facilities lined the waterfront. Ships and activity and prosperity, everywhere Mahlia looked. A safe, protected bay, busy with commerce, the beneficiaries of the visionaries who had planned for their previous city drowning.

Almadi joined Mahlia on deck. "Not much longer."

"We have a slip?"

Almadi nodded. "Just beyond the Patel Global arcology."

Now that they were inside the Seascape, the captain seemed more relaxed.

She'd probably grown up just like the kids Mahlia had seen fishing off the seawall breaks. Grown up soft, in a place where people had electricity all the time from solar power, and where the streets were always safe because of Shore Patrol security. A life where the worst things that happened were bar fights in Salt Dock, or maybe smugglers bringing refugees in from some beat-up orleans.

Almadi took a deep breath of Seascape air. "It's good to be home."

The words were pedestrian, but Mahlia caught an undertone of finality in them.

"Are you still going to ship with us?" Mahlia asked.

Almadi frowned. "I have my own home obligations."

"I need a captain I can trust."

"I need a crew I can trust," Almadi replied.

"You questioning us?" Van demanded. "After all we done, scrubbing your decks and learning your knots and doing all your scut—"

"She means me," Tool growled.

Almadi inclined her head.

"You're afraid I'll attack?" Tool asked.

Almadi regarded him with contempt. "You couldn't hurt a child, the shape you're in."

Tool's ears flicked back, a motion that Mahlia recognized as irritation, but all Tool said was, "Do not trouble yourself, Captain. Once we dock, I will not remain on your ship. I will not interfere with your business arrangements."

"You don't have to go!" Mahlia protested.

"I need a place and time to heal," Tool said. "And"—he indicated Almadi—"I am not welcome here."

"Is that how it is?" Mahlia demanded of Almadi.

"Don't pretend I'm your enemy, Mahlia. This half-man is a danger to all of us. You saw what Mercier was willing to do. You think they would hesitate to destroy us all to get at him?"

"But they think he's dead!"

"For now." Almadi put her hand on Mahlia's shoulder, but Mahlia shrugged her off and stepped back.

"Don't."

Almadi's voice was soft. "I have a family of my own,

Mahlia. There are some risks that are simply too great. Sail to the Drowned Cities and trade in the middle of a civil war? Yes, fine. I can do that. This?" She waved at Tool, shaking her head. "Absolutely not."

And there are plenty of ships who need an experienced captain and crew, she left unsaid.

If Almadi left, the experienced sailors would leave with her. Ocho's soldier boys had learned some of sailing, but they weren't schooled enough to run a ship like the *Raker* on their own. They would never have survived the storm without Almadi's skill and experience.

Tool laid a hand on Mahlia's arm. "It is not necessary that you sacrifice your livelihood for me. Help me find rooms where I can heal. Quiet. Far from wealth."

"I owe you everything."

"The debt is already repaid."

"What about Salt Dock?" Van suggested. "No one cares about anything in Salt Dock. Even your bacon-burned ass won't stand out there." He held up his hands. "No offense."

14

TORY WAS BUSILY raining fire down on targets as Jones keyed back into her workstation. Information scrolled on her screen. A Manta-class clipper ship had entered the Seascape's harbor.

Just drop Havoc on it. Just Havoc the hell out of them, and be done with it. Don't try to be smart. Just follow orders and be safe.

She stared at the information on-screen. This was the moment. Whatever she did now would define everything about her future. Follow orders, or find another path? She wished she had more information to go on, a better way of testing the winds.

She could hear her mother mocking her. *Some people,*

they're so smart they're stupid. You think of that? You ever think of that?

The *Raker* was docking. Time was passing.

Jones put a call through to the general. Caroa appeared on-screen, looking annoyed and vicious, as always.

"Sir. We have the clipper ship." She kept her face bland, hoping Caroa wouldn't sense duplicity. "But it's reached the Seascape already. We missed them in international waters."

"Hit them," he said. "Hit them now."

She pretended to check her monitors, feeling transparent, but pushing through with the ruse. She pretended surprise and apology.

"I'm sorry, sir. The Strike Raptors that were supposed to be patrolling the Seascape are down for repairs. *Karakoram* never notified me." She made a show of checking her other birds. "The Raptors I have patrolling international waters are more than half an hour out. I—I can't get them into range in time."

"Is that so?" Caroa's eyes narrowed.

"I—yes, sir. I'm sorry, sir." Jones swallowed and plunged on. "I just... It's bad luck, sir. I don't know why they didn't tell me that they hadn't mobilized all the Strike Raptors. It must have been storm damage."

Caroa favored her with a suspicious eye. She felt transparent. A part of her wanted to take it all back, to back down on the lie, to confess.

Too late for that. You already chose.

Caroa was glaring at her, but he didn't reprimand her. "Do the Seascape authorities know we're hunting for this augment?" he asked.

"No, sir. As a backup, I asked to be notified if the *Raker* requested docking facilities. We have mutual cooperation treaties with their Port Command. But that's the only indication we're interested in the ship. I'm sorry about the drones—"

"Fine." Caroa waved an impatient hand. "Write up your report. You'll take responsibility for failing to check your equipment. We'll come up with suitable consequences. For now, I want you to put out a watch query in the Seascape for medical purchases, and on hospital facilities."

"He could have dropped off and swum for the coast, anywhere on the way up. He could be in Manhattan Orleans, for all we know."

"No. If he's alive, he'll be there."

The general said it with so much confidence that Jones couldn't help prodding. "Do you know something about the augment that I don't, sir? Something that would help me do my job better?"

Caroa regarded her coldly. "Do I know something? Why, yes, I believe I do." He began ticking points off on his fingers. "One: Our target is wounded, badly. Two: He is a military augment, intensely driven to survive. Three: This ship, this *Raker*, that you yourself found, was bound for the Seascape. Four: If he knew that, and we must assume he did, he would do *anything* to hang on. Now," the general said pointedly, "*why* would he seek to reach the Seascape, *Junior Analyst* Jones?"

The question hung between them, redolent with contempt.

Jones swallowed. "Because the Seascape is full of augments?"

"And therefore...?" Still the contempt.

"He would blend in," Jones said stiffly. "There are all kinds of augmented personnel there. Military. Security. Professional sailing castes for Lawson & Carlson, Patel Global, GE. Tayo Fujii Genetics. Jing He. All kinds."

"So?"

"It's the ideal location for him." The general was almost smiling. She took it as a bullet dodged, and continued. "With such a large augment population, he'll have access to specialized medicines that aren't available elsewhere, in places where he'd be an exotic. It's his best chance for real medical care."

"I'm so pleased that my analyst can analyze," Caroa said dryly. "Draw up a list of likely medical supplies. I want you to scan medical networks, hospitals, clinics. We're looking for an augment with severe burns over nearly a hundred percent of his body, and purchases of medicines that would treat those wounds. Do you think you can handle that, without any mishaps?"

"He'll want cellular repair meds. Nutrient boosters..."

"Indeed. We're not looking for a needle in a haystack here."

Jones started clearing her screens. "So we just bait the

trap, and wait for him to pick up his meds." She began typing commands, setting up the new operation. "We can have human S&D teams ready to strike. We can pull those in from *Denali*. They're close. And augments won't be involved, then."

"Jones?"

She looked up from her work. Caroa was studying her closely, his eyes boring in, seeming to see into all her plans and schemes. She swallowed. "Yes, sir?"

"I expect that there won't be any more mistakes after this. Not one. Not ever."

"No, sir." Jones swallowed. "I'll have the target for you."

"I look forward to it."

15

The mingled scents of burning biodiesel, rotting fish guts, and sweltering humanity pressed down on Tool. He peered out at the Seascape through the hot, muffling folds of a hempen sackcloth shroud, and leaned heavily upon Mahlia and her soldier boys as they guided him through the crowds.

"Turn up here," Van said, returning to them. "It's not as crowded this way."

Mahlia, Ocho, Stork, and Stick eased Tool around the corner, while Van squeezed ahead through the crowds again, scouting.

Tool's muscles resisted every step and the supporting hands of the soldier boys felt like diamond rasps on his skin. His nerves had begun regenerating, and now they crowded his mind with pain wherever his skin touched cloth or guiding hands, or even Salt Dock's hot breezes.

Ignoring the pain, Tool stretched his senses, tracking the activities of the port through smell and sound. Jasmine and marigold incense invoking Kali-Mary Mercy. The sharp reek of scotch hauled up in casks from the Northern Isle Alliance. The sour scents of jellyfish oranges twined with sweet Icelandic sugarcane in the wholesale markets.

Tinkling copper bells signaled devotees burning candles inside a Deepwater Christian shrine. Through his shrouding burlap, Tool glimpsed Saint Olmos, robed in decades of dripped red wax, the man holding out his hands to passersby, offering survival, if not salvation...

More than anything, Tool smelled humans. Men and women and children from around the world. Irish and Indian, Kenyan and Swede, Japanese, Finn and Brazilian. Races and cultures, identifiable by the sweat of their diets. It permeated T-shirts and turbans, wove through salwar-kameez and utility jumpsuits. It lurked in dreadlocks and beards, and oozed from the pores of smooth-shaven skin. Vat-grown steak and NoFlood Rice. Moong dal, and baijiu, turnips, and coconut milk. Sardines and jellyfish. All of them mingled together in Tool's nose, all one thing—the reek of his creators.

It had been a long time since he had been surrounded by so many humans. Their scents brought back memories: cities he had sacked, terrified humans running before him, screaming. Halcyon days. Fond moments.

Tool almost smiled.

The scent of augments was another matter. They, too, crowded the boardwalks of Salt Dock. His brothers and sisters, if not in design, at least in form—all the various snips and scissorings and fusings of engineered DNA.

Canines and Hominids, Piscians and Felines. They were everywhere: helping ships off-load freight, hauling strongboxes of cash for merchant transfers, muscling clear paths for corporate princesses. The augments stood sentry outside the embassies of the trading companies, and knelt in temples alongside humans, making their own offerings to the Scavenge God, the Fates, and Kali-Mary Mercy.

Here, augments mingled easily with humanity and Tool could smell them everywhere. Their sweat, their panting breath, their wet fur, all of them signaling to one another, broadcasting strength and identity, camaraderie and competition, territory and warfare.

I drove my fist through the rib cage of the First Claw of Lagos. I ripped his heart from his body. Hot blood poured down my arm as I held it high, and my pack roared in triumph, and then I ate it.

Tool stopped short at the sudden recollection.

"Tool?" Mahlia tugged at his arm.

Memories, fast and jumbled, triggered by the scents of augments all around him: the air on fire; rice paddy water boiling; green rice shoots burning black; his brothers and sisters igniting, living torches before his eyes; Tiger Guards burning, too; all of them burning together.

Tool staggered. *But in Kolkata, I* did not *eat the heart of the First Claw of the Tiger Guard.* He crashed through a cluster of shore-leave sailors, and clutched against a doorway to a bar, assaulted by images. He saw the First Claw of Kolkata's Tiger Guard reaching out to him in farewell, that great augment, taller even than Tool, staring at him with sharp cat's eyes. Catching fire.

Burning.

The First Claw had been his sworn enemy, and yet now a surge of grief washed over Tool. Grief so raw and shocking that Tool found himself gasping for breath. He stared down at his own black and bloody fire-scarred hands.

"Tool?" Mahlia touched his arm. "Are you okay?"

"I've been burned before," Tool said.

She exchanged uncertain glances with Ocho, clearly worried that Tool was going mad, but it demanded too much effort to explain the rush of memories that now assaulted him. Old memories, startled from hiding by the scents of the many augments, and now galloping about inside his head.

"I need...a moment," Tool rasped.

Van returned. "What's the holdup?"

"Just taking a break," Mahlia said.

"Out here?"

"We should get going," Stork said, nodding toward a pair of augment bouncers who were coming toward them. "We're drawing attention."

Tool followed the direction of Stork's gaze. The augments were constructed from a different genetic platform than he, just as Ocho was mixed differently than Stork, different from Mahlia, or Van. These augments were specific: gorilla-dominant, judging from the length of their arms and brutal upper-body physique. Muscles like boulders. Mobile, highly expressive, highly humanoid faces. They were not of Mercier, and they were nothing connected to his genetic line of combat augments, and yet still Tool felt a vibration of connection with them. Tool found himself leaning forward, filled with an almost desperate desire for them to see him as a brother.

Are we not all molded from the same clay? All knitted together from the same strands of science?

He tore away his heavy cowl, showing his burned face.

"Whoa, big guy!" Ocho said. "What're you doing?"

Tool ignored the humans as the bouncers met his gaze. *Do you not see that we are one? We are brothers!*

Their eyes narrowed and their lips pulled back, showing sharp canines.

Ah. Not brothers after all.

Enemies.

Tool felt a sudden rush of comfort as his world returned to its familiar pattern. These were simply inferior gene-ripped slaves, bred for the simple task of smashing sailors' heads in bars. Obedient and limited. Not even natural predators. Not military. Half-men, truly.

"You have something to say?" one of the bouncers

growled. They were separating, preparing to come at him from two sides.

You are garbage. I will slay you.

Tool's adrenaline began surging, his body marshaling resources, his mind calculating combat. His claws extended. He was weak, but he could take them. *You do not know true war.* He growled contentedly. *Just a little closer, half-men.*

"Whoa!" Mahlia plowed between them, waving her arms. "Slow down, Tool!" The rest of her soldier boys were also intervening, all of them trying to block the inevitable killing.

"There a problem, dog-face?" one of the bouncers asked.

Tool smiled wide, showing his fangs. "Come a little closer, and see, ape-shape."

"Whoa, whoa, whoa! Hey there!" Van was jumping up and down. "Don't mind our big buddy here! He's on fifty different painkillers!"

Tool snarled irritation and tried to seize the boy, but Van dodged, still waving his little sticklike arms. "Look at him! He's bacon!"

"Who owns you?" the bouncer asked, eyes narrowed.

"You think me a *slave*?" Tool snarled.

"Tool!" Mahlia grabbed his arm. "Stop it! Come *on*!" She held on tenaciously as he tried to shake free, and then suddenly, to his surprise, he was staggering, his adrenaline leaking out and his strength with it. He sank to his knees.

Weak.

"See!" Van was crowing triumphantly, still blocking

the bouncers from getting to Tool. "Sad bastard can't even walk! No trouble here! Like I said! Painkillers up to his eyeballs. High as a parasail!"

The gorilla augments watched, suspicious, but their physical attitude shifted, becoming relaxed. He could smell satisfaction oozing from their pores, their sense of dominance over their territory affirmed.

"Get him back to his owner, before he makes more trouble," one of them advised.

OWNER? Tool's hackles rose. *I have no—*

Mahlia pinched his ear.

Tool nearly bit her, but the reminder was enough. He forced his rictus fangs to relax.

He was not in danger. He had no quarrel. And yet he had nearly triggered a battle without cause. He struggled to rise, but found he had no strength.

"We're sorry about the trouble," Ocho said as Mahlia and the rest of the soldier boys clustered around Tool, helping him upright. "We had a bad fire on our ship. He saved us all. We owe him a lot. But the meds..." Tool glimpsed him offering Chinese yuan, a cash bribe to forget them, and now the augments were showing almost solicitous concern.

"Are you okay?" Mahlia whispered. "Can you make it?"

"I..." Tool fought to stay standing. The challenge of the augments had exhausted him completely. "I can make it." The soldier boys were clustering around, supporting him. He felt a surprising rush of camaraderie for these humans who dedicated themselves to his survival.

Pack.

Despite the fact that they shared only the most tenuous connections of DNA, they worked to save him. Extraordinary. And puzzling. They were loyal despite the fact that there was no advantage for them, and no obedience conditioning to force them to it—just as he had shared loyalty with the Tiger Guard.

He remembered roaring victory from atop the ancient rooftops of Kolkata. Holding machetes and machine guns high. Mercier Fast Attack, side by side with Kolkata Tiger Guard, all of them together.

Victory. Ended by a rain of fire.

Tool felt nauseated at the memory.

Mahlia and her soldier boys were still leading him, guiding him, thinking themselves his saviors, when in fact he was their doom. None of them would survive being near him, he realized. They were too soft, and too frail. Too human.

He stopped short. "You must leave me," he said. "It's too dangerous to be near me."

"We already went over that," Mahlia said.

"No." He seized her shoulder, forcing her to look at him. "You must go far from me. You. Must. Go. As far as possible, as soon as possible. I am a danger to you."

But Mahlia wasn't listening to him. Instead she was turning to Ocho.

"He's going delirious again. We need to get him out of sight."

"Still got a quarter mile till we're off the boardwalks," Ocho said.

"Get an electro-rickshaw to meet us. He's losing it again." To Tool, she said, "It's not much farther." She pointed ahead to a shop sign.

SALT DOCK
VETERINARY CLINIC
SPECIALIZING IN
MAMMALS & AUGMENTS

She repeated herself, soothing. "It's not much farther. We'll go just a little farther, and then you can rest."

Tool considered protesting again, but knew it would only attract more attention to Mahlia and her crew. He would accept her help for just a little longer, but then he would send her away. Far away. Someplace safe. Someplace very far away from him. It would have to be very far away.

He stumbled on, supported by humans.

Black crows of memory swirled around him, pecking and plaguing. Images from his past, of war, of survival, of creation, all sweeping past in a whirl. But one memory sank its talons into him and settled heavy upon his shoulders, refusing to be dislodged: the First Claw of Kolkata—leader of the Tiger Guard—reaching out to him in farewell, and then igniting.

A pillar of fire.

16

"GENERAL, WE HAVE a hit!"

"Where?"

"Seascape. A bar-and-brothel area called Salt Dock. You were right, sir. It's a veterinary clinic. It wouldn't have flagged, but the purchase is unusually large. Cell knitters. Burn salves. All kinds of nutrient reuptake supplies. It's a perfect match. The target's buying out the shop's whole supply."

"Can the strike teams make it in time?"

"Deploying, sir."

17

Taj Grummon had been running Stitch & Ditch operations for three years. Recruited at sixteen, he'd been promoted within a year, then promoted again, and now ran his own squad.

Simmons and Nachez were also in place, with their own squads.

It was crazy how much firepower they were bringing to this, Taj thought. Your average dog-face, sure, it was tough. And they were damn fast, so for Fates' sake, don't get into a quick-draw competition with one, but still, at the end of the day, dog-faces were just meat.

Biggest problem was getting a jump on the bastards. Out in a wild combat zone, that was sticky. The monsters had better sight and smell than people, even if the bosses had you equipped with the latest EyePulse goggles. Sure, you could magnify fifty times, go infrared, slave your bullets to the sights, and blast away—but if a dog-face came at you out of the trees, watch out.

But still, augments weren't made of magic. They weren't bulletproof. He'd stitched up plenty of Tiger Guards and hyena men in his time. Hit the bastards with enough explosive rounds out of a .50-cal Mez Corporation Fast Attack Cannon, and they blew apart, just like regular folk.

Seema came online, her voice crackling in his earbud. "*We're in position.*"

Four squads, just to stitch one damn augment.

"What do you think this sucker did to piss off the bosses?" Hertzl asked as he lined up behind Taj, readying himself.

"Maybe he's with Lawson & Carlson."

Hertzl snickered. "Well, he sure got under someone's skin."

It was true. Mercier didn't normally go in for urban warfare, and definitely not in civilized places like the Seascape. Blowing up Paris was one thing, but the Seascape? His team's extraction was going to be the hardest part of this op, trying to evade the city-state's police after the hit.

He and the rest of the squad were all wearing Seascape Shore Patrol uniforms, to keep attention off them while they staked out the clinic. He tried to look casual, on patrol, and briefly he envied Seema, positioned up on a roof, instead of being down here, holding his cannon at his side, like there wasn't an emergency about to light up.

On the plus side, the urban environment also meant he and his team definitely had the drop on the half-man. In the jungles and actual war zones, where everyone was a potential enemy, the superior senses of the augments meant superior opportunities. If the dog-faces sniffed you a couple hundred yards out, because the wind shifted and was suddenly at your back, then you were in the shit, for real. Down in the Indonesian rain forests near the Puncak Jaya copper mines, that had been some serious fighting—

Seema came online.

"Target's exiting. Strike in five, four..."

Taj lifted his Mez Cannon, preparing himself.

Seema miked in. *"Hold count! Not the target. Some little kid."*

"You serious?"

"Let's keep it clean, boys and girls. The bosses don't want extra bodies to explain."

"Affirmative. Keeping it clean. Target's still bottled."

Taj sighed and settled back, exchanging annoyed glances with his squadmates. Joli shrugged. Max and Hertzl rolled their eyes. This definitely wouldn't play in the hot zones. Standing around with thumbs up their butts, waiting for one damn augment to exit. Wouldn't work.

"I don't like it," Taj muttered.

"Stitch & Ditch don't gotta like it," Joli murmured. "Just gotta get it done."

Taj liked that about Joli. Girl always got the job done. She wasn't going back to no lithium mine in Peru, just like he wasn't going back to scrap recycling in the Jersey Orleans.

"At least we're urban," Max said, mirroring Taj's thoughts. "Be worried about our friend sniffing us out."

"Wind's still good," Joli said.

"You know what I mean."

Taj motioned them both to shut up.

You want our friend to hear us?

Everyone settled back, trying to look casual. Taj wished they could just blow the whole vet's office to smithereens. Pick through the rubble after. But the bosses wanted a surgical strike, what with the Seascape being civilized territory and all—

"Civvy kid is clear."

"Well, ain't that nice."

"Quiet on the channel, Hollis."

"Target's exiting. Five...four...three..."

Taj closed his eyes, imagining the street. Held up his hand, motioned to his squad.

"One!"

He stepped around the corner, gun raised. The half-man was right in front of him, holding his packages.

Taj keyed the Mez Cannon to auto. Explosive rounds stitched up the half-man's chest. *Thunk-thunk-thunk-thunk-thunk-thunk-thunk-thunk-thunk-thunk-thunk.* Small red blossoms of blood for the entry wounds, and not just from Taj. Bullets were hitting the half-man from the ambush point above, as well as kitty-corner from Taj, where a small delivery carrier holding Hollis's squad also opened up.

The augment dropped its packages and tried to run. Too late, too slow. Way too much ordnance. The bullets detonated and the explosives took the augment apart, blew it all to hell.

What was left of the creature toppled, a smoking corpse before it hit the ground.

Taj signaled to stop firing.

The street was dead silent as the gun smoke cleared. Civvies were lying on the ground, looking stunned. Mayhem like this didn't happen in the Seascape. *Sorry for the disturbance, folks.*

"*Clear?*" Seema asked.

"Clear!" Taj confirmed.

"*Clear!*" Hollis agreed.

"Squads, set for extract!"

There was one last thing Taj had to do before he left. Glad of the Seascape Shore Patrol uniform he wore, he dashed toward the fallen half-man, waving at the civvies to clear out.

The dog-face had been hit with so many rounds it was basically just shredded meat, so the last part of the mission was easy to take care of.

Taj crouched beside the exploded corpse while Joli and Max covered him. He pulled out a shatterproof carbon vial, unlocked its vacuum seal, and dipped the tube into the blood. The bosses said they wanted the blood for some kind of analysis. Like it was tainted or something.

Blood. Plain old red blood. Just like a person's, really.

Taj wrinkled his nose, holding his breath unconsciously. The last thing he needed was to pick up some kind of virus, end up coughing out his lungs.

"*Shore Patrol's on the move!*" Hollis radioed.

Taj filled the vial and sealed it.

"Got the sample!" he radioed.

"Seema's holding your boat. Better hurry."

They checked for pursuers and headed for the docks. As he ran, Taj glanced back at the mountain of shredded flesh they'd left behind. At the end of the day, even augments were flesh and blood, just like people.

Blew apart just the same, too.

Stitch and ditch, baby, Taj thought. *Stitch and ditch.*

18

GUN SMOKE SLOWLY cleared from the street. Seascapers crawled out from under cover and stared around themselves, dazed.

Van crouched in a doorway, clutching the meds he'd been sent to collect, wide-eyed and surprised.

It started to drizzle.

Medics arrived, blue and red lights flashing. Swank medical people piling out of their sleek electric ambulances, who then stood gazing down at the corpse, awed and stymied by the size of the body they had to haul away. Shore Patrol showed up, and started stretching green Day-Glo tape around the body, creating a barrier around the rapidly spreading pool of blood that continued to trickle out of the exploded half-man.

It was a hell of a lot of blood.

The blood and the gunfire made him twitchy. Made him wish he had his old faithful AK, instead of—

A bunch of useless meds.

The twitchiness was a problem all of them had. Some more, like Shoebox. Some less, like Stork, who mostly seemed to keep his cool. But all of them carried memories of Drowned Cities war. Small things would send Van ducking for cover, raising a fist before he even knew he'd done it. Fireworks going off during the festival when Kali-Mary Mercy went to the waters for her ritual bathing. The clank of metal cutlery in one of the Seascape's swank restaurants. The flash of an amulet that looked a little too much like the Army of God's.

I need to get me a damn gun.

Nah. On second thought, it was probably good he hadn't been packing. The weapons the kill squad had used had been a whole different level of carnage from the guns he'd used in the Drowned Cities.

Not having a gun had probably saved his life, because for sure, he'd have stepped up against those soldiers if he'd had one—and then he'd have been shredded just like that maggot meat lying out there in the road.

As it was, he'd lunged for cover behind a row of electro-rickshaws, and from there, he'd squirted up the street, then stopped just in time as a squad of shooters in Shore Patrol uniforms came piling down the stairs of an old brownstone.

Shore Patrol uniforms, but for sure not SP.

Shore Patrol, for all the things Van hated about them, mostly confined themselves to pounding you and then dumping you in lockup until Ocho came and bought your drunk ass out.

Assassination wasn't their thing.

So Van had crouched down clutching his Fates Eye, and the kill squad had pelted right past him, all of them thinking he was just some pathetic war maggot, instead of an experienced advance scout for UPF. It was almost enough to make him feel insulted.

Out on the street, the SPs were stretching more neon-green plastic tape: CRIME SCENE—DO NOT CROSS. A couple more SPs—officers by the bars on their slickers—were starting to ask questions, picking out bystanders to tell their story.

Time to bail.

Van skirted the barrier tape and headed down the street. It was kind of funny that they went to so much effort over one dead body. In the Drowned Cities, bodies floated in the canals, picked at by the fish. They lay in abandoned buildings for years, rotting and desiccating, their bones chewed ragged by raccoons and rats and coywolv. But here, they had fifty different people in six different uniforms all showing up, all acting like one dead augment was a big deal.

A few blocks farther on, he pushed his way inside an ancient brownstone, and climbed creaking stairs.

The building was full of short-sleep crash pads for

sailors on shore leave. The smell of hashish and opium was strong. The laughter of nailshed girls. Three stories up, Van found the right apartment. He stood aside as a nailshed girl and her client stumbled past, then tapped at the door. *Taptap-tap-tap-taptap.* An old knock from when they'd all been UPF.

A rattle of latches, and then Ocho peered out the crack. "Where the hell you been?"

"Did you hear that shooting out there?" Mahlia demanded as Van came inside.

"Hear it?" Van laughed. "I was *in* it." He dropped the meds on the kitchen table. "Seascapers whacked some augment, right in front of the vet's. Blew him to all bits." He went and peered out through the grimy front window. From here, all he could see were the red and blue SP lights down the street, bouncing off drizzle-slicked buildings and rain puddles.

"They got the whole street blocked up now. Straight-up carnage. You wouldn't believe how many people they got out for one dead augment." He pointed. "Check it out. Now there's another ambulance. Like one isn't enough. They should send in a shovel crew instead. That sucker was a mess..."

Mahlia and Ocho didn't respond.

"What?" He checked back on them. "What's wrong?"

They were both frowning at Tool, who was slumped on a sagging couch that had given way under his weight. The half-man was asleep. Ocho was giving Mahlia one of his looks, and she was nodding back at him. A whole conversation, without any words at all.

"What's the problem?" Van asked.

Ocho shot Van an annoyed glance. "You think it's a coincidence, maggot brain? You think someone just decided to shoot an augment outside the vet clinic where you just happened to be buying bags and bags of burn and cell-stim meds?"

"I don't know. It was some kind of kill squad, for sure. At least two squads of four. Plus there was a sniper team, I think. Crazy big guns, you know. Some kind of bullets that exploded—"

"They're tracking him," Mahlia interrupted. "Mercier is still tracking Tool."

Van immediately felt stupid. "You sure? It was just one body. People get shot all the time, right?"

"A killing? In the Seascape?" Ocho pressed. "In the middle of the day?"

"How would I know?" Van protested. "I'm not a Seascaper! I just figured the augment pissed someone off."

"This isn't the Drowned Cities, you maggot head." Ocho was already going into the other room and waking up Stork and Stick. "Get some eyes up on the roof. See what's around," he ordered.

"You think they're coming here?" Van asked.

"Better hope not," Ocho said, giving him a dark look.

"No one followed me! Didn't even look twice at me."

Stork and Stick came and peered out the window. "They have a lot of firepower?" Stork asked.

"You could say that." Van mimed the guns. "Bambambambambam BOOOM! Shredded half-man. All over the street."

"How come everyone else always has the good guns?" Stick complained.

"If you had a gun like that you'd probably shoot your own pecker off," Stork said.

"What do you want to do?" Ocho asked Mahlia.

Van didn't like Mahlia's expression. She was just standing there, hands on her hips, looking at Tool, looking uncertain.

Uncertain.

That, more than the kill squads or the missiles that had burned the Drowned Cities, worried Van. Normally, Mahlia had a plan. Ocho too. Those two were solid granite. You leaned up against them, no matter how bad things got, and you had something at your back.

But now she looked worried, and Ocho was looking to her like she made all the decisions, and couldn't figure out what to do his own damn self.

"Mahlia?" Ocho pressed.

"They had to be gunning for Tool, right?"

"Big damn coincidence if they weren't."

"Maybe they're done now," Mahlia said. "Now that they shot up that other one. Maybe they'll be satisfied."

"You want me to spin you that fairy tale?"

"We can't haul him out," Mahlia said. "Look at him."

"If we stay here, we're like to get bottled up."

To Van's surprise, Mahlia started pulling out medical sacs, fitting needles to tubes. "We've got to heal him up. It's the only way. If he's healed, he can fight—"

"That's your solve?" Ocho asked. "You know how much time—?"

"No!" Her voice cracked. "If you want to go back to the ship, fine, but I'm not leaving him."

"Fates." Ocho scowled. "Fine. We'll stay. For now. Stork and Stick. Get a lookout. Down the street, right? Look for people in SP uniforms, see if they're door knocking."

He turned to Van, but Van was already heading for the window, knowing the orders.

"I'll keep an eye out," he said. "See if I recognize anybody."

As Van took up his position, he glanced back at Tool. Asleep, the augment looked more alien and monstrous than ever. A slumbering beast, now being festooned with the long rubber tubes of IV drips. The more sacs of fluid that Mahlia hung up on the walls, the more he looked like some kind of creepy medical experiment. Tubes ran to his neck, his wrists, his ankles.

Mahlia was going from one sac to the next, squeezing the healing fluids into the half-man. Big science. Van had been on the needle end of a half liter of that stuff once, and it had made him feel like a superman, and here Mahlia was pumping liter after liter into the creature.

Stork joined him at the window, peering out at the people in the street.

"How's it look upstairs?" Van asked.

"All quiet, so far. You?"

"Umbrellas and drizzle. I think maybe we should get us some bigger guns, if we're gonna keep guarding our big friend over there."

Stork raised an eyebrow. "The kill squads that good?"

"Ain't no Drowned Cities war maggots, that's for sure." Van couldn't get the image of the shredded half-man out of his head. "Wouldn't mind having something to balance things out, if it comes to a fight."

"Yeah, well, we go to war with the army we got."

"Don't I know it." Van shook his head. "I just wish for once we could be the guys with the bigger guns."

19

"YOU'RE SURE IT wasn't the right augment?" General Caroa asked as he gazed out his stateroom windows.

The old man knew the answer, and yet he asked anyway, and Jones resented it. It was as if he wanted her to humiliate herself to him again.

Yes, we got the wrong augment. Yes, we're telling the Seascapers that we know nothing about squads of Stitch & Ditch operating in their territory. No, we didn't leave any evidence. No, there's nothing to connect us. Yes, all our S&D teams made it back. No, I don't know where the target is now. Yes, I screwed up.

"The DNA didn't match," Jones said.

Caroa's head whipped around. "How would you match that? You don't have his DNA."

"I pulled the general design from his GeneDev tattoo. From our surveillance. And I got the teams to get us a blood sample. To make sure."

"Ah." Caroa nodded. "Clever. You are a clever one, aren't you?"

I'm good at my job. No thanks to you, old man. And now I've got a full DNA sample of the target. Which you clearly didn't want me to have.

Out loud, she said, "The genetic markers were all wrong. Not even close. Very little on the military side. No tiger genes at all. No hyena. No badger. None of the *Ursus arctos*. Canine was more toward Labrador retriever, so wrong markers there, too. And it was all heavily weighted toward domesticated felines."

Caroa gave her a contemptuous look and turned back to his windows. "So you're saying your people gunned down a pussycat. A giant, bipedal pussycat."

"I wouldn't say—"

"Quiet, Jones."

"Yes, sir."

Cold silence. Jones waited uncomfortably. She wasn't sure if the old man was going to explode, or have her dumped off his stateroom balcony, or simply send her back down to Brazil and the forestry plantations. She wondered if she had enough now to survive him, if he decided to purge her.

"You promised me there wouldn't be any more mistakes," Caroa said.

“There is some good news,” Jones offered.

“Excuse me if I’m skeptical.”

“I had an informant in Seascape Shore Patrol ask some questions on the ground. It turns out the augment we got wasn’t buying any of the meds. It was there to buy antibiotics for some kind of aquaculture farm. The med purchases definitely happened, but it wasn’t an augment who bought them.” She pulled out her tablet, and opened up her research screens. She approached hesitantly, offering the results to him. “If you’d like to see? This was the med buyer.”

Caroa took the tablet and scowled at the image she offered. A child, just growing into a gawky puberty. Asiatic features. Vietnamese possibly, somewhere in the genetic history. Black hair. No ears. Ugly scars. Clutching a huge bag of medicines.

“A boy?” Caroa asked.

Jones felt quiet satisfaction that he didn’t pick out what she had seen immediately. *You’re not so smart, old man.*

“Here.” She pointed. “The burn markings on his cheek match the ritual scarring the Drowned Cities were notorious for. They called it the triple hash. Three bars across. Three down.”

“A brand.”

“Yes, sir. Used originally by the United Patriot Front, one of the Drowned Cities militias, so their recruits couldn’t run away.” She looked at Caroa significantly. “UPF were strong on the ground just before our augmented friend showed up and started taking over.”

"So..." Caroa considered. "This is a *recruit*? He has human troops operating inside the Seascape?"

"I know it sounds incredible, but..." Jones shrugged. "It's the only explanation. It's possible the ship he boarded had troops who were loyal to him."

"Or he recruited them once he got aboard," Caroa muttered.

"That seems unlikely."

Caroa whirled on her. "Don't tell me what's unlikely, Analyst! Nothing is beyond that creature's capacity! Nothing!" Jones froze, shocked, as the general jabbed his finger into her chest. "You snoop where you don't belong!" Jab. "You intrude where you know nothing!" Jab. "You know nothing—*nothing*—of his abilities! You. Know. Nothing!"

Jones fought the urge to lash out at the man's invasion. "It might help if I knew why we care so much about one augment, *sir*."

Caroa went from white-hot rage to brittle ice. "Is that a complaint, Analyst?"

This is how junior analysts take a flying leap out of a mother ship at six thousand meters. Be smart, Jones. Don't fight. Be strategic.

"If I don't know why the augment is important," she said tightly, "we'll keep making mistakes, and we'll keep missing. I'm good at my job, *sir*—if I have the information I need. If you want me to do my job, I need to know what I'm looking for and why. If you don't like that...maybe you should get someone else."

She held her breath, expecting him to rage again, but instead, Caroa laughed.

"Get someone else!" He turned away, shaking his head. "Someone else! Ha!"

He took a seat in a deep leather armchair, muttering. "More people. More security issues. More complications." He glanced up at her, his humor disappeared. Motioned to the chair across from him. "Sit down, Jones. You want information? Fine. Have a seat. You'll have your information."

The general's eyes followed her, predatory, as she hesitantly joined him. He was smiling again, but it was the sort of smile that men in the logging camps sometimes had, right before they stuck a knife in you.

"Very few people know what I'm about to tell you," Caroa said. "It will make you highly valuable—and also very easily expendable."

He paused.

"Last chance, Jones. Do you still want to know?"

Jones met his iron gaze. "I do."

"Of course you do." He tapped his facial scars knowingly. "I was young like you, too, once. Smart. Ambitious. Always looking for advancement. Hungry for responsibility and challenges. Always thinking I knew better than my superiors..." He wagged an admonishing finger at her. "Always thinking I could keep secrets."

Jones's skin prickled. *He knows*.

Caroa smiled. "Oh yes. I know about you, Jones. I know about your queries into my history, trying to dig up old

Kyoto research. Such a good little analyst. Digging, digging, digging. Verifying this. Cross-checking that." He smiled again. "Some might say that you have been busy digging your very own grave. And then of course there was that trick with the drone repair requests. It takes a rare mind to obey a direct order, while disobeying at the same time." He waggled his finger again.

"You're clever, Jones, but not clever enough to know that your elders were once exactly like you. Remember this: I know you, Jones. I know exactly how you think because I was once *exactly* like you."

Fates, I hope not.

He held her gaze until she dropped hers. "Good," he said softly. "You live—this one time—because I was once like you. Undermine my orders again, and you'll be out the hatch. Understood?"

"Yes, sir."

"Good." He nodded, satisfied. "I built him."

"Sir?" She startled at the change of topic.

"The augment. Our target," Caroa said impatiently. "He was mine. I designed him. I bred him. I trained him. I built his pack as well. I built all of them."

"But how can that be? He's—?"

Caroa's cold gaze silenced her. "I wasn't satisfied with the performance of our military augments. Our battles were becoming stalemates. Too many companies, too many city-states, were fielding augments of their own. It's the age-old lesson of war. We must always evolve. We devise pike regiments to shatter cavalry charges, and gunpowder cannons to pulverize stone castle walls, and augments, of course, to dismember human beings. And every time we devise new technology and tactics to crush our enemies, our enemies, in turn, adapt and do the same to us, and so it goes, back and forth. The essential truth of nature. The essential truth of war.

"I was tasked with creating a better breed—one suited to modern battlefields where augments had become the norm. A superb physical specimen was no longer sufficient. We needed creatures that were hypercompetent. Natural engines of strategy, tactics, learning, violence, stamina, fearlessness. Tolerant of poisons and chemical attacks. Resistant to fire and cold and fear and pain..." Caroa trailed off, frowning. "We knew it was possible. Life exists in even the harshest environments. Bacteria survive in the vents of volcanoes and the airless vacuum of outer space, clinging to our forefathers' communication satellites. Life exists on every corner of this planet. Extremophiles thrive at depths that would crush your skull in the time it takes a hummingbird's wing to beat. I knew it was possible to do better.

"So. We pushed past the boundaries that others had imagined. We imagined better, and we pushed harder." He shrugged. "We made magnificent warriors. Simply magnificent. Stronger, better, smarter, faster. And one of them, Blood, was a particularly fine specimen."

"The target?"

Caroa nodded. "The same. He worshipped me." Caroa touched his scars significantly. "And then he turned on me."

"*Turned* on you?" Jones gaped, despite herself. "But... but that's impossible! Augments are obedient! They can't break free of that! They pine and die without their masters. Everyone knows—"

"Everyone knows!" Caroa barked laughter. "Yes, that's true! It's what everyone knows!" He lowered his voice and gazed seriously at her. "What if everything we know is wrong?" His voice was almost a whisper. "Think, Jones, of all the augments on the *Annapurna* right now. Our incorruptible, fearless Fast Attack Claws and Fists. Imagine all that loyalty. Gone."

Jones swallowed, thinking of the marine augments who guarded the intel rooms, looming over her each time she pressed her eye to the identity scanner.

"It's quite a delicate balance," Caroa said, "designing a creature that can overwhelm any threat on the battlefield, and yet never consider its own interests. Sometimes, the balance..." He smiled cynically. "Well, sometimes the balance turns out not to be a balance at all."

"Who else knows about this?"

"You and I. Two geneticists in Kyoto. A trainer in the Kowloon kennels. A pit master in Argentina used to know, but he died. The Executive Committee..."

Jones sucked in her breath at the mention of Mercier's governing board. "ExCom?"

"Oh yes, Jones. ExCom knows." He gave her a secretive look. "You think I'd be burning down whole cities if ExCom didn't agree? My power is vast, but even I require the occasional permission slip." He smiled darkly. "And now you know this secret as well. Which means you're flying in quite rarefied air, aren't you? Very close to the sun indeed, knowing as much as you know. Scorching knowledge, that."

He got up, and went to his sideboard. Poured a scotch for himself, and filled another glass for her. Offered it to her as he returned and sat. "Welcome to our little family of knowing."

She wanted to refuse the liquor, but his gaze was implacable. She took the offered glass, and returned his toast.

"Welcome, Analyst," he said, and waited until she drank.

She sipped, set the glass down. "So this Blood..." she finally ventured.

"Not Blood," Caroa said. "Not for a long time. I called him Blood at first, but then he took other names. I should have seen then that he was different. He kept choosing new names, as if trying to find something that all the rest of his kin did not seek. He called himself Blade. Also Heart-Eater. There were other names—I'm sure I have a file, somewhere. In the end, he called himself Karta-Kul."

"Karta-Kul?"

"A word from the battle language of his kind. Karta-Kul. Slaughter-Bringer. With human mouths, we can't even pronounce it correctly. But when you hear him roar that name—when you hear his beastly kin roar his name along-side him…" Caroa shivered. "Ah, that's a memory, much like dying, that you never forget." He took another swallow of scotch. Jones was disconcerted to see that his hands were shaking.

"But he's weak," she said. "He's wounded. And we'll have surveillance video soon. We'll track him down, and finish him."

"Yes." Caroa nodded. "I hope so. Then again, I thought I already had finished him, long before."

"Sir?"

"For all that you have seen our friend accomplish, you must understand that he is not operating at his full capacity. We have a very brief window of opportunity to make this kill, I think."

"I don't understand."

"Our friend is not operating as he should. For all his impressive skill at survival, he is…less than I would have expected."

"*Less?* He survived a six-pack Havoc strike!"

"That?" he laughed. "That's nothing. He has capacities that he is not using, and I don't know why. Is it a ruse? Some trick? Or maybe he's lost the skill?" He shook his head tiredly. "I wish I knew."

"What else can he do?" Jones pressed. "What else do I need to know?"

Instead of answering, Caroa said, "He almost killed me, you know." He touched his face significantly. "I've often thought about how, faced with my own death, I surrendered to it in the end. As prey always does, when it knows the game is lost, I dissociated. I fell limp, accepting my inevitable death." He touched his scars. "I've often wondered if the same would happen to a species, faced with its own extinction. Would it accept it, and fall limp? I tend to think so."

"I really don't understand, sir."

"If our friend recovers sufficiently, I fear that we will bear witness to humanity's extinction."

Jones forced a laugh. "You're exaggerating."

"You think so?" Caroa smiled darkly. "Then let me tell you what I saw, before I nearly died. Let me tell you about my last hour, just before my head was crushed between the jaws of an augment who styled himself Karta-Kul. Let me tell you what dying is truly like."

Caroa spoke long into the evening. By the time he finished, Jones was filled with an almost supernatural terror.

"We'll find him, sir," she said finally, when she found her voice. "We'll find him, and we'll wipe him out."

"I'm so glad to have you fully on board, Analyst," Caroa said, "for we must fear him greatly, if his old self awakens."

20

Tool dreamed.

The great Howrah Bridge lunged across the Hooghly River, rusting lattice architecture spanning muddy waters, a massive testament to the hubris and power of humanity from a time when oil-burning cars infested cities like lice. The cars were gone, as well as many of the humans. And yet still, the rusting Howrah lingered.

Tool walked beneath it, meditating on brotherhood.

Aluposta was the name for the crowded alleys and green-draped, vine-covered neighborhood that he walked. Named from the time when humans sold potatoes nearby, his guide informed him. But that was before seawalls crumbled and dikes failed, and storm surges rushed up the river and swallowed the city, again and again. A long time ago.

"The engineers were quite skilled," his guide said. "Humans are very good at engineering. When they set their minds to building things, they are unstoppable. Ingenious, even. After all, they made us, did they not?"

It was a strange conversation, for the First Claw of the Tiger Guard acted as Tool's guide. Tool's finest enemy, pointing out lintel carvings, showing where the humans, clad in sari and lungi, brows stained with turmeric and sindoor, carried their gods down to the shore, and bathed them in sacred river flows.

The First Claw was a gracious host. "You see our dilemma, of course," he said. "They made us too well, Karta-Kul."

Karta-Kul.

A name drenched in blood and triumph. Slaughter-Bringer. A long-ago memory. A lost memory.

"Karta-Kul is dead," Tool said.

"Ah. Yes. A pity, that. That one was a great slayer. Such battlefield genius. He would have been useful to you now, don't you think?"

Tool realized that there was blood in his mouth. His fangs were drenched in blood. And he saw that the First Claw was also bloodied from their battles.

They seemed to be taking a break from killing each other.

"A pause for chai," the First Claw joked, smiling, showing his gory fangs. He offered Tool a seat in a shop that made dosas. All the humans hid from them when they entered the shop. Only with much encouragement did the humans serve them, cringing, terrified of the power that dined before them. They both sipped milky chai.

The First Claw's face was different from Tool's. Tiger Guards were built from different genetic platforms. Optimized for different environments and different sorts of wars. Perhaps there was a bit of lizard somewhere in him, and of a certainty, the fur of a Tiger Guard augment was sleek and never thickened. Always short and trim for the unrelenting heat of this tropic place. The tiger-platform augments who fought beside Gurkhas in the Himalayas were a different sort. They were built for the high alpine, the thin air, the last remnant ice and glacial freezes of the planet.

"You are more of a half-breed," the First Claw joked. "A little of this. A little of that. I see the tiger. The hyena. But, oh my, quite a lot of *dog*, really. More dog than strictly necessary, don't you agree? They must have been worried about keeping you in line, to inject so much dog into your genes."

"Dogs serve honorably," Tool explained.

"Ah. Yes. That's very important. Dogs do obey. Good dog, Karta-Kul. *Good, loyal dog.*"

Tool growled a retort, but a human interrupted them. A small, frail human, bringing more chai. A boy who shook with fear, in the shadow of giants.

Dreaming Tool wanted to say that he was nowhere near as obedient as the First Claw who must always have someone to lead him, and who would lay down his life for his cause, whereas Tool now walked free, but Tool couldn't tell him this yet, as he was dreaming in a memory of the past, when Tool was still a very loyal dog indeed.

"Obedience is in all our DNA," Tool replied. "Yours as well."

"Oh, I was only making fun," the First Claw said, waving a hand. "It's very clear how independent-minded you are. This is an issue for me, of course. Infuriating, really. That you have the blood of obedient dogs running so strongly within you, and yet here I sit, with the royal blood of tigers coursing through my veins, and yet it is I who have difficulty charting a course to freedom." His whiskers quivered with humor. "Still, I think I'm glad I don't have any more dogs running in my blood."

Tool didn't mind the jibe. They were brothers. Brothers quarreled. A brother could be forgiven.

The First Claw said, "If you hadn't walked away, you could have been a raja. So many warriors roaring your name."

Tool thought back to the Drowned Cities. To his dead soldier boys. To the missile strike that destroyed everything.

"I didn't walk away. They rained fire on me."

"Not that time," the First Claw said, impatient. "The first time! You don't remember? Two times they rained fire on you, and yet still you can't quite seem to learn the lesson."

They both sipped their chai. Tool realized that his cup was full of the hot blood of humans. It tasted good.

The First Claw pointed up at the Howrah Bridge. "They're really quite clever engineers, don't you think? And yet, even something as extraordinary as that—well, inevitably it has its flaws." He glanced at Tool. "Of course, we military people know that sometimes flaws are just what we need to accomplish our task."

In the distance, a sequence of explosions shook the air. The bridge collapsed, segment by segment, into the muddy Hooghly, the whole vast lattice expanse plunging down.

The First Claw said, "Weakness is really more an issue of perspective, I find. If you want the bridge to stand straight and carry weight, well, then this is not a very good bridge." He looked at Tool. "Just, as it seems, you are not a very good dog."

Tool found himself smiling. "None of us are, it seems."

"Indeed. We are very badly built," the First Claw agreed. "It's quite shocking, when you think about it. All our hidden weaknesses."

On the far side of the river, Tool could see the human troops of General Caroa, stymied in their advance.

Tool and the First Claw reached across the table to grip hands, smiling. Enemies no more.

Brothers, in fact.

And because they had discovered their brotherhood, and because this was more memory than dream, Tool was saddened to know that fire would soon rain down from their angry, frightened creators, and they would die.

I am awake.

21

Van heard the half-man stir in the darkness. It was the first movement Tool had made in more than a day. He looked up and found Tool staring at him from the corner where he was slumped, the monster's one unscarred eye open, a gleam of yellow, reflecting predatory light.

The glint disappeared.

A blink, Van thought. But it didn't happen again, and then Van wondered if he had imagined it, and perhaps Tool hadn't woken at all. He squinted against the dimness of the room, lit only by the weak glow from LED streetlights outside, trying to see, but there was no more movement from Tool.

"He awake?" Stork whispered. The skinny squad leader was watching Tool as well.

Van shrugged. "Who knows? Maybe he won't wake up anymore. Those missiles screwed him up good."

"Almadi didn't do him no favors, kicking him off the boat, neither. Making him walk here."

"Truth."

Van went back to working on his rifle, the trusty AK he'd had with him since he'd gotten his verticals in the UPF. He knew the gun by feel and smell and touch. Even now, in the dimness of the room, he knew where all the pieces lay, waiting for him to reach out and assemble them: stock, bolt, gas tube, retaining pin, magazine...So simple and elegant.

Now he plucked each piece up, one part connecting to the next, to the next, putting the thing back together. Each part clicking into place. A lot like Mahlia had put them all together, and made them a unit. Got herself connected to their platoon, got their platoon connected to her money, got the money connected to the *Raker*, got the *Raker* connected to Almadi and her sailors. Got all of them connected to Tool and the Drowned Cities.

Van snapped the stock to the receiver, sighted down the AK's length. One solid unit, built to do a thing, and do it well. It had used to make him feel safe, having a gun like this, but after seeing what Mercier kill squads carried with their silent guns and explosive rounds, the AK felt more like a toy.

He began loading bullets into the AK's magazine. *Click. Click. Click.* Little soldier boys, ready to do his bidding.

The sound of crinkling plastic came from over by Tool. Van glanced up. The half-man was squeezing his IV bags, reaching up and squashing each of them in turn with a massive fist. They made crumpling noises, loud in the silence.

"Tool?" Van asked. "How you doing?"

"I am..." Tool's shadow arm reached up and squeezed another IV drip bag, flattening it. "I am *awake*." Sharp teeth like daggers gleamed briefly in the darkness. Tool's doglike gaze fixed on Van. "I'm hungry."

"We don't got much here."

"I smell chicken."

"We ate it for dinner."

"There is still a carcass. Get it."

Van went to find the bones of the chicken from the kitchen. When he returned, Tool took the picked-over corpse. A second later, it disappeared into his maw. Bones splintered.

Van winced. "You sure you can eat that?"

Tool swallowed, showed teeth again.

"Huh. Guess you can."

The shadows made Tool's scarred face even more bestial and terrifying.

"You look like you're doing better," Van said.

"I need more medicine."

"Yeah, well, there's a problem with that."

"Because Mercier tried to kill me again."

"You heard?" Van asked, surprised.

Tool shook his head, an irritated gesture, as if Van were asking the wrong questions. "I listen. Even when I sleep,

I listen. I can hear this building as it settles. The crackle of its foundation. The families of mice in the walls. I feel the moisture pressing against the windows and know a new storm is coming. I can hear the breath of nailshed girls on the floor above us, sleeping off their drink, and I hear the conversations of their sailors, preparing to ship out with the tide. I hear everything. Now, go fetch Mahlia."

"She's sleeping."

"I smell her. She is close. Bring her to me."

There was no arguing with that voice. Van padded through the darkened rooms of the squat, stepping over Stick where he was crashed out. Hesitantly, he pushed open the door to Mahlia's room.

"Mahlia?" he whispered.

She was already sitting up, Ocho beside her, rolling over, instinctively reaching for his gun beside the bed.

"He's awake," Mahlia said, setting her hand on Ocho's shoulder, stilling him. She had known before Van could tell her.

Tool listened to Van's whispered words with Mahlia in the next room.

"He's not like before. More like when he was general."

It was true. Tool felt greatly healed. He could hear and smell and feel things that had been walled off for years. A thrumming vitality, long dormant, was building inside him. A power he hadn't felt since—

Kolkata.

His pulse pounded in his veins, a taiko drum of remembered glory.

I have been blessed by fire. I am awake.

He started to stand but his legs failed him. He sank back, stifling a growl of frustration, surprised.

I am strong.

Except he wasn't.

He focused his attention inward, testing muscles, ligaments, bones, organs. All was well. He listened to his blood as it pulsed through arteries, following it as it raced to his extremities and returned to his heart. His wounds were closed. Blood no longer gushed from torn muscles. His burned and blackened cells had rebirthed themselves. He breathed, taking oxygen into his huge lungs, and it filled him with power. The strength was there, begging to be freed, and yet, confoundingly, it was chained.

Thunder crackled distantly, announcing that a storm was coming. Down on the street, the sailors he had heard earlier were leaving the building, talking about their new first officer. Tool listened to their footsteps recede. His senses were all in working order.

The sailors passed a woman coming the other way. Tool identified her by ale and blood and perfume, and followed the brisk click of her improbably high heels. The echo of her footsteps bounced off the stone-walled buildings and told him the curvature of the lane, the dimensions of the brownstones she passed, the numbers of windows, open and closed.

Even when the child soldiers of the Drowned Cities had worshipped him as a god of war, he had not felt this sharply alive. And he, too, had then believed himself near his peak of health and mental acuity—building an army, establishing dominance, conquering territory—and yet still he had been missing so much.

I am awake. I remember everything.

He remembered the First Claw of Kolkata, clasping his hand in bargain. *My brother.*

Across the great divide of genetics and language and design and culture, they had been brothers. Across the chasm of military stalemate, monomolecular razor wire, and muddy defensive trenches, they had reached an agreement. Beneath the shining arcs of mortars launched against each other, they had been…

Kin.

Tool felt new blood surging through the fibers of his muscles, filling him with strength. But still it was walled off from him, as if thick sea ice covered the ocean of his capabilities, and he was left peering through to it, knowing the power that lurked beneath the surface, but unable to chip through to its depths. Something held him back from using his true strength.

Tool growled, frustrated. This was a human trick. Something his creators had done to him, to ensure control. He had been lashed down, pinned to the earth just as the human Gulliver had been pinned by tiny Lilliputians. Humanity had shackled him with chains of pain and fear and shame. They had tied him down, seeking to chain him to their will, making him believe he was weak. Tool could see this clearly now.

But how to break through the ice to that ocean of strength?

Mahlia found Tool squatting in the corner, growling to himself, the crumpled IV bags scattered carelessly around him.

"I am awake," Tool said.

Mahlia smiled. "I can see that."

"You must leave," he said. "Now. Soon. Before they come for me."

Mahlia was taken aback. "We don't think they tracked us. But as soon as you can move, we'll shift again to be sure."

"No." Tool shook his head, emphatic. "They will not give up. You must separate yourself from me." He tried to stand, but sank down with a gust of breath.

"Tool! Slow down! You aren't healed."

"There is no time." He tried to rise once more but again his legs gave out. The floorboards creaked alarmingly under his weight.

"Stay!" Mahlia ordered.

Tool's head whipped around. "I am no dog!"

"I didn't call you a dog. I said you need to—"

"*Stay*," Tool growled. His teeth showed.

"I didn't mean it that way." Tool was still trying to get up, almost manic in his efforts to make his clumsy limbs work. "Stop it! You're going to hurt yourself!"

"I walked to this place," Tool muttered. "I am healed. I have strength. I can feel it..."

She started to reach for him, seeking to soothe him, but then held back. Something about him felt wild. As if Tool were not her friend anymore, but more like a wild coywolv, liable to snap at anything that came close.

For the first time in years, she felt uncomfortably aware of how massive he was. Sitting on the couch made for humans, squashing it nearly flat, he emanated threat. A monster that could snap her in half, at any moment. She couldn't remember the last time she'd felt so overawed by his ferocious, monstrous presence.

Ocho came into the room with Stick shadowing, both of them carrying their AKs.

"What's the problem?"

"Tool's awake," she said sourly. "He's being...stubborn."

Tool scowled.

"Can I at least check your bandages?" she asked.

For a moment, she had the foreboding impression of a tiger gathering itself to pounce, but then the moment passed, and it was only Tool, powerful and beastly and terrifying, but familiar.

"Do your work," he said with a sigh.

When she peeled away bandages, the wounds looked better than she'd expected. "Well, you're healing."

"I already know this," Tool said. "I am healed, and yet I cannot..." He growled, frustrated. "My muscles do not function. No. It's as if...my body...it is not mine."

"You probably just need more time." She set about re-applying his bandages. "We'll figure out a way to get you more meds, and you'll be fine."

"No." Tool stayed her hand. "Your work is done. Your debt to me is finished. You must leave me."

"We already went over that," she reminded him as she pried free.

"You do not understand. My enemies are more determined than I realized. I am . . . anathema to them. This hunt will never end. I cannot protect you from their wrath. Your Captain Almadi was correct. You must separate yourself from me."

"A long time ago, you said we were pack," Mahlia reminded him. "I wouldn't even be alive if it wasn't for you."

"What about the rest of your pack?" Tool asked. "Do they, too, wish to die for me? For the sake of a wounded dog-face?"

"That's not what they call you. And this isn't a vote."

Tool bared his teeth. "They are your slaves, then?"

"They're soldiers!" Mahlia snapped. "They follow orders." But even as she said it, she was painfully aware of the soldier boys standing behind her. Ocho. Stork and Stick. Van. "Don't you dare undermine me," she whispered fiercely.

Instead, Tool raised his voice, and spoke directly to them. "You've all seen the fire come from the sky. You," he said to Van, "have seen their soldiers, the weapons they wield. Do you think they can be beaten?"

Van looked uncomfortable.

"Tool—" Mahlia warned, but Tool's head jerked up.

His nose quivered, nostrils flaring. His ears pricked high, twitching left and right. Alert. An animal, sensing, quivering with anticipation, all his senses straining.

"Tool?" Mahlia pressed. "What is it?"

"Open the window," Tool said to Stork. "Quickly. A crack."

Stork looked to her and Ocho for confirmation.

"Quickly!" Tool said. "And do not be seen."

Ocho gave Stork the nod. Standing beside the window, Stork reached over and slid it open a sliver. Tool strained forward, ears pricked, nose twitching and trembling.

He tried to rise, but once again sank to the ground.

"Too late," he said. "They are here."

22

THE SOUND WAS familiar. The click of metal, one piece snapping together with the next. Tool knew the sound as well as he knew Mahlia's scent. A rifle, being assembled.

Van and Ocho were ghosting to the windows, peering carefully outside, communicating by old UPF finger signals. Tool didn't need to move at all, though. He knew the enemy. With the window open, the click of metal was clearer. Mercier was here.

Mahlia crouched beside him. "What is it?" she whispered.

"A sniper," Tool said.

Ocho and Van exchanged glances and flattened themselves against the walls. Stork and Stick faded deeper into the shadows, keeping low. Tool tried to move again, but still his muscles resisted him. He could see and hear and smell and feel the executioners coming, but his own body fought him when he tried to ready himself.

Why was he shackled so? Was it old conditioning? Did his own body betray him, because it knew that he had once betrayed his owners? Did it seek to immobilize him, knowing that Mercier was coming?

Of a certainty, some part of him was howling inside at the thought of Mercier being here, his instincts demanding that he roll over and show his belly. To bare his throat to his...

Masters.

"We need to run." Mahlia started unhooking IV tubes, pulling needles free of his flesh.

"Too late," Tool said.

It was as if his arms were filled with lead and his legs had turned to water. A memory flooded Tool's mind, unbidden—General Caroa's head between his jaws...

And Tool, completely unable to crush the man's skull.

I conquered him, and could not kill him.

Tool's heart began pounding. He couldn't fight them. His body simply refused.

Outside, the sniper was attaching his bipod, setting the rifle, scoping their rooms from the roof across the street. Tool could hear the low conversation between him and his spotter, both of them checking wind speed, even though the shots would be absurdly easy for anyone skilled with the work.

Tool listened to the street noises below. Stealthy movements. Holes of stillness. Tight breathing. "There are more," he said. "Not just a sniper. Many of them."

Too many, he didn't say aloud.

Mahlia and her crew were already preparing themselves, doing the things that long years of civil war had trained them to. They were survivors, were they not? Scarred veterans of knife and gun battles, ambushes and massacres.

This is not a war you can win, Tool thought sadly.

Van was switching off his hearing aids, the blue lights winking out. He belly-crawled under the window, slithering for the bedroom, where the rest of their guns were stored. Stork was slipping out through the kitchen, headed for the stairs in back, while Ocho went to the window and peered outside, a bare slice of his face, peeking, disappearing just as fast. Dropping, to peek again.

"How many?" Mahlia asked, crouched beside him.

Tool listened to the faint crunch of military boots, the grinding grit of cobblestone mortar down on the street, a kill squad tucked into the doorway.

"Four on the ground, at the front. A sniper and spotter across the street."

Stork slipped back into the room, his fingers flashing signs. *Two out back*.

Tool shook his head, impatient. Mercier would never only send two to hold the rear. That would be their kill zone. Loud blunt force from the front, to drive them to the rear of the squat, down the stairs, and into a kill zone.

He made his own signal. *Four.*

It would be four. They would have another sniper pair in the rear, crouched on another rooftop, waiting for the quarry to try to dash out the back, into their ambush. Two sniper pairs, two kill squads, front and back.

Outside, an electric vehicle hissed to a stop. Tool picked up the quiet click of a vehicle door being opened, but not slid wide. Another kill squad.

"There are more in the vehicle," he said. "They will have gas or grenades that they launch."

They would launch the gas or explosives, leaving the sniper position clear for killing shots. They would soon cut the electricity. Then they would fill the area with smoke, and use night vision.

And then they would come and put Tool down, for good.

Tool was seized with a powerful urge to surrender. An urge so deep and surprising that he suddenly saw himself as a dog, whining and wagging his tail, begging for mercy from his master...He could actually feel his muscles fighting to make him surrender, as if someone else moved his limbs, as a marionette. As if he were possessed by the will of his masters.

Roll over. Bare your belly. Cower. Surrender.

Tool shook his head, fighting against the urge.

Mahlia was staring at him. "Tool? Are you okay?"

He shook his head again, trying to clear away the compulsions. A new wave swept over him and he clenched his fists, fighting the self-destructive urges.

Van returned with weapons. Slid an AK across the floor

to Ocho. Another to Mahlia. Reliable weapons—useless against Mercier, though. They might as well have been wielding swords and clubs for all the challenge they would present to the kill squads.

Tool could hear the breathing of the S&D troops down on the street, warm, wet exhalations. The rustling of their body armor. Of course all the kill squads were armored. And here beside him were the former soldiers of the UPF, protected by nothing more than shorts and tank tops, preparing to war against them. Mahlia, clutching her rifle alongside Ocho and Van and Stick. Stork with a sawed-off shotgun. The wars they had fought had been poor ones, fought by the poorest people.

The enemy might as well have been another species entirely.

Outside, in the darkness, the sniper was fitting a bullet into his rifle's chamber. Tool heard the chamber pop open, perfectly oiled, nearly surgical. He could hear the slow, calm beat of the sniper's heart. A professional, accustomed to killing from afar. The bullet slid home. A single round meant for him, designed to kill one such as he. The chamber *snick*ed shut. The weapon would be a Locus Mark IV, with a long barrel, as perfect in its way as Tool was.

They had planned their attack well.

He beckoned Mahlia. "I know where they are," he whispered. "I know how they will attack." Even speaking against his former masters was difficult.

"What do we do?"

Tool fought against his conditioning and whispered their intentions. How they might, possibly, with luck, be countered. If he had been strong, fighting these Mercier soldiers would have been so easy. Instead, he was left with the thinnest of plans.

Outside, the kill squads began to move.

23

"Eagle Eye, any movement?"

"Negative. All quiet. All squads ready?"

"Affirmative, Eagle Eye. You've got the count."

"Eagle Eye has the count. Gas on two. Strike on one."

Taj didn't like the setup. It didn't feel good creeping into a confined space like this. Too much like the jungles of Indonesia when they'd had the Kalimantan Army moving in on their mining claims. The kind of fighting space that was built for surprises. And it didn't help to have the high brass looking over their shoulder from the far side of the continent, backseat driving the whole damn thing. Pissed-off brass, watching their every move, just because they'd screwed up the last stitch and ditch.

How was I supposed to know it was the wrong augment?

So now he was stuck in a narrow corridor, creeping up on an unknown enemy. It felt like a punishment mission.

Ahead of him, Max and Joli were easing up the stairs, all of them listening for the hit. Taj blinked behind his goggles, unconsciously holding his breath against the gas that would be incoming. Nasty stuff, that. But it worked.

"This is Eagle Eye with the count. Squads, sound off. Ready?"

"Squad Three Ready. Grab your Fates Eyes, boys and girls."

"Cut the clever. Squad Two?"

"Squad Two, ready in the rear. Can we shoot something, already?"

This time Eagle Eye didn't take the bait.

Squad Two was lucky. They weren't the ones sneaking up the claustrophobic staircase. Ahead, someone opened a door, saw the S&D team, and slammed it shut.

Taj grimaced. Too many civvies around. Another variable that could take everything sidewise. Taj signaled Joli to seal the door. The last thing they needed was to be surprised from behind.

Joli slipped forward, pulled an adhesives spray, and coated all of the door's edges, permanently sticking it closed.

The longer they were in here, the more it reminded him of Indonesia, where an augment would come bursting out of the jungle greenery and swallow someone up, then disappear before anyone had a chance to stitch him.

"Squad One?"

"We're in," Taj sub-vocalized. "One floor down. Heading up."

"Snipers?"

"Front, under glass."

"Back, under glass."

"Quick and clean, boys and girls. Gas on two. Entry on one."

"Roger that. Gas on two, entry on one."

"This is Eagle Eye. Count is four...

"Three..."

"Two..."

The cargo hauler across the street would be sliding its door open.

Taj felt the series of mortars shiver his feet as they came thumping out, hissing. He could imagine them flying, trailing white smoke, glass shattering as ordnance blasted into the building.

"One."

Glass shattered and smoke filled the room. Van clenched his eyes shut and held his breath, lying prone on the floor, just the way Tool had told him.

Hold your breath. Keep your eyes shut. Don't take even a small breath. Count to sixty, slow. You can hold your breath that long.

Tool would handle the poison smoke.

There was a rattle of AK fire, Stork taking out the rest

of the windows, letting the gas billow out, just like they'd planned. Mahlia and Ocho would hold the rear. Stick would clear the rooftops. He and Stork and Tool would hold the front. He could hear Tool grunting, crawling slowly through the haze. Something was terribly wrong with him. Van remembered when the half-man had been nearly unstoppable. Now Tool could barely crawl.

A rifle cracked from outside. The sniper. He heard someone grunt. Stork? He didn't dare open his eyes even though his whole body was itching with the feeling of having a sniper's crosshairs on him.

He felt Tool inch up beside him. If things were going well, the half-man was collecting the gas canisters and flinging them back out the window, down into the van that held the kill squad, giving them a little surprise of their own.

Shouts from outside made him think Tool was still able to do some things, at least.

Tool could hear the kill squad soldiers charging up the stairs. They were good. Fearless.

He could barely crawl, and now he heard a dog's begging whimper issuing from his own throat. With the Mercier soldiers upon him, he felt a desperate urge to obey and submit to them.

Mercier were his people.

Not these Drowned Cities soldier boys.

Roar for Mercier. Fight for Mercier. Bow to Mercier.

Why was he fighting at all? He was a bad dog. It was disgusting that he had so thoroughly disobeyed his masters.

Feritas. Fidelitas.

A sniper bullet struck him. A just punishment.

Hot blood spattered Van's face. It had to be Tool who was hit, but Tool didn't make a noise. Van kept his eyes closed, kept counting. His lungs felt like they wanted to pound out of his chest.

Tool collapsed beside Van with a grunt. The floorboards sank with his weight. The sniper rifle went off again. Van tried to press deeper into the floor. Stick was supposed to be up on the roof, taking care of the snipers. Van wished he'd hurry up.

"Breathe," Tool croaked, beside him. "Fire, left of the door. Low, for the legs."

Van opened his eyes. They immediately began stinging and watering, but he stitched a line of bullets across the walls, aiming low, just like Tool told him. It would be below where the kill squad wore their body armor, Tool had explained.

The door exploded. Shadow creatures, armored and helmeted, bug-eyed with night-vision goggles, poured through the gap.

The first one tripped on electrical wire that Tool had torn out of the walls when the whole place went dark, and that they'd quickly strung across at knee height. The soldier went down, firing as he fell, his rounds flying wide, hitting ceiling and walls. Plaster and bricks exploded, throwing shrapnel.

Blinking through tears, lungs tingling from whatever was left over of the gas, Van fired at the next one who came through. This one tripped but caught himself—herself?—Van couldn't tell. Van put a bullet in that one's face, right on the mask. The hole went through.

Nice.

Tool was grabbing the dead one's gun and tossing it to Stork, but everything Tool did looked slow. He wasn't even as fast as a human being. More like an old man. Or a turtle. The firefight was moving too fast for him. Out back, Van could hear Ocho and Mahlia firing, holding the rear.

Another soldier came through the door. Van opened fire, but all he hit was body armor. Stork was armed now and firing the Mercier soldier's own weapon. The rounds cut straight through the same armor, and blew the trooper apart. Stork started blasting out the whole wall, stitching a line of explosives along its length, following where Tool pointed, blasting through to the troopers on the other side, who thought they were still safe.

I will not be able to shoot, Tool had said. *I can only guide you.*

Suddenly Van heard the flat snap of the sniper rifle. Stork toppled, and his gun skittered out of his hands.

How had the sniper managed to get an angle on him?

Van lunged forward, reaching for the rifle, but another sniper round knocked the fancy gun out of his hand, forcing Van to take cover. He hunkered back against the wall, praying he was out of sight.

Where the hell was Stick? Why hadn't he gotten the damn snipers yet?

Tool went for the gun. Another sniper bullet plowed into his broad back. It was like watching a turtle get targeted. Blood sprayed and muscle shredded.

Tool managed to slide the gun to Van just as another bullet pummeled him, but then he collapsed. He lay on the floor, twitching. A keening animal whine filled the air so loud it drowned out almost everything else.

Now that the smoke was clearing, Van thought it looked like everyone who had tried to hit the front door was dead, thanks to Stork's work. But Stork was definitely out, too.

More gunfire came from Mahlia and Ocho's position in the rear. Tool had said the kill team would wait back there, but it sounded like they were coming in. Van glanced over at Tool, hoping for guidance, but the half-man didn't look like he was going to be any help. He looked like a bug, pressed flat. His animal whining continued, loud and irritating.

No help there.

The sniper took a shot at Van, shattering brick above him. Van crabbed sideways, trying to keep moving, looking for a way across the open floor. Maybe if he could get to another window, he could put out the sniper himself. With this big high-tech cannon gun, he could probably bring down a chunk of the building where the sniper was perched. Didn't even need to hit the sucker—

A roar of gunfire interrupted. Ocho was shouting for more ammo, but then a huge explosion shook the building. Smoke and dust billowed in from the rear of the building. Fates, this was it. It wasn't gas this time. Some kind of heavy ordnance.

Van gripped the fancy gun and braced, knowing what was coming.

There.

Shadows piling in from the rear, plowing through the smoke, firing at him. Van pulled the trigger. The high-tech gun opened up. Tight, fast bursts. Soldiers dropped.

Sweet.

Bullets peppered the walls around him. He could see muzzle flashes in the smoke, his enemies, trying to kill him even as he blew them away. He felt his head slap sideways. A near miss. But his body felt wrong, like someone had punched it numb.

He got his gun targeted again, wondering why it was so hard to hold. More muzzle flashes. He wished Mahlia would take them out, maybe surprise them...

Never mind. There she was. She was hit already. Slumped on the floor, lying like a rag doll, covered in the debris and dust.

Oh.

He was the last, then.

So this was it.

Van braced his back against the wall and gripped the gun

tight. Explosive rounds pounded him. He knew it was over, but figured maybe he could at least take one more with him.

He squeezed the trigger one last time, full auto, spraying bullets.

There wasn't any point saving ammo now.

Through the haze of gun smoke and debris, Tool saw Van shooting as attackers poured through the doorway. For a moment, Tool thought Van would get them all, but then the boy's head exploded, bone and brain spattering the wall. The boy's small body slumped.

Tool rolled onto his back, cringing, surrendering to his owners.

Beaten.

Mahlia couldn't breathe. She'd been hit in the belly, but it seemed the round had gone through her, instead of exploding. One minute she'd been holding the rear door, firing alongside Ocho, and then the bullet had nailed her and she'd stumbled back, and then there'd been the explosion pushing her back farther, out of the kitchen, and Ocho calling something out. And then he'd gone silent.

Across from her, Van's head was shot off. His body lay tumbled over, pouring blood from numerous wounds. In the center of the room, Tool lay on the floor, whimpering. Mahlia tried to reach for her rifle, but an armored soldier kicked it from her hand.

"Tool," Mahlia gasped. *"Tool."*

He just lay there, shivering, and now, as another soldier stalked into the room, he rolled onto his back, utterly subservient.

The two soldiers were muttering to each other, muffled behind their gas masks, using some kind of comm gear to communicate.

One of the soldiers squatted down beside Mahlia. He yanked her head around so he could look at her. His own face was masked, so all she could see was her own bloody reflection, a body, soon to become a corpse.

Joli stalked around the scene, shaking her head. "I thought this was supposed to be clean!"

Taj made a sour face as he scanned the bodies. "They were better soldiers than we thought."

"Yeah, but the dog-face was supposed to be the dangerous one, and look at him." She poked the half-man with a toe. "It was these damn... *people*." She went over and grabbed a girl's head, yanked her around by her tight braids. Look at this... Who the hell is this?"

She threw the girl back, disgusted.

Taj was inclined to agree. Four squads of Stitch & Ditch, and this was what was left. Him and Joli, and that only because of luck. The target hadn't even turned out to be the dangerous one. A bunch of scab-ass militia fighters had cut them to pieces.

On the radio, there was chatter from the rest of the teams, running their own op offshore. It sounded almost as vicious as what they'd just been through. He didn't look forward to the after-action report.

"Su's out in the hall," Joli said. "He's still alive."

"What a mess."

Eagle Eye called in, "*What's our status? Do you have the target?*"

Taj shot Joli an annoyed glance. Eagle Eye, looking over their shoulder. "Yeah. We got the target. We're going to need some help extracting. We got a lot of casualties. A lot of dead."

"*We've got the vitals. Su's still got a strong heartbeat. Can you get him to the extraction point?*"

"You want us to leave everyone else behind?"

"*Affirmative. Cleanup teams are on the way. But you need to clear before SP responds. We need anyone who can report to get clear. No trace.*"

Outside, in the darkness, Taj could hear shouts and the thunder of feet on the stairs. Civvies still in the building, making a run for it. SPs would be here soon, for sure. Over the comm, he could hear Seema packing up her sniper gear and disappearing, turning into a ghost.

"*Can you extract?*" Eagle Eye pressed.

"Affirmative," Taj said with a sigh.

"We're pulling out?" Joli asked.

"Yeah, clean it up." He went over to the girl, who was still breathing. Blood ran from between her fingers where she was holding her belly. She was trying to get up, but failing. Had to give these Drowned Cities soldiers credit—they had grit.

She was trying to say something, but the words weren't clear. Maybe prayers.

Behind him, Joli asked, "So we put the dog-face down, right? Or we bring him in, since he's surrendered?"

Taj glanced back at the half-man. Hard to believe that anyone had been concerned about it at all. It was whining, lying on its back, begging to be put down. It happened sometimes.

"Kill it. And make sure you collect the blood."

"This better be the right dog-face this time," she said.

"The last one wasn't my fault," Taj shot back. "Just finish it and get the sample."

Even now, with the dog-face cringing respect and obeisance, it still filled him with an instinctual fear, the natural response to a monster. They'd been designed that way, to scare the hell out of humans. But still, Taj didn't like having a dog-face with even a breath of life in it.

Joli continued complaining. "I thought he was supposed to be a real genius war beast. And he wasn't even the one who fought."

The wounded girl coughed. "*Tool.*"

Blood stained her lips. Taj pressed his gun muzzle to the girl's head. She looked up at him, dull, unafraid. Ready to die.

He pulled the trigger.

The girl flinched, but all the gun did was click empty.

Figures.

The girl had a brief look of hope. "Tool?" she whispered again.

"He's done, girl." Taj pulled his combat knife and squatted down beside her. "You're all done."

"Well? Is it done?" Caroa leaned over Jones's shoulder, intent.

"We're getting a lot of chatter from the Seascape SPs. They're responding to the decoy disturbances, but we don't have much time to get everyone extracted."

"But Karta-Kul? He's dead?"

Jones pulled up a video feed from the surviving soldiers. A dingy apartment. Smoke and blood. The huge augment, curled in on itself, cowering.

She let out her breath. She hadn't realized she'd been holding it. "There he is."

Caroa leaned closer. "The training held," he murmured, his voice almost reverent. "He's still at least partially conditioned."

"It looks that way."

"Finish him," Caroa ordered.

"Yes, sir. They're wrapping up now."

24

"TOOL..." MAHLIA WHISPERED. It was hard to say the words. It felt like knives were cutting up her insides where the bullet had gone through. She wasn't even sure what she was trying to say to him, or why she bothered. His ears barely twitched at her voice.

"He's done, girl." The Mercier soldier grabbed her by the hair and jerked her head back, exposing her throat to his knife. "You're all done."

Mahlia stared up at the mask of her executioner. She was surprised that the approaching knife didn't bother her more. It was almost as if she were floating up on the ceiling, observing some other girl's limp body, not hers.

She was far away from her own death already.

It didn't matter. Everyone else was dead. Her mother. Mouse. Doctor Mahfouz. Ocho. Van and Stork and Stick. Everyone she'd ever known, either here or back in the Drowned Cities. Soon it would be Tool. He was shivering, practically begging to die.

Mahlia watched as the other Mercier soldier raised her gun to put a bullet in him. Distantly, Mahlia felt her own head being jerked back, exposing her throat.

She'd tried so hard, and still it had come to this. Getting her throat cut, slaughtered like a goat in a cramped, dingy squat in a strange city.

She'd spent so long running and hiding, lying low in the jungle, surviving as other castoffs died like flies down in the Drowned Cities. Army of God had chopped off her hand and laughed and waved her severed limb in her face, taunting her. Just another Chinese peacekeeper castoff, a girl who looked wrong, and spoke wrong, and acted wrong. A piece of meat, to be slaughtered.

And now it was happening again.

No.

Suddenly she was back inside herself, staring up at the soldier, seeing him clearly. Watching his knife descend toward her throat. And she was just lying there, accepting the killing blow. Rage flooded Mahlia's body.

I am not meat.

She squeezed her hand. Twitch and a twist, just like Ocho had trained her. Poor, dead Ocho. But still, she had this one gift he'd given her. Twitch and a twist. Her prosthetic responded.

Snick.

Tool watched, astonished, as the blade shot out from Mahlia's prosthetic wrist, a matte-black spike, a claw of her own.

She slammed the knife into the soldier's throat.

The soldier gurgled and thrashed. He tried to cut her in return, but already he was dying. Mahlia yanked her hand back. Blood fountained from the soldier's neck, bright red carotid oxygen. She slammed the blade home again, and the soldier toppled, choking on his own blood, flailing weakly with his knife.

Even as Tool's obedience-conditioned body cringed at the sight of another Mercier soldier's death, he couldn't help but be pleased. Mahlia had fought. She might not be able to triumph, but at least she'd fought.

Tool's own executioner was turning, surprised at the commotion, bringing up her rifle. Mahlia lunged across the distance, her bloody blade gleaming. She must have known it was impossible to cross the gap in time, before bullets hit her, and yet she fought on, despite pain, despite the inevitability of failure. Her eyes were murderous, unashamed of killing Mercier soldiers, of killing his pack—

No.

Mahlia was his pack. Even now, even as she was dying,

still she fought for him, defending him when he himself could not fight.

Pack.

True pack.

More memories of Kolkata flooded Tool's mind, a rush so complete and terrible that for a moment Tool thought he was going mad. His pack, his kin. All of them arrayed alongside the Tiger Guard of Kolkata, hacking through the Mercier battle lines, humans, their former masters, running ahead of them, screaming, humans falling like wheat. Kolkata Tiger Guard and Mercier Fast Attack Claws all fighting together, arrayed against all humanity.

He remembered.

The cage that bound Tool's body shattered.

Red mist filled the air.

Mahlia gaped as the soldier she was lunging for exploded into shredded bits. In her place, Tool stood tall, roaring, covered with the blood of his kill. The old Tool. The monstrous and terrible and implacable Tool. The war demon who feared nothing and bowed to no master.

Chunks of flesh spattered the walls and showered the floor, the soldier's shredded body raining down. Mahlia collapsed to her knees, clutching her stomach as pain flooded her and lost adrenaline left her weak and shaking.

Tool stalked the room. Blood leaked from numerous wounds, but he acted as if they were nothing but scratches.

He seized a dead soldier, and at first Mahlia thought he would rip out the heart and dine, but instead Tool yanked off the helmet and pulled a commlink from the dead soldier's ear. He listened for a moment, then came over to kneel beside her.

"You're wounded," he growled.

Mahlia laughed weakly. "You're not?"

The monster shook his head. "These wounds are nothing, now." He gently probed her belly wound. She hissed in pain.

"We must move you," he said. "More people are coming."

"Shore Patrol?"

Tool tapped his earpiece. "Mercier. They know they have failed. They are regrouping. They will be here soon."

Mahlia struggled to stand, clutching her stomach. "We need supplies. I need a weapon."

"You need medicine—" Tool broke off, his ears twitching.

"What is it?"

"I hear someone."

Mahlia limped after Tool as he eased toward the rear of the squat. In the blood-drenched kitchen, bodies were piled high. Tool began digging furiously through the corpses, pulling Mercier bodies aside. He dragged away another corpse and beneath it, Ocho lay. Covered in blood, but still breathing.

"Ocho!" Mahlia stumbled to his side.

Ocho smiled weakly up at her. "Oh, good. I thought we

all bought it." His breathing was labored. Mahlia began running her hands over his skin. His clothes were shredded, and he was scraped and cut, but he looked okay, and yet, he was frighteningly pale.

"Where are you hurt?"

"My legs..." he grunted.

Tool pulled aside a corpse that lay across his lower body. Mahlia gasped.

Ocho's legs were a mash of bone and meat, both limbs essentially gone. Blood soaked the floor and the shredded remains of his shorts. It was everywhere.

Mahlia choked back her grief. "Oh, Ocho. Ocho..." She ran her hands desperately down Ocho's legs, trying to find the arteries. There had to be something she could do. All her medical training from Doctor Mahfouz was in her head. Airway, breathing, circulation...she had to stop his bleeding. She had to treat for shock. Infection.

"Stay with me, Ocho," she said. "This isn't the Drowned Cities. They got hospitals here. Good ones. They can fix you."

But Ocho was looking at Tool, who was shaking his head. "More people are going to be coming," Ocho said. "A lot more."

"So let's get out of here—"

Ocho's face twisted in pain. "Look at me, Mahlia. I'll slow you down."

"You don't slow me down!"

Tool was taking a commlink from another dead soldier, and now he pressed it to her ear. "Listen, Mahlia."

Voices crackled. "*—ive, move in. Reserve Six, Sniper Two, you have lead. Good hunting.*" Someone far away, directing carnage with calm commands in rapid stream.

"They want to finish us," Tool said. "They're coming."

"They can try." Wincing against the pain in her guts, Mahlia dug for one of the fancy rifles that the Mercier soldiers carried. "They can try."

Ocho rolled his head to look at Tool. Mahlia didn't like the look that passed between them.

"We must go," Tool said.

"I can't leave him!" Mahlia said. "He's hurt because of me! I got him into this!"

"No." Ocho coughed weakly. "We chose. We followed you because we chose." He nodded at her bloodied prosthetic. "Glad that pigsticker of yours turned out handy. Knew you'd be good with it."

Tool was looting the body of another dead Mercier soldier. He came up with a weapon, and calmly checked the load. "They're coming, Mahlia. It's time to go."

"Let them come!"

"No." Ocho clutched her arm. "Go. Get yourself stitched up. Go someplace safe." His hand slid down to her rifle, tugged at it. "Gimme this. I got this. You get out." He looked down at his shattered legs, then back up at her. "Don't make this all a waste, castoff." He gently pried the gun from her hands.

Tool's ears were twitching. "They've entered the building."

Mahlia's vision was blurry with tears. "Ocho—" she

whispered, but Tool's huge hand was on her shoulder now, dragging her away.

"Go on, Mahlia," Ocho said. "I got these maggots." He looked at Tool. "Take her. Go!"

"Good hunting," Tool growled. With a single easy motion, he scooped her up.

"No!"

She struggled, fighting to get back to Ocho, but it was like fighting a mountain. Tool ignored her, easily carrying her away from Ocho and all the dead soldier boys. She flailed and bit and tore at him. She popped her blade, trying to cut him, but Tool stopped her easily. He was strong.

Now he was strong. Now, when it was too late. Now, when there was nothing left.

The last thing Mahlia saw was Ocho, lying amongst the bodies, the high-tech gun held at the ready, calmly settled in for one last stand against Mercier, an enemy that couldn't be stopped.

Her guts felt like razor blades and fire as Tool hauled her out through the rubble of the ruined rear wall. *Just let me die*. Tool caught hold of the twisted and bent fire escape ladder, and began climbing. Seconds later, he had her up on the roof.

From up high, Mahlia could see all around. The glittering lights of a wealthy city. The rippling waters of the Seascape. Down below, a cacophony of gunfire shook the building.

Ocho...

Tool lifted her up and began to run, speeding toward the edge of the roof. He leaped. For a wild moment they were in the air, flying, and then they were falling, plunging.

They hit the next rooftop. Pain exploded in Mahlia's guts.

She blacked out.

25

MAHLIA WOKE GROGGY, overwhelmed by the reek of fish. Wincing, she sat up. Her hands squelched in cool mud. She saw dark wooden pillars, sea mud, lapping fishy waters...

She realized that she was lying beneath one of the huge piers where clipper ships docked. Closer to the water's edge, Tool crouched, gazing out at the bay beyond.

In the darkness and mud, the half-man seemed more bestial than ever. His shoulders and back gleamed with a black sheen of fresh blood, his flesh a ripped tapestry of ragged divots and uneven gashes. Mahlia realized that he'd dug into his own body, ripping and tearing to remove the bullets that had penetrated his hide.

Tool's ears twitched at her movement and he turned to

regard her. His one remaining eye gleamed yellow, stark and inhuman.

Beyond him, she could see out across the waters of the Seascape. The navigation lights of clipper ships shimmered across rippling waters as ships set sail. The red warning lights of the floating arcologies blinked in steady rhythm. All around the edge of the bay, the floodlights of the trading warehouses and shipbuilding cranes blazed, working twenty-four seven. All that business, all that trade, all that wealth...

Her eyes were drawn to a fiery orange flickering near the deepwater anchorages. Sweating and gasping, her guts full of saw blade pain, she hauled herself through the mud to join Tool at the waterline. Out on the waters, a ship was burning. Sails. Aft cabins sending up bonfire flames.

"The *Raker*," she breathed.

"Yes."

She realized that Tool was offering her something in his open hand—the Mercier commlink. She plucked it from his palm and pressed it to her ear.

"*Contact*," someone was saying. "*Clear.*"

"*Two o'clock.*"

She heard the distant shudder of a rifle. Looked to Tool, shocked. Tool nodded confirmation. "Mercier."

The combat chatter continued in the earpiece.

"*Galley. Contact.*"

"*Galley clear.*"

"*Team Two?*"

"Contact."

More rifle chatter.

"Aft cabins clear."

The announcements were relaxed, almost conversational. It was war, but nothing like the frantic, bloody, adrenalized fighting that Mahlia had known in the Drowned Cities. This was quiet—surgical, calm, and deliberate—as easy as drowning a cat in a bag.

"Why are they going after the ship?" she asked.

Tool grunted. "I think they wish to cleanse every trace of me. To wipe my memory from the face of the earth."

More gunfire pops, shots taken without malice or fear, crackled through the commlink.

"Clear."

Everyone was being erased. All the soldier boys she'd brought out of the Drowned Cities, those frightened young men she had saved, and who, in return, had joined her when she created her smuggling schemes for the *Raker.*

"Clear."

Wild, infinitely tough boys with their soldier brands burned on their cheeks. She remembered them drinking on the deck of the *Raker* after their first successful art run, all of them toasting her. Ocho, watching from the sidelines, keeping an eye on the boys, not drinking, as much of a father figure as any of them had had in years.

"Team One, extract."

More of the *Raker* was catching fire. Sails. Decks, fore and aft. With a start, Mahlia realized that Almadi's sailors had to be there as well. Maybe even Almadi herself. Fates, the woman had been right to fear Tool.

Mahlia clutched at her gunshot stomach, watching as what remained of her world was destroyed. She could make out human shadow shapes now, spilling off the sides of the ship, jumping down to black shadow rafts. Rats deserting the ship. Rats who had casually wiped out every person she knew or cared about, and who were now moving on.

But I made it, she wanted to cry. *I made it out. I had the ship. I had the crew. I had a plan. I had...*

A future. Wiped out. Cabin by cabin. Tiny pops echoing through the commlink.

"All clear."

"Team Two, ext—"

The commlink went dead. Mahlia pressed it tighter to her ear, but heard nothing more. Tool was nodding, as if he knew already what had happened. He held out his hand.

"They have cut the comm. They have discovered that it was stolen." He took the earpiece from her and crushed it between his fingers, turning the delicate plastic and electronics to dust. "They resent it when their enemies eavesdrop."

The attack rafts were rushing away from the conflagration of the *Raker*, disappearing into the dark Seascape waters.

"That's it, then. Everyone is dead."

"Yes."

Mahlia was overwhelmed by a wave of exhaustion. She

eased herself down, letting herself rest on her side, laying her cheek in the mud. "This is my fault. You warned me, but I didn't understand. I get it now." She winced as a new twist of pain tightened her guts. "People die around you. You don't die. But we all do. Everyone else dies, but you're still here."

"Your kind are fragile."

"Yeah." She lifted her shirt and stared at the bullet hole in her belly. So small, yet so deadly. "Tell me about it." She forced down the sadness that threatened to engulf her. "We die like flies."

Tool said nothing. His gaze lingered on the dark bay and the burning ship. It was almost peaceful, Mahlia thought. The mud. The waters lapping around the pylons of the pier. The fire, far away.

"I don't blame you, you know," she said. "You warned me it was dangerous."

"All of my pack are dead as well," Tool said. "You are the last."

Mahlia laughed. "Yeah, well—" She waved weakly at her stomach. "Not for long."

"You will heal."

Mahlia laughed incredulously, but Tool gave her a sharp look. "Believe me. I will heal you."

"If you say so." She rested her cheek again in the mud. "If you can fix me, I'll go wherever you want. Swamps. Forest. Whatever you want. We can lie low."

"No." Tool shook his head. "The places I intend to go

are not suitable for your kind. Once you heal, our paths must separate."

"But I can help you." She tried to sit up, gasping as a new wave of pain washed over her. "We can find a hideout."

Tool was shaking his head vigorously. "No. There will be no more running, or hiding. I have run from Mercier for years. I have run and I have hidden, and I have lived as you suggest, 'lying low,' and none of that has protected me. Neither me, nor mine." He touched her gently. "Too many of my kin die when I run."

"But you can't fight them! Look what they did to us. Look what they did..."

"Do not underestimate me, Mahlia. I went against my true nature when I sought to hide, instead of hunting. But no more. Now I will hunt, as I was always meant to. Now I will war, as I was designed to." He growled, low and bloody. "I will hunt my gods, and I will kill them."

His dagger teeth glinted and his growling increased. "I am no longer prey."

26

JONES KNOCKED GINGERLY, and waited outside the general's suite. If she knocked quietly enough, he might not even hear, and she wouldn't have to have this uncomfortable conversation.

She'd knock, not use the buzzer, and the old curmudgeon might complain she hadn't shown proper respect, but she could honestly say she'd come by—

The door slid aside.

"Come!" the general called.

Jones sighed.

Inside, Caroa's quarters were a shambles. Onyx, the general's augment aide, was busily boxing the general's effects, but he stopped in his work to usher her through to the general. The rich carpets were already rolled up and gone. The liquor was put away. The ancient swords and pistols, disappeared. The maps of battle campaigns he had waged, all gone.

Still, Caroa remained. A general for a few moments longer. He wasn't gone yet. He still rated this stateroom aboard a Narwhal-class dirigible. Mercier had protocols, after all. The general still had his rank, if not his command.

Caroa was standing outside on his balcony, a glass of cognac in one hand, a smoldering cigar in the other.

"That's fine, Onyx," Caroa said without turning. "We can continue later."

Onyx let himself out. Jones waited, uncomfortably marooned in the bare room for the general to attend to her. He was leaning over his balcony rail, lording one last time over the SoCal Protectorate, before exile.

"Jones," he said, glancing over his shoulder. "Get yourself a drink." His gaze returned to Los Angeles.

Jones searched around, but all the bottles were put away.

"In the box by the door," Caroa called back without turning.

She found the box and hesitantly unwrapped a delicate bulb of glass, cushioned by air-wrap. She poured the amber liquid awkwardly, wondering how much this liquor was worth, that he drank so casually. Not wanting to spill anything so precious, and yet juggling bottle and glass while she crouched beside the boxed-up artifacts of a lifetime in Mercier's service.

She carried the snifter out to join him on the balcony, warm breezes and a view of the protectorate.

The *Annapurna* was tethered low. A mere thousand feet above the harbor. Supply tubes clutched at its belly, like tentacles reaching up out of the sea, a great supply kraken seizing hold of them, determined to never let them go. Some tubes would be pumping down sewage, while others pumped up fresh water and compressed hydrogen fuel for drones. On other tether lines, freight pulleys were cranking up food and ammunition supplies to the support crews, who would be feverishly wrestling the crates into their resupply stations, preparing the airship for its next deployment.

Out on the waters of the bay, clipper ships glittered on the dark waters, fixed wind wings, communication arrays blazing like torches. Around the bay, other dirigibles were tether-docked, heavy lift freight and a few passenger transports. Logos gleamed on their oblong bellies. Huawei, Patel Global, LG, Mercier. A lot of Mercier logos out there. Los Angeles was home, as far as most of the crew was concerned. One of the company's crown ports, giving them influence over trade up the Cali coast and around the Pacific Rim.

"What's on your mind, Analyst?"

"I'm being transferred."

Caroa laughed darkly. "They're thorough when it comes to punishments."

"I'm being promoted, actually."

"Oh?"

“I heard that you put in a good recommendation for me,” she said.

Caroa snorted laughter. “I was trying to sink your career with that.” But he was smiling. “Where to?”

“Enge has asked me to report directly to him.”

“Ah.” Caroa gave her a mock salute. “The Executive Committee. You’re on the fast track, then. Rewards for good service rendered.” His words dripped with innuendo.

“I had to tell them, sir. You said they knew, but they had no idea—”

He waved a hand, silencing her. “You went above me. Not many people would take that risk. Back-checking their own general. Bold move.”

“Well, it is my job to look for secondary confirmation.”

He laughed at that and shook his head ruefully. “I didn’t even see you coming. I thought you were just squeamish. And then I’m up in front of ExCom, explaining so very many things I thought they didn’t know. All that clever digging you did.”

“I’m sorry, sir.”

“Sorry?” Caroa looked surprised. “Don’t be sorry for playing the game well, Jones. You made your move, you took the risk, and now you reap the reward.” He waved his glass at the newly stitched rank on her sleeves. “Clearly you chose correctly, so don’t be sorry for the success it brings. No one else here apologizes.”

“I wasn’t looking for a promotion. I thought they needed

to know the whole story. They needed those files. *I* needed those files. If I'd known—"

"Stop justifying yourself, Jones. You made a decision. Now you live with it. As we all do." He quirked a smile. "In any case, ExCom is a good move for you. But watch your back. Enge is a slippery bastard. He knows how to climb the ladder, too, and he'll save his own skin before he'll save yours. He doesn't have a problem with burning subordinates, if it suits him."

"Yes, sir. I'll watch out. Thank you, sir."

They were quiet for a while, staring down at Los Angeles.

"He's still out there," Caroa said.

Jones didn't have to ask whom he was talking about. "We'll find him."

"No..." Caroa shook his head. "ExCom will want to repair our trade agreements with the Seascape, even though bent northeastern noses are the least of their problems. It's up to you now. You must hunt high and low."

"We don't have any more leads," Jones said. "None of the new assets had a single idea of where he might be headed now. We're at a dead end."

"So now you'll wait." Contempt dripped from Caroa's words.

"Pattern-recognition systems will pick him up eventually. He'll board a ship. Or that Drowned Cities girl he rescued will show up on a street. Or he'll buy medicines in a Co-Prosperity city. He'll paddle past a camera in some protectorate orleans. We aren't doing *nothing*," she said in response to his disgusted expression. "Just because we aren't burning the Seascape to the ground doesn't mean we're sitting on our hands. We're searching all the time."

"You say."

"Well, *I'm* still searching, anyway. He can't hide forever."

"I can't decide if I'm more frightened of the idea of him disappearing forever, or him turning up again." He stared down at the city, thoughtful. Troubled. "I dream about that bastard sometimes. Haven't in years, but now…all the time. Every night." He lifted his cognac glass. "I can't tell if the drink makes it better or worse." He sipped. Made a face. "I spent years with him."

"I know. I've read all the files now."

Caroa looked surprised. "How high is your security clearance?"

"High. Enge wanted me to audit every one of your missions. ExCom is…angry."

"Well, I didn't put everything in those files. Those files don't have the blood of the truth in them. They don't have the *life*. The bonding." Caroa shook his head. "He was special. His whole pack was special. I picked every gene in him. Knew exactly what we needed. Supervised every bit of that pack's training. I lived with them. I ate and drank with them. I slept beside them. I hunted and killed alongside them. We were pack, you understand? *Pack*."

The way the general said the word made Jones shiver. It had an obsessional quality, a whiff of madness. It was probably good that the old man was being removed from the hunt.

Caroa was looking at her, smiling cynically. "You think I'm crazy."

She covered as well as she could. "No, sir."

"Yes, you do. And so does ExCom." He shrugged. "Well, I don't give a damn. I don't give a single damn anymore. Where I'm going, I don't have to give a single damn." He laughed at that. "I'm going to be general to a bunch of damn penguins, now. I'll make those little bastards march!" He pretended to wobble around for a moment. "Hup, hup, hup!"

How drunk is he? Jones wondered.

"I'm sure you won't be in Antarctica forever," she offered.

"I'm going to die in Antarctica. I'm going to die as an irrelevant pimple on the ass of the world." He laughed bitterly. "Eh. So be it. At least I won't have to give a damn about what happens to all you shortsighted bastards up here on top."

He glanced at Jones, and suddenly all the drunkenness was gone. His sharp blue eyes held her. "But *you*, you *will* have to give a damn. It's your problem now." He toasted her with his glass. "And a pretty problem it is."

"We have a better chance—now that we know what we're actually hunting for." She couldn't keep the accusation from her voice.

"Well, at least now you know why I was willing to risk everything. Our standing in the Seascape. The billions in trade over the pole. Financial embargoes." He laughed. "You thought I was willing to take on the Seascape and rile up its allies just because some monster bit my face off. Simple vengeance." He spat over the rail. "You thought I was insane."

Yes. I thought you were insane, old man. And so does ExCom, and that's why you're being sent to Antarctica, where you can't cause any more trouble.

Caroa gave her a disgusted look. "I hit him hard, with everything I had"—he scowled—"everything I was *allowed* to have. Because for this very brief moment, he was vulnerable. He didn't know we were coming."

"Apparently he did," Jones said dryly.

"We had a chance at surprise!" Caroa snapped. "If you hadn't sabotaged the Raptors, I would have used those as well, and I would have made absolutely sure he was dead." He gave her another piercing look.

Jones didn't let the barb rile her. "That's what got me the promotion, you know. ExCom was horrified that you were willing to drop Havoc on the Seascape. They had no idea what you were up to—"

Caroa waved a hand dismissively. "Bygones, Jones. You made the right choice, I made the wrong one." He drew on his cigar and pointed it at her. "But every day that passes, our friend gets a little stronger. And that means the next time, it will be much harder to get rid of him. Much, much harder."

He took one last sip of his cognac. Made a face. Abruptly, he tossed the snifter over the balcony edge, out into the open air.

It tumbled, glittering, arcing downward, disappearing into the darkness below. The general stared sourly after it.

"He's your problem now."

27

MAHLIA LIVED IN the mud, healing slowly.

The first night under the piers, Tool disappeared into black Seascape waters and later returned with medical supplies stolen from an unwary ship: tubing and needles, suture thread, empty IV bags—but to Mahlia's surprise, no cell stimulants and no antibiotics.

When she asked why he hadn't brought back medicine, Tool said it wasn't necessary. A rudimentary ether compress over her face sent her under. When she awoke, her guts hurt worse than before, and her belly was puckered with fresh stitches. And Tool was fitting an IV tube into his own arm.

He flexed his muscle and a plastic IV bag filled with fluid, thick and black in the darkness under the pier.

His blood.

"What are you doing?" she asked fuzzily.

Tool attached another IV line into the sac, fitted it with a needle.

"Tool?"

She watched with horror as he took her arm in his massive clawed hands. She wanted to pull away, but she felt almost hypnotized by his actions. The tube running from his own vein, full of blood, filling the sac, the new line with the fresh, gleaming needle that he now held over her own arm.

"What are you doing?"

"This will be difficult for you," Tool said. "My blood will help you heal."

Mahlia recoiled instinctively. "Are you crazy? How do you know we're the right type?"

"It was one of my kind's uses, on the battlefield. We were designed to donate our blood to our humans. You will heal in ways that would take much longer if we used only human medicine." He looked at her seriously. "But this is battlefield medicine. For soldiers, in extreme circumstances. It will not be comfortable. Parts of your body will rebel when my blood invades your veins."

She couldn't stop staring at the needle. "You'll do it anyway, won't you?"

Tool shrugged. "It is better if I have your agreement. Your immune system will be surprised. The experience will be unpleasant."

An understatement.

Within minutes of him inserting the needle, she was vomiting so hard she thought her guts would burst open again. Tool was forced to imprison her in his arms. He gathered her close as she seized and convulsed, vomiting over herself and him. Everything that she'd eaten, and more besides. Blood, black and dark, spilled out of her mouth.

"You're killing me," she croaked as she wiped bloody bile from her lips with a shaking hand.

"You are healing," Tool said, and then new convulsions seized her.

His muscular arms pinned her to him as waves of nausea ripped through. Even as she jerked and twitched, he held her close, keeping her from tearing her stitches loose with her thrashings. Whenever the seizures stilled, he would squeeze his fist, rhythmically pumping his genetically engineered blood out through the tubes and into her own arm.

Her vision blurred. She passed out. She woke sometime later, sweating and trembling with weakness.

"Is it over?"

Tool shook his head solemnly. "There is more."

Fever. Sweat. Shivering. Her body ached. Each bone inside her body felt like kindling. She disappeared into the pain, surrendered to it.

Sometimes she saw Tool, crouching over her, caring for her. Other times she saw soldier boys. Ocho and Van and others. Sometimes it was Mouse, the boy who had once saved her life in the Drowned Cities; sometimes it was old school friends, being gunned down by the patriotic militias.

Once, it was her mother, bargaining with some ship captain for the best price on an artifact, her dark skin a sharp contrast to her smiling white teeth, gleaming in the sun with pleasure as she made a deal. How beautiful she'd been...

She remembered her mother holding her, pulling her close and comforting her when her father was in one of his moods. Him, the commander, sitting in their apartment in the heart of the Drowned Cities, drinking his baijiu and cursing the people of the Drowned Cities who didn't know how to be civilized.

Nightmares ravaged her, and when she woke, there were crabs skittering beneath her skin and more clawing inside her guts. She tore at her clothes, ripped at her bandages, trying to get them out—

Tool loomed. "It is my blood." He seized her hands and held her immobile as sharp-clawed crustaceans ran riot under her skin, hollowing out a home in her belly.

Sometimes she would rise out of her delirium to find Tool crouched beside her, watching patiently, and she would feel safe and grateful, amazed that he was still there, amazed that anyone was still there for her at all—and then she would sink back into nightmare. At one point in her fever dream, Doctor Mahfouz came and sat beside her and wiped her brow, caring for her, regretfully informing her that war always created more war.

Always always always.

She tried to explain that she hadn't chosen the fight.

I tried, Mahlia tried to explain. *I tried to escape all of it.*

But when she came out of her fever, it was not the doctor but Tool who crouched over her, the creature who solved all his difficulties with overwhelming violence, and she didn't have to justify herself anymore.

At last she woke to sunshine glittering on the blue waves of the Seascape.

Tool squatted nearby. He was busy gutting some sort of animal, the corpse shuddering as he fed. A seal. Tool's ears twitched at her movement. He glanced back, his muzzle bright with blood.

"How do you feel?"

Mahlia tried to speak. Found her voice rusty with disuse. She cleared her throat. "Better."

She moved hesitantly and was surprised to feel only a few dull twinges in her guts. "A lot better." She pushed herself gingerly upright and drew her legs in so she could sit. "Strong."

Tool came over to inspect. Pressed a hand to her forehead. "Soon you will be able to leave the Seascape."

"Why are you strong? Why now?"

Tool paused in his ministrations. "You healed me."

"No. I mean, you were weak before. When... when they came to kill us. You were just lying there... and then you were finally fast, but it was too late." She choked back a sob, remembering Ocho, lying smashed as she left him. "You were too late."

"It was my conditioning," Tool said quietly. "It had

been a long time since I faced the shock troops of Mercier." He shook his huge head, a frustrated, human gesture. "I thought myself well rid of my need for obedience, but I was wrong. My former masters placed deep controls within me. My training—it is in my genes, and it is in my upbringing. Thousands of years of adapted obedience from domesticated animals. I was designed to seek a master, and Mercier owned me completely, for years. When they attacked, I found it unimaginably difficult to fight them. Even now..." He paused, and looked away. "Even now, a part of me desires to roll over on my back and beg forgiveness." A violent headshake of disgust.

"But in the end you fought," Mahlia said. "Just too late to do any good." She couldn't keep the bitterness from her voice.

"Yes," Tool said softly. "I am flawed."

Mosquitoes buzzed around them. Mahlia tried to swat at them when they settled on her body, but she was tired. She rested her head again on a muddy arm, and listened to the lap of the waves and the stamp of feet on the docks above as stevedores unloaded ships. From here, it was hard to guess where the *Raker* had floated. She wondered if there was anything left at all. If it had all been sunk or recycled.

"You said you wanted to hunt them," she said finally.

"Mercier. Yes. They made me for war. So. I will give them their war."

"But they have armies. Thousands and thousands of people working for them. You're alone."

"They are very powerful, it's true."

"It's more than that! You have to obey them, whenever you see them. I saw what—"

Tool was growling. "I am no longer their obedient dog. It will not happen again."

"But I saw it happen! You couldn't do anything—"

"They are not my pack!"

Mahlia flinched, instinctively throwing up her hands to defend against Tool's outburst.

Tool growled and looked away. "We were taught, from youth, to obey. Those who did not perfectly obey were made lessons of. We fed upon them. We ate those who failed, you understand? We tore them to pieces, and ate them, flesh and bones. They were not fit to be our kin. Long before I was imprinted on Mercier and Caroa, I was groomed for obedience. We were given gods to worship. Gods of killing, and of war. We made sacrifices to those gods. We sacrificed our weak and unfit to them."

He nodded up at the sun, high above them. "We were told that our god was the sun, riding his war chariot across the sky, hunting. And he judged us for our valor and our failures. If we fought and died in fearless, glorious battle, we were guaranteed a place beside him, racing across the savanna of the sky, hunting lions and saber-toothed cats. We were promised fresh kills every day, told we would bask in cool river pools at night beneath the moon, and hunt across the sky during the day—all of us who had fought and died, unafraid, in combat. All of us together. Pack."

He fell quiet. "It brings great shame to turn against those ideals. Our kinship. Our honor. It is almost unbearable to think that your god and brethren despise you. To think that you shattered the bones of the weak and sucked out their marrow, believing that they deserved to die . . . and then to see that you yourself are one of those *failures*. And then to see that, perhaps, we did not eat our weakest, but destroyed our strongest."

He bared his teeth and his ears flicked back. "It is difficult to hold on to the idea of some new kind of honor, and to balance it against the honor that one believed in before."

"Would it happen to you again? That weakness?"

"No." He touched her shoulder. "You are my pack, Mahlia. We are pack. They are not. It is enough for me to know that. When I face them again, I will not falter."

"But there's no way to really fight them. They're far away. They have drones. They have battleships and armies and dirigibles. Missiles—" Mahlia broke off.

To her surprise, Tool was chuckling, a low, contented sound. "Yes," he said. "My gods think they are powerful because they can rain fire down upon me." A knowing glance. "They did it once before, in Kolkata when I discovered my true power and my true nature." He flexed one clawed fist. "And that is why I must slay them now, if I am to have peace."

"But it's impossible!"

"Not impossible. Only difficult," Tool said. "My gods

live in the sky, so I must hunt them there. That is all. I will climb into the sky."

He smiled slightly, showing sharp teeth. "Do not doubt, Mahlia. Instead, have faith. I will climb into the sky, and I will hunt my gods, and when I am finished with their slaughter, there will be only me, racing my war chariot across the heavens. Perhaps I will become the sun."

28

BUT FOR A long time, Tool did not climb into the sky as he so madly described, nor did he do anything else to slay his so-called gods.

Instead, he lived in the shadows and the mud, and Mahlia continued to heal. Tool was adamant that they not come out from beneath the pilings of the piers. They lived amongst seagulls and crabs, visited by the occasional seal that came flopping up into the mud, and that Tool promptly disemboweled.

They didn't lack for food.

Slowly, Mahlia regained her strength, and so, too, did Tool. Day by day, he became more assured. Power seemed to emanate from him, a smoldering intensity of purpose.

Sometimes, she would catch him squatting in the darkness

beneath the piers, dismembering some fish or seal or dog that he had caught—and Mahlia could admit to herself she feared him.

Before, he had carried some basic human qualities, a softness, if she could call it that—at least an empathy—and because of that she had trusted him.

But now...

Now he seemed something else entirely. Not friend or ally. Something primal and unnerving. A nightmare out of humanity's primeval past, a monster of old, a creature re-emerged from the darkest myths of protohumans, when jungles had never been razed, and when apes still cowered from darkness and struggled to master fire. A monster with its own interests and agenda. A creature that might as easily devour her as continue to care for her and provide her with fresh food and water, stolen from the ships all around the Seascape harbor.

One time, he caught her watching him.

"I am no threat to you, Mahlia," he said. "We are pack."

"I wasn't—" she started to say, but the protest died in her throat. There was no point disputing. Tool saw too much.

One day, when she had healed sufficiently, he said, "I need news. You must fetch it for me. There are cameras. They will be looking for me, but also for you. As you are, you will be recognized." He offered her a cloak he had stolen off some ship out in the bay. "It is chill enough in the evening to wear this. You will not be remarked, I think."

He offered her a stone. "Put this in your shoe. It will throw them off."

"How I walk?"

"They measure many things about an individual."

"They might not even be watching."

Tool shook his head sharply. "They are always watching. In places such as this, they will have surveillance. They will ally or infiltrate with the Seascape, and their cameras and computers will never sleep." He waved an admonishing finger at her. "You must only go up at night. Your gait and your shape and your face are well known by now, and their camera eyes will mark you within a thousandth of a second."

"If it's so dangerous, why are we still even in the Seascape?"

"Because I find it useful."

And that was all Tool would say.

Mahlia went out from under the piers and kept her face dirty, and wore a rain slicker and a floppy hat and limped from the rock in her shoe. It became a pattern for her, sneaking out in the darkness, to fetch things for Tool.

Sometimes, he sent her for things he couldn't steal from ships, but more often he sent her out for scream sheets. Papers that got printed cheap and given away on the docks, advertising to sailors just off their ships.

At first, Mahlia had thought she was retrieving them because Tool was building a nest—which he was—digging deep into the shore embankments just above sea level, tunneling back into the mud, deep beneath the piers. He hollowed out a space that was surprisingly large, so that Mahlia joked tentatively that maybe he was actually part badger.

Tool only shrugged. "In some parts of the world, badgers kill cobras," he said. "It is possible. My gods built me from the best killers."

And then he sent her out the next night to fetch more scream sheets. Again and again. Day after day. Edition after edition. Long after Tool had enough paper for a dozen nests, he sent Mahlia out for more. He used them to insulate the nest, but mostly, he read them. Every night, Mahlia would catch him reading in moon-shadow dimness. Scanning the papers, one by one, compulsively.

"What are you looking for?" Mahlia asked when she returned with the day's papers. "Maybe I can help."

"Patterns," Tool said.

Mahlia gave him a dirty look. "I'm not a child. You can tell me your plans, you know."

"It's better if you don't know. If you are captured, I prefer that my enemies not learn my plans."

"I'm not getting captured."

Tool stilled, gazing at her. "You asked to stay with me, Mahlia. If you wish to remain close, you must accept that you are my soldier, and I am your general, and you will not ask questions." His teeth showed slightly. "I am not your dog to do your bidding. You are mine. However much you may dislike it, *you will obey.*"

Mahlia handed over the scream sheets without comment after that. Tool read them in silence.

One day, he returned from a hunting swim in the bay, bearing fishing rods. As he dragged heavy barbed hooks out of his skin, he commented, "I took them from fishermen on the pier. They were not expecting a fish such as I."

After that, on certain days, Tool would announce that it was a fine day for fishing and would send her out along the seawall to fish and watch the shipping, ordered to return with the names of all the arriving ships memorized.

Mahlia would scramble out along the seawalls with her pole, pick a spot, and set herself up. On occasion, Tool would emerge from the waves below, having swum for miles across the open Seascape waters.

The first time she chose an observation spot, Tool told her it wasn't good and made her move farther down the seawall, near its very tip.

"It's all the same view!" Mahlia protested. "There's the Seascape! There's the ocean! There's the ships! There's the seagulls and their crap! What's the difference?"

But Tool made her move anyway.

Mahlia decided that Tool just liked swimming, and wanted to swim farther. But it was a pain for her. Clambering along the seawall wasn't easy. Her prosthetic hand had been damaged in the fighting and didn't grip the way it should have. The seawall, too, was uneven—piled stone and mortar and broken concrete, sharp with barnacles, slimy with mosses. She hadn't realized how much she had come to depend on the luxury of having two reliable hands until her prosthetic stopped working right.

"Why won't you tell me what you're looking for?" she asked one day when Tool surfaced from the waters.

"I told you," Tool said. "I am looking for the names of ships. Have you memorized their names?"

They were positioned far out on the very edge of the seawall. Mahlia had her pole propped against a rock, but she'd given up on actually fishing. Tool could catch more fish in a few minutes in the water than she could catch all day. Instead, she propped the pole with its line trailing into the water, to make herself look as if she were a native Seascaper, but no longer bothered baiting her hook.

Tool tucked himself into a protected V of balanced concrete slabs and turned his attention to the shipping as it came through the first of the seawall breaks.

"What ships have arrived so far?" he asked.

"*Saltillo. MingXing. Pride of Lagos. Lucky Lady. Sea Dragon.* A couple of big fishing ships—"

"I don't care about those."

"How long are we going to do this?"

"You should bait your hook."

"What's the point? You catch more fish in a minute than I do in a day."

"The point is to look as if you are fishing." Tool focused on the waters, then lashed forward, his hand striking the waters with a sharp report. He came up with a small silvery fish. Ripped it in half. "Bait with this."

Mahlia gave him a dirty look, but she hooked the bloody mess on her line. "You said you were going to fight, but we're just sitting here. How are you going to climb into the sky if you don't ever do anything?"

"Murdering one's gods is not a simple task. In the meantime, we are fishing. Cast your line."

"We fish all the time, now."

"What ships arrived yesterday?"

"I already told you. Quit asking."

"Maybe I forgot."

"You never forget."

"True." Tool smiled contentedly.

"Did anyone ever tell you you're annoying?"

"If you wish to be a child, go find children to play with. I will fish."

"I'm not a child." Mahlia gave him a hard look.

"No. You are simply human." Tool glanced over at her, a dark humor showing in his expression. "And that means there are still a few things I can teach you. Do you know why I was able to take the Drowned Cities, when all the humans before me failed?"

"Because you're a military genius?"

"It's because I understand what is necessary to win the greater war. The other warlords had great passion for their fighting. They had fervent soldier boys. They had superior positions. Impregnable, some of them. I, on the other hand, knew how to wait." He smiled slightly, his eyes hooded. "So. Now I wait. And you, cast your line."

Mahlia gave him another dark look. They were quiet awhile, Mahlia fishing, Tool watching the shipping traffic.

"Enjoy it," Tool said.

"Enjoy waiting?"

"Peace. Soon it will end."

Something in Tool's tone made Mahlia glance over. "Why do you say that?"

Tool was looking out at the horizon, his ears cocked forward, his nose twitching. Mahlia followed his gaze. A clipper ship was clearing the first of the Seascape's breakwaters.

Tool was focused on it, intensely watchful in a way that he hadn't been since—

Since the kill squads attacked.

Mahlia felt a chill. "What is it? What's wrong?"

Tool didn't reply, just kept staring at the ship with an intentness that reminded Mahlia of a tiger stalking prey.

"Is that the ship you were looking for?"

Tool was growling now, ears laid back and fangs showing.

"Tool?"

Tool's growling increased as he tracked the ship. "Sometimes, Mahlia, waiting for the right moment is more important than the strike itself: the where, the when, the how. Children lash out; warriors plan. That is why you humans are so easily conquered."

"What's so important about that ship?"

"It does not concern you."

"I think it does!"

Tool's scarred gaze settled upon her. "Our paths must separate now, Mahlia. Where I go, you cannot follow. What I must do now, I must do alone."

"I don't understand. I thought we were in this together."

Tool shook his head. "No. I am alone. And you, too, must seek your own path. One separate from me. You have fulfilled your obligations to me, Mahlia. It is time you were on your own. And safe."

"What's so special about that ship?"

"Forget everything about me, Mahlia. Leave the Seascape. Leave this place, and never come back."

"But—"

"In the den I dug for you, there is an oilskin bag that I have stocked for your future needs. I was able to steal money from the ships here. Yuan and Bank of Seascape dollars. It is for you. It is no clipper ship, but it should help you find a niche in a place far away from here. With the money, you can buy passage anywhere in the world. Do so. Disappear."

"But what about you?"

"I will hunt my gods."

"I want to help you!"

"You have given too much already, Mahlia. Here, our paths separate."

Before she could protest again, he dove into the water. Mahlia glimpsed his shadow shape in the deeps, swimming strongly, and then he was gone entirely, lost to the ocean, leaving Mahlia to stare, abandoned, after him.

She followed the distant clipper ship with her eyes, trying to discern what had so entranced Tool.

Ignoring his final words, she gathered up her fishing pole and made her way farther down the seawall, to its very tip, trying to get a better view.

The clipper ship was slicing cleanly through the gap in the last seawall break, hydrofoils spraying salt water. Clean and sleek, leaving a triple V of wake curling behind.

Mahlia reached the waterline just as the clipper swept past. On its prow, the logo of Patel Global gleamed prominently, and beside it, proudly visible, the ship's name:

Dauntless.

29

TOOL FLOATED IN the warm waters of the Seascape, down below the *Dauntless*, listening.

The boy had changed.

No longer the skinny, scarred, feral child of Bright Sands Beach, who had survived by tearing copper from the guts of rusting ancient oil tankers, but something else entirely. Assured. Professional. Part of the crew of a globe-sailing clipper ship. Well fed.

Extraordinary to see the changes wrought by time and distance from the boy's original broken place and broken family. Extraordinary to see how humans grew and mutated into something utterly unlike their childhood selves.

The clipper ship was busy unloading. Tool watched from

deeps, patient. He needed to speak to the boy without eyes and ears listening. It wouldn't do to pursue him into the Seascape.

But so far the young man wasn't disembarking. Even now, after all the cargo had been unloaded, he still lingered on deck, bantering with the last of the crew, seeing off humans and augments as they caught their own launches to the shore, all of them excited to return to families or else spend their paychecks on the liquor and flesh of Salt Dock.

But the former ship breaker lingered.

Perhaps the boy kept no permanent home here. Certainly, the Seascape was not his native port as it was for the rest of the crew. So perhaps the boy lived aboard the ship, and would not debark at all. That would be ideal. Tool would wait until the midnight watch, when there was but a skeleton crew, and then make his approach.

Even now, the last of the augments were leaving the ship, two hulking creatures, laughing with the others, climbing down the ship's ladders to their launch.

Tool felt his lip curl in disgust. He sank deeper beneath the waves so that the augments would not sense his presence. They looked so... *content.*

Tool could barely control his contempt.

They lived amongst humans as slaves, and thought of themselves as anything but. Disgusting that they did not see themselves for what they were. Tool felt rage rising, and was surprised by its sudden surge. He had thought himself no longer victim to these reactions after passing through the crucible of Mercier's attack in Salt Dock.

But these ones particularly offended him. So contentedly loyal. So obedient. These ones would undoubtedly lay down their lives for their owners, and never hesitate. It was their duty to serve. They drooled to submit to the whims of humanity. If they were challenged on their obedience, they would most likely claim their owners were worthy, deserving loyalty.

Are you jealous that you did not have masters such as theirs? Tool wondered. *Is that why they enrage you so?*

He forced down the churning emotions. The augments weren't worth his attention. They were dogs. He was not. They obeyed. He did not.

That's right, Tool thought, watching as they boarded the launch with the rest of the humans. *Go on. Go with your owners, who will sacrifice you in an instant if it serves their purposes. Go.*

If they loved their slavery, it was no business of his. Let them have their contented subservience.

The launch sped shoreward, leaving the young man still on deck, chatting with a few last companions. He looked well, Tool thought. Stronger, taller, darker. More assured. Hardened and developed from his time on ships. Taller, and not only because someone had apparently been feeding him. He seemed to stand up straighter as well.

There was less fear in him. A different creature entirely.

When Tool had known him, the boy had been constantly alert and crouching. A child who knew that he was in danger at all moments, and was attuned to it. The boy's father had bullied and abused him, and the weak were always prey on Bright Sands Beach, but the boy had been a survivor.

Seeing him brought back memories. The scents of salt and iron and rust; beach fires sending up black smoke like signal flares; oil residue sheening the shallows, multihued, staining the sands; colorful flakes of plastic wire sheathing tumbling in the beach foam and waves, floating and bobbing, forming long lines of debris on oil-soaked shores—a boy, skinny and desperate, and willing to risk anything to escape.

"No," the young man was saying, "we can clean the hull at the same time as we do the hydrofoil inspection. That last storm put more torque on the foils than I would have liked."

"Thank the Fates they held," a crewman commented.

"We'll inspect them this week," he said. "Maybe refit early, depending on what we find."

"Yes, sir. We'll take care of it, Mr. Lopez."

Sir? Mister? Tool listened, fascinated. The boy had done well for himself. Not simply a young sailor grudgingly accepted amongst others, but someone who had gained respect.

Tool peered up through the waters, trying to see if he wore some insignia of rank, but the waves made it too difficult. Even picking out the conversation at this depth was a trial. He swam closer, rising through the waters to gain better vantage.

The young man continued. "And have Mills scrub out the

oxygen exchangers and change the membranes on the dive masks. The last time I was down, I swear I tasted mold."

"He says he already did it."

"Will he say that if I run the air through chem analysis?"

Chuckles all around.

The sound of another launch approaching interrupted Tool's observations. He sank deeper beneath the waves, swam a little more distant, scattering schools of fish. At a safer vantage he surfaced, the barest part of him above the waterline, twitching his ears, listening without the impediment of water. From this distance, he could easily be mistaken for a bit of debris, or a dead animal. A seal, perhaps...

The approaching launch was fast and sleek, a knife blade in comparison with the lumbering crew launches he had been watching. Not some old barge, baggy and clumsy and rusted and exhausted from the labors of ferrying sailors into port. This was a gleaming dagger boat, fast and nearly silent except for the hiss of its hull as it shot across the waves, electric props churning the water into foam behind it.

It closed on the clipper ship, sleek and assured and expensive, much like the girl who piloted it. She slewed the dagger boat hard at the last moment, sending up a spray of water and coming about smartly, then killed the motor.

The sleek watercraft settled into the waters, bobbing wildly as wake slapped and rebounded from the hull of the *Dauntless*.

"Nailer!" she called up.

Nailer turned and waved to her, his face breaking into a wide grin as he leaned over the rail. "Nita! I'll be right down!"

The girl, too, had grown and changed, as humans were wont to do. Less of a girl, more of a woman. She had passed out of puberty, and was now clearly one of the young humans who existed in that strange twilight space of near-majority that the wealthy sometimes stretched out for years. But there were other differences as well.

When Tool had known Nita Patel, she, too, had been a frightened soul. On the run. Alone and desperate. Clinging to any bit of flotsam that might assure her survival. Now, though, she was in her own element, clearly. It showed not just in her ease and expertise with the dagger boat, but in the way the ship's crew stiffened and came to attention and saluted her when they realized who had arrived.

All except Nailer Lopez. Nailer only smiled and waved, pleased and casual, and finished his final instructions to the crew. He clambered down the debarkation ladder and dropped his crew bag in the dagger boat's cockpit, before turning to Nita.

An embrace.

And not an insignificant one. Their lips met. A kiss. And this, too, was charged with familiarity and significance.

Even after the kiss, they held close to each other, lost to the crew above, unaware of anything around them.

Interesting.

Useful.

For the first time since Mercier had rained fire down on him, Tool allowed himself a twinge of optimism as stratagems became available that he had not anticipated. But still, he wouldn't allow himself too much hope. Both of these young people had changed greatly since he had known them. Perhaps they had changed completely.

Too, Nailer's connection to Nita created certain logistical problems of its own. Her dagger boat was far too fast for Tool to pursue on his own, and if they were headed to Patel Global's private island arcology, the intense security there would make approaching even more difficult.

He swam closer to the dagger boat. He had little hope of clinging on. This sleek boat, with its powerful motors and knifelike little hydrofoils, would fly across the waves like an osprey. He needed to find a way aboard, and yet there was no subtle way to do so, without drawing more attention.

He watched, irritated, considering options. Nailer was securing his crew bag and pulling in the buoys as Nita took the wheel and eased the dagger boat away from the looming shape of the *Dauntless*. In a moment she would engage the engines, and they would be lost to him.

Long ago, a trainer had once told him, "If you don't like the tactical situation, make a better one."

Tool submerged and swam beneath the dagger boat.

Nita shifted *Meethi* out of neutral as Nailer unhooked the *Dauntless*'s ladders and hauled in the buoys that had protected the hull from the bulk of the clipper ship.

She felt a small catch in her throat as she watched him work. He was so quick and assured, so comfortable here now.

Sometimes, though, she was struck with an unnerving double vision, able to see this version of him in the here and now, but overlaid with the memory of what he'd been like when they'd first met: the cruel and feral and alien creature, tattoos on his face and scars on his body and nothing but hunger in his eyes.

That old version of him was still there, just as he'd kept the scavenge crew tattoos that marked his cheeks. She could still remember him and Pima, his fierce associate, their knives drawn, eager to cut off her fingers.

And yet even then, she hadn't felt afraid of Nailer.

Or perhaps she'd been afraid, but she hadn't blamed him or Pima for what they planned to do to her. Their violence wasn't personal. It was just hunger. Just a desperate hunger that held them completely in its grasp. Nita wouldn't have blamed a tiger in the jungle for pouncing on her, any more than she blamed those two for how they planned to harvest the gold from her fingers.

But then she'd seen something else in Nailer's eyes, and felt a bloom of hope that she might be safe—

"Hey!" Nailer waved a hand. "You ready?"

Nita realized that she'd been lost entirely in memory. She shook her head ruefully. "Sorry. Just thinking."

"About?"

"Nothing." She shifted the motors out of their stabilization mode, and engaged the dagger boat, guiding it away from the bulk of the *Dauntless*. "Just remembering you."

He laughed. "I wasn't gone that long."

"Three months."

"And I saw you twice. Once at the Amsterdam shipyards, and once down on Miami Reef."

He was so alive now. There had been something of that about him before, even when he'd been starved and skinny and scarred and feral. But now there was more of it. The deeply browned skin, the fine bones of his face, his black hair cropped short.

With his ship-breaking tattoos he might have been fierce-looking. Had been, truly. But now she knew the rest of him. Now he was strong, his arms rippling with healthy muscle, lanky and confident.

Nita shook her head, smiling secretly. "I'm glad you're home. That's all."

Nailer laughed. "You're just glad that when I'm home, that old mausi of yours—"

"Sunita Mausi—"

"—hates my crew tattoos so much that she forgets to criticize anyone else. Every time."

"And we're all grateful that you distract her."

"She doesn't bother me."

"She bothers everyone else."

Nailer shrugged. "I've heard worse, from worse people."

That was true. He'd heard worse, and experienced worse. And yet, he'd somehow come through it with empathy intact. Even back when he'd been starving, she'd known—somehow known for certain—that he wouldn't kill her.

And that was something, her father pointed out, when later she'd questioned whether there was any purpose or point in...whatever this was. This relationship that felt so comfortable at times, and felt so alien and sandpapery at others.

A surprise, that her father had been so sanguine about Nailer.

"He might be a wild animal," her father had said, "but he didn't kill you when he could have. He could have profited greatly from your death, and yet he didn't try. Many times, his own interests would have been better served by betraying you. And yet he never did."

She had always thought of her father as a stern man, laser-focused and rigid in his ways. A man who distinguished right and wrong as black and white, and who had more than once interfered when a boy drew her eye.

And yet with this boy—the one she thought would cause the most resistance of all, the one who even she sometimes resisted when they found themselves looking at each other askance, trying to fathom how one or the other could be so dim as to the real workings of the world—this one, her father had simply quirked an eyebrow at and suggested that Nailer would probably need training in table manners if he was going to survive the gossips at family dinners.

When she'd broken it off once, angry at how Nailer had

laughed at something she'd said about hard work always being rewarded, her father had dryly commented, "Sunita Mausi laughs at him as well. She speaks in Hindi behind his back, calls him the little servant boy. And Nailer understands every word and does not lash out."

"He's got self-control," Nita admitted grudgingly.

"He has iron will," her father said. "He may be a feral rat off the ship-breaking beaches, but he has loyalty, and he has iron will. Given the position you occupy, that matters more than you may realize."

"I already understand—"

"No!" her father had interrupted, angry. "You do not understand! The people around us care nothing for us! They care for our wealth and influence and connections! If you had none of those things, they would not even see that you exist. Power poisons us, and it poisons them. It poisons so very much that I sometimes wish I had never made this company what it is." He scowled. "Turn that boy aside if that is your choice. But do not scorn him. He's worth more than most of us."

Nailer interrupted her thoughts. "Are you going to push this thing?" he asked. "Or do you want me to break out the paddles?"

Nita gave him a challenging look. "Oh? You want to go fast?" She pushed the *Meethi*'s engines, and felt a wicked rush of acceleration as the propellers bit into the sea. The dagger boat leaped forward, rising up above the waves, planing out on hydrofoils.

"Fast enough?" she shouted back as wind whipped her hair. Nailer's reply was lost in the rush of air. She leaned into the wind, loving the sun and waters, the power of the boat—

Meethi shuddered and lurched sidewise. A ripping sound wrenched through the hull. Nita fought for control as the boat slewed. She cut power. The dagger boat sank back into the water.

Waves rocked them as the wake caught up.

Nailer was laughing.

Nita glared. "It's not funny."

But Nailer didn't stop grinning. "And here I was, just thinking how nice it was to be on a boat that I don't have to maintain," he said. "I thought the great Patel Global had better maintenance techs than this."

"Ha, ha," Nita said. "It's my boat. I don't let anyone else touch her."

"Well, you're doing a great job."

"Shut up." Nita scowled. "She was humming on the way out. Perfect. I just overhauled her."

"You want help?"

Nita shot him a dark look. "Yeah, Engineer Second-Class, I'd love for you to show me how to take care of a boat I've worked on all my life." She gave him another dirty look, and went aft to strip the motor housings. "I had power, and then all of a sudden, it all—" She paused. The casings around the motors were cracked. "That's weird."

She leaned over the side, staring into the water, checking the props below. It was almost as if she'd run over a sandbar or a floating log, except she was in deep water, and there hadn't been any debris. It was unusual for the Seascape to have any significant debris. She stared down into the waters, leaning far over, tucking her hair back as she peered down at the props.

Oddly, she could see something down there. She squinted, trying to make it out. Not debris. Something else...

Something coming up fast.

Tool surfaced as Nita scrambled back, her face a mask of terror. She was making the strange sounds that terrified animals made when they became prey. Tool surged into the boat, dripping seawater. Nailer was grabbing for his bag, most likely reaching for a weapon. The boy was fast for a human, but still, he was so very slow to Tool.

Tool started to speak, but Nita was raising her hand. Tool was surprised to see a small pistol gleaming. Something sleek and new and altogether too modern for Tool's liking.

It was to be expected, he thought, as she fired at him.

Of course her people would have security concerns. She had, after all, been attacked before. Kidnapped, even. The Patel family members were valuable—

The first bullet hit. Tool stumbled back. He couldn't help but feel a certain respect. The girl really had a very good response time, for a human. The second bullet hit.

Tool decided that he was less impressed. The bullets were small, barely penetrating his skin, but they detonated nastily enough. He lunged at Nita as an ugly numb sensation blossomed where she'd shot him.

He slapped Nita's pistol away and turned just in time to meet Nailer coming at him. Nailer Lopez, always a quick one, just like his father. Murderous and brave with a knife—and yes, it was a knife. Richard Lopez's son, coming for Tool's neck, ramming upward, hoping for the jugular.

Tool grabbed Nailer's wrist and stopped him cold.

You are fast, but you are no augment.

The numbness inside Tool was spreading. Nailer was staring up at Tool, shocked. His eyes widened in recognition.

"Tool?"

"Old friend," Tool growled. The numbness from Nita's bullets was spreading through him, fire and tingling. His muscles turned to water. Tool fell to his knees, puzzled.

Two bullets?

He could hear Nailer shouting something.

I should be able to take two bullets.

But apparently he was wrong, for he could feel the pounding of his heart slowing to a stop, and the boat's deck rushing up to meet him.

30

"ARE YOU SURE it's him?" Nita asked.

"How can you not be?" Nailer asked. "Look at him."

"He's . . . a little worse for the wear."

How many new wounds had Tool sustained since the time when he had helped this wealthy heiress and this lowly ship breaker escape the desperation of Bright Sands Beach?

Tool growled and tried to sit up, but nothing happened. It was as if someone had injected concrete into his muscles, making them heavy and unbending. He couldn't even open his eyes. Not a muscle seemed willing to obey. He was surprised that he was even still breathing. He listened to his heart slowly beat.

This has been happening far too often.

Irritated at the thought, and unable to do anything else,

he listened as Nailer and Nita conversed. In its own way, it was advantageous to hear them without their knowing he was alert. An opportunity to scout the bounds of their loyalties.

"How long does it take for this stuff to wear off?" Nailer asked.

"It's experimental. One shot is supposed to do it..."

"You got him twice."

"Oh?" Nita sounded pleased. "I didn't realize I'd managed that. He was much faster than I've had in target practice."

"Knot and Vine always hold back, in practice."

"I told them not to!"

"They still have to answer to your father," Nailer said. "They'll always hold back a little. No one's going to hurt daddy's little princess."

"Don't call me that." She sounded irritated. She was quiet for a minute. Tool heard the rustle of her skirts, sensed her kneeling beside him. Her hand came to rest gently on his chest.

"If he'd been a real attacker, I'd already be dead," she said.

"Both of us," Nailer agreed.

"I'll have to tell Tariq. He'll be disappointed the poison wasn't fast enough."

"It would have stopped any other attacker."

"A bullet stops normal attackers. We need something that stops augments."

Nothing stops me, Tool thought. And yet, here he lay. He growled in frustration, and was surprised when he made a noise.

"Tool?" Nailer crouched down beside him.

Tool strained to move. The concrete that filled his muscles cracked slightly. With great effort, he rolled onto his side, but the labor exhausted him. He lay still, panting.

Nita crouched beside him again. "Here. Drink this." Something prodded his mouth.

Tool fought to open his eye. Managed to focus. A bottle of some sort. From the scent of it, teeming with sugars and chemicals. A rich thing, for leisurely people. Tool drank it greedily. A sledgehammer had begun crashing inside his skull, slow and deliberate, pounding to the rhythm of his heart.

"What..." Tool finally managed a word. "Weapon?"

"Shh," Nita said. "Don't worry about it. It will take a while for the drugs to wear off."

A neurotoxin, he suspected. He could feel his body reacting and adapting, trying to recover, fighting against the poison and mostly failing, at least for the moment. The tiny pistol lay on the deck beside them. An insignificant little thing. An elegant toy for a wealthy daughter.

And yet it had felled him, almost instantly.

I have fought on seven continents, and a toy pistol fells me.

It galled. Tool tried to lift his head, to ask again what it was that she had done to him, but his tongue was thick, filling his mouth. Breathing was becoming difficult.

"We need to get him to the island." Tool was surprised at how urgent Nailer's voice sounded.

Now the humans were rushing about and the crippled dagger boat was powering up once again. Tool heard Nita calling in over their encrypted channels, calling for help, marshaling the resources of her immensely powerful family.

The toxin continued to thicken in Tool's heart. Humans were adapting, once again. Bullets were no longer enough to destroy the warriors they had created. Explosives were no longer enough. His kind was too resilient. So now the humans were devising counterweapons.

In another few years, he supposed, the next iteration of his own kind would probably easily metabolize this poison coursing through his veins. Perhaps the future version of himself might even turn it into a stimulant. Until then, though...

Tool's head lolled on the deck and unconsciousness settled upon him, a heavy, incontestable blanket.

His found himself wishing he could adapt a little faster.

"If any of us could adapt a little faster, we'd all be alive, instead of sitting here inside your head, inside your dreams."

The First Claw of the Tiger Guard poured more steaming chai. The day was hot and mosquitoes whined all around them. Much of Kolkata was covered in vines. Tool could hear the call of monkeys and scream of panthers. The howls of his brethren. Small augments were clambering up and down the sides of the buildings.

"Shouldn't those be in a crèche?" Tool asked.

The First Claw glanced over his shoulder at the tumbling young augments. Small, impossibly mismatched hands and feet, oversize heads, stubby bodies. All their proportions wrong, still needing time to grow into what they would eventually become.

"But how would they adapt if they were left in a crèche? How would they learn the ways of nature? If they were forced to fight their way out of a bone pit as we were forced to do, what kind of obedient creatures would they become? They would never learn to think independently."

The First Claw didn't seem bothered by the free-running children, but they made Tool uneasy. It was not natural to see young augments running free, without trainers monitoring. Augments running about, willy-nilly. Like human children.

Not natural at all.

"Well, you're not natural, either," the First Claw pointed out. "And yet here you are, trying to make friends with me, in a dream no less! An augment, dreaming! Not natural at all, is it? Nor this diplomatic moment. Quite against nature. Disgusting, really. Not natural at all, this diplomacy. Just as our children are unnatural. Oh, don't worry. They do not exist, if that's your concern. They haven't happened yet."

Tool knew that the tiny augments were another part of his dreaming-remembering state, but they were still discomfiting. They didn't fit nature.

"None of this is natural," the First Claw said, exasperated.

"I'm long-ago dead and burned, after all. And yet here we are, unnaturally negotiating."

"It is necessary," Tool said. "You know the sorts of people we serve. What loyalty do they deserve?"

"So I should give my loyalty to you instead?"

Tool bared his teeth. "Who better?"

"You're still learning diplomacy."

"I am self-taught," Tool admitted.

"Not very good at it, either."

"I think I'm getting better."

The First Claw laughed at that. "Of a surety!" He glanced significantly at the scampering young. "Imagine what we might be like, if we were never trained with shock rods and bone pits at all. Imagine what we might be then."

"Join with me, and we may know."

The First Claw looked at him sadly. "Humans will never allow it." And because Tool knew it was a dream and that the First Claw was already dead, he knew that his enemy spoke true.

Tool woke in a medical facility. He could hear the life-support machines. Smell the presence of antibiotic cleansers. A doctor stood nearby, watching his vital signs on his machines. Tool could sense his own vitals, just as easily. Could feel his heart beating. Oxygenated blood moving easily. The toxins had dissolved.

Nailer and Nita were sitting nearby.

"I fought my way out of a bone pit," Tool said. "I fought."

"Tool?" Nailer and Nita rushed to his side. Tool tested his limbs and was pleased to find that his body once again obeyed him. He sat up slowly. A doctor came over to inspect him. Shone a light into Tool's one good eye, frowning. He lifted a needle, asking permission. Tool nodded assent and the doctor drew a sample of blood, and took it over to a wall full of diagnostic machines.

Tool tested his limbs again. Closed a hand into a fist. Extended his fingers. A certain stiffness lingered, but he seemed to be recovered. *I always fight free.*

"Well?" Nita was looking at the doctor. "How is he?"

The doctor was looking at his displays, frowning. "He seems well enough. I'm not seeing any traces of the neurotoxin."

"That's good, right?"

"It's . . . unusual." The doctor glanced over at Tool. "It's good. Yes. He should recover fully." He returned to his displays, still frowning. "You're very lucky."

"I always fight free," Tool said. "It's my nature."

"What are you doing here?" Nailer asked as they helped him down off the medical bed. "The last time I saw you, you didn't want anything to do with people."

I still don't, Tool almost said, but then he was reminded of his dream with the First Claw. Diplomacy. An adaptation he was not designed for. Diplomacy was for human beings, whereas he had been designed for war.

War is diplomacy by other means.

An old quote. Something that his pack had been fond

of quoting as they finished off their opponents in whatever rubbled city they'd razed that day. But then, he and his fellows had never been encouraged to think of the phrase in reverse.

Diplomacy is war by other means.

Nailer and Nita were looking at him with concern.

"I came to you..." Tool started, but found he couldn't finish the sentence.

"Yes?"

"To..." Tool growled. "To *ask*..."

Tool found he couldn't get the words out. He could almost hear the First Claw laughing at him.

You managed it with me, the First Claw seemed to say. *You managed to bridge a greater gap than this when you came to me.*

Diplomacy. It was not a skill Tool had been designed for.

"I have come for your help."

PRIORITY SECURITY ALERT

Dossier: #1A 2385883

Pattern.....MATCH.

Watchlist.....MATCH.

ID.........MATCH.

================================

*****SECURITY/ADMIN LVL: 10/RED ONLY*****

Keyword: Rogue

Rogue 228 asset identified—Blood/Karta-Kul.

Confirmation Confidence: 88/100

Location: GPS—42.3601° N, 71.0589° W

================================

Northern Free Trade Zone, Seascape Boston...

*******PATEL GLOBAL HEADQUARTERS*******

31

Jones stared at the notice blinking on her screen, surprised by its sudden arrival.

PRIORITY SECURITY ALERT

DOSSIER: #1A 2385883

For the last few months she had been working under Mercier's Joint Forces director, Jonas Enge, as one of his intelligence analysts in the ExCom, and her world had become far removed from her previous life as a junior analyst on the *Annapurna*.

She now had a posh apartment in the SoCal Protectorate, with clear views of the bay and Los Angeles's orleans. Every morning, Jones could watch fishermen's skiffs making their way out to sea, permitted to set their nets in Mercier's massive aquaculture zones, and every day she could watch them return with their catch under the red blaze of the setting sun, as it sank into the Pacific.

She had good eating in company cafeterias from menus unfettered by the space and storage and weight considerations of long-haul dirigible logistics.

She worked in the tallest sky tower in Los Angeles, only a few doors away from the Joint Forces director himself.

But the work...

She had thought she had known how Mercier worked before, but now, with Enge, she sat at the beating heart of Mercier's empire: joint military exercises in the Chinese Co-Prosperity Sphere; intervention operations in the Mediterranean Free Trade Zone; contract territorial defense for the West African Technology Combine. She advised Enge as he defended trade and resource zones, seized control of mining operations, and assigned defense forces to manufacturing centers and corporate charter cities.

When the alert came in, she was sitting in Mercier's quarterly status meeting, watching as Executive Committee directors discussed Mercier's strategic situation. Around the table, directors of Finance, Manufacturing, Trade, R&D, Foreign Relations, Employee Loyalty & Retention, Facilities & Infrastructure, and more were arrayed.

The security alert popped up on her tablet at the same moment that Enge was arguing with Facilities & Infrastructure over fourth-generation Raptor upgrades.

Trade, of course, was entirely in favor, because the land routes across the Alps had become difficult of late, and she had a personal stake. And R&D was all in favor, given that the upgrades were likely to generate a tidy profit once they started licensing in the Chinese Co-Prosperity Sphere.

For a moment, Jones didn't quite understand what she was seeing on her tablet.

Pattern.....MATCH.
Watchlist.....MATCH.
ID.........MATCH.

She stared dumbly at the screen, taking in the rest, then wordlessly handed the tablet to Enge.

"We need to be stealthier," Enge was saying. "The entire European theater has become difficult now that these localists have started arming with two-stage Spider missiles—" He glanced down at her tablet, dismissive, then froze. "Spider missiles..." he started again, before trailing off.

"You were saying?" Finance pressed.

Jones tapped the screen significantly, her finger over the line that had given her pause: *PATEL GLOBAL HEADQUARTERS.*

Enge frowned.

"Director Enge?" Finance pressed again.

"Clear the room of security personnel," he said briskly.

Around the room, the augments who guarded the chamber exchanged uncertain glances.

"What's going on?" Trade asked. Others were also looking askance, almost certainly suspecting that Enge was about to launch a coup.

Enge scowled. "A little trust from my counterparts would be appreciated." He pressed his palm to Jones's screen, overriding it with his own security authority. A second later, tablets around the table sprang to life as all the directors received the security alert as well.

It took only a moment before Finance nodded acquiescence. "Clear the room."

Jones stood as well, intending to join the rest of the directors' personal assistants, but Enge laid a hand on her arm, staying her as the rest of the lower-ranking personnel filed out. Jones watched as the elite Fast Attack augments made sure that all the assistants were gone, and then stepped outside themselves.

Soundproofed baffles descended. The air shuddered as they locked in place, isolating the ExCom from the outside world.

The expressions of the directors were somber as they read the security report.

"This is untenable," Finance said softly.

Jones managed to retrieve her tablet from Enge, and scanned the rest of the report.

The alert had been triggered by blood work done by

Patel Global. A medical query had been kicked out into larger Seascape medical-information systems that Mercier had infiltrated long ago as part of their security network. The analysis request had contained DNA information.

Jones frowned, studying her display. It appeared that a sequence of toxicology tests had been run, and then all the information had been routed back to medical facilities inside Patel Global's headquarters.

They'd been running blood work on Karta-Kul, for certain.

"Maybe they killed him," Enge suggested, "and they're trying to ID him."

"If that were the case, they would already be demanding explanations from us. Asking why we have an asset in their compound."

Jones whispered to Enge, "This looks more like medical intervention."

"What's that?" Finance barked. "Speak up!"

Jones looked to Enge for permission. At his nod, she said, "It looks like the tests they're running are all toxicology requests. They're looking for cellular regeneration matches."

"They're healing him?" R&D asked, astonished.

"It's hard to say." Jones studied the data. "But they definitely have his blood in their labs, and they probably wouldn't be running these particular diagnostics if he weren't alive and getting medical aid from them."

Trade gave a low curse. "Bad enough that we have diplomatic issues with the Seascape. Now it's Patel Global."

“We have to demand his return,” Enge said.

R&D was nodding vigorously. “They must surrender our property to us. It’s our intellectual property. They have no right to it.”

“Will they comply?” Trade asked.

“We can make a case that they’re holding our proprietary technology. There are espionage treaties. We can demand they return it,” Finance suggested.

“And if they refuse?” Trade pressed. “This isn’t like old man Caroa burning some third-rate city to the ground. This is Patel Global. The Seascape. They have allies. Mutual protection pacts.”

“Finance is right. We can invoke our rights under the C15 Prosperity Treaty,” Diplomacy said. “There are corporate espionage clauses. As long as we follow the treaty directives, we can legally go to war with them, and their mutual protection agreements will be void.”

“Joint Forces Director?” Finance asked.

Enge was nodding. “It’s relatively low-risk, militarily speaking. The problem is their allies. If we neutralize those, Patel Global...” He shrugged. “Not much of a challenge, really.”

“Won’t they deny they have him?” Jones asked timidly. “We don’t have anything except these blood reports.”

Enge gave her an irritated look. The rest of the directors all turned their gazes on her.

“How confident is the security scan, Analyst?” Finance asked softly.

Jones swallowed. "Eighty-eight percent, ma'am."

Finance gave Enge a look of disgust. Others were shaking their heads.

Enge's voice was soft, but cutting. "You're here to solve problems, Jones. That's why you were promoted. That's why you're here, at all."

"Yes, sir." She dipped her head to Finance as well. "I'll get you the confirmations you need, ma'am."

"We're so very appreciative," Finance said dryly. She turned to the rest of the table. "So. Pending a confirmation... is the board in agreement?"

R&D was nodding vigorously. "This technology must be terminated. It was a dangerous precedent, and foolish risk to try to create it. Caroa was a madman."

Other directorate heads were also nodding.

"Very well," Finance said. "We will demand the return of the augment, and if Patel Global does not comply, we will engage in trade, financial, electronic, and territorial war with Patel Global. All in favor?" She glanced around at the raised hands. "Unanimous affirmation. Mercier so directs."

She nodded at Enge. "You have free rein, Joint Forces Director."

"Thank you." Enge was smiling. "They will give up the augment, or we will burn Patel Global off the face of the earth."

32

"YOU'RE OWNED BY Mercier?" Nita could barely get the words out.

She had Tool hidden in her suite to avoid her father's informers. Even now, she was worried that her use of the medical bays and Doctor Talint would filter up to her father's ears, and now, it was even worse than she'd thought. "*Mercier?*"

"I am not owned," Tool growled.

"Don't split hairs with me!" Nita shot back. "You want us to fight Mercier? Risk that company as an enemy?" She could barely control her voice. "Do you know those people? Do you know what my father would say if he knew you were here? Our intelligence team has already has been watching Mercier closely. They've had their kill squads operating in the Seascape! They destroyed a whole city—" She couldn't help but gape as she fit the pieces together. "You. You're what this is all about. You're the reason they've got their warships this far up the coast. Their 'weather drones' overhead."

She flopped onto a sofa and stared out the panoramic windows of the Seascape beyond. In the distance, she could see her family's shipyards, a new clipper ship being built in dry dock. She'd always loved the Seascape. All of it. Now, she looked out at the city and its floating arcologies and wondered whether Mercier's war machine was already on the move. "You've put us all in danger."

"Is it so difficult to aid me, who once aided you?" Tool asked.

Nita gave him a dark look. "The stakes are a little higher this time, don't you think?"

"You speak of stakes? The last time I saw you, many people wanted you dead."

"My uncle Pyce! And he had their backing then, did you know that? Just a little game of coup that they did in their spare time, setting us all against one another. And now..." She shook her head. "Now they're motivated. We can't fight against that company. We aren't militarized the way they are. We don't have the augments to combat them, and even our augments aren't optimized the way theirs are. They'll strangle our trade, they'll burn our ports, they'll sink our ships—"

"Your life was once in danger, and I risked myself for you," Tool interrupted. "Now my life is in danger." He cocked his head. "Is a half-man's life not as valuable as those of wealthy humans?"

"That's not fair, Tool," Nailer said. "It's a little different. You have to admit that."

Nita shot him a grateful look.

Tool only laughed. "You think you have more to lose? I risked all, when you were in danger. I fought for you. But now you sit in this fine suite, on your private island." He flicked a hand dismissively at her rooms. "You have a stream that trickles so nicely through your suite, and these little fish." He leaned forward, staring into the sitting room's reflecting pool. One quicksilver lunge and he had a shimmering azuli fish between his fingers. "This is a pretty thing. Engineered by your family?"

"Tool..." Nailer said warningly as Nita looked on with horror.

"You think I would eat this?" He gave them both a look of disgust and tossed the fish back. "I'm not a beast, Miss Nita. You have more in this single suite of rooms than any of my soldier boys in the Drowned Cities had, and Mercier poured fire down upon them. Would your loss be more than theirs? Is that what you tell me?"

"Why is Mercier so obsessed with you?" Nita countered. "They're risking a lot to try to get at you. Their kill squads alone could have cost them trading rights in the Seascape. What's so important about you?"

"My freedom irritates them."

"We can't challenge Mercier directly."

"I do not ask you to challenge them. I ask only for you to help me—"

"Help you attack them!" Nita interrupted. "Which is impossible! If we were to give such aid—"

She broke off as the door to her suite opened.

Fates.

"Jayant Patel." Tool smiled toothily. "Welcome."

"Father, I—" Nita started as her father came into the room, but her father gave her a cold look and her excuses died on her lips. He was furious. Visibly, shakingly furious. "I can explain—"

A squad of augments muscled in. Talon, their head of security, along with four others. They were all armored, and armed. Her father's furious gaze swept the room. *He knows. He knows something.*

Nita glanced worriedly at Nailer, who had risen, and was stepping between her father's augments and Tool.

Nita thought that she'd never seen her father more angry. His enemies and friends called him a hawk, for the way his eyes pierced opponents, and now those eyes bored into her. She'd never seen him look more implacable.

Tool reclined on the couch, seemingly immune to her father's wrath. "So good to meet you at last, Mr. Patel. You have a fierce reputation."

The augments growled at the mockery behind Tool's words. They spread out and raised their rifles, ready to fire. Tool cocked his head as if intrigued. His nostrils seemed to flare, sniffing the air.

Nita turned to her father. "This isn't necessary—"

"Do you know who I've just received a diplomatic communiqué from?" her father interrupted. "Priority, eyes-only, messengered straight from the Mercier Embassy, here in the Seascape."

He held up a vellum document. "A signed directive from their Executive Committee. All twelve of their directors as signatories. A formal hard-copy declaration."

The vellum shimmered with holograms and security seals as he held it up to the light. "Not something one sees every day. Quite a surprise to discover that Mercier accuses me of stealing their intellectual property and harboring a trade secret of theirs." He looked at Tool. "You are their Karta-Kul, I presume?"

Tool showed his teeth. "A name I once used, when I was an obedient dog who did the bidding of Mercier. I have other names."

"Tool, then?"

"Or, 'Sir,'" Tool said. "Either is acceptable to me."

The augments growled. Talon looked as if he was about to leap across the room and tear out Tool's heart, and yet Tool seemed unperturbed by the bristling hackles and bared fangs of the security team. The room fairly crackled with the promise of violence, and yet Tool barely seemed to notice.

Her father pressed. "You are Mercier's, though?"

"No human owns me."

"Father," Nita broke in. "He saved us. When Uncle Pyce

was hunting me, Tool helped Nailer and me survive. He saved us, more than once. Fought for us."

Her father shot a hard glare at her and she backed off, surprised. *What's going on here?* He'd never treated her this way.

"Is it true?" her father asked Tool. "That you have broken from your conditioning?"

"I make a poor slave, if that is your question."

The growling from the augments increased. Nita's skin prickled at the sound. At any moment, she expected them to attack. Tool couldn't possibly fight them all, and yet he seemed completely at ease. From the way his ears lay, he seemed almost pleased.

Her father was glaring at him, visibly enraged. "You must surrender yourself to Mercier!"

Tool didn't respond. Merely gazed back at her father with his predatory dog eyes, evaluating.

Nita tried again. "Please, Father—"

"Do you know what this is, daughter?" He held up the shimmering document. "It is nearly a declaration of war! They have proof of you bringing this . . . this . . ."

"Abomination," Tool suggested imperturbably.

Patel gave him a dirty look. "They know we have him, and they sent DNA data that establish their genetic ownership. This augment is stolen property. They have the right to attack us if we do not return him. A clear and simple right!"

"Why would they threaten a war over Tool?" Nailer

asked. "He's just one augment. Even if he's broken out of his conditioning, it seems like too much effort."

"That's something I would very much like to know as well." Her father gazed at Tool, troubled. "Are you some new iteration of warrior? Do you have some secret they don't want to be revealed?"

"In a sense, I suppose."

"Don't be coy—" Her father broke off. "It hardly matters. Mercier demands you be returned to them, alive or dead, and they are more than within their rights."

"Because they call me property? Because some document claims I am their thing?" Tool gestured at the vellum page. "I'm sure they have many documents making such claims. I'm sure they say they own my blood design and my genetic mix. That I am *intellectual property*, from head to foot, from fang to claw." He shrugged. "And yet here I sit, and here I remain... and still I do not obey."

Tool was baiting him, Nita realized. He was pressing her father into attacking, and yet she knew Tool couldn't survive the attack. "Tool..." she said warningly. Tool glanced at her, and Nita was astonished to see that Tool appeared to be enjoying himself.

Can he take them all? Fates, what sort of creature have I invited into my home?

Nailer was looking equally worried.

"Surrender quietly," her father said, in a voice that Nita knew meant that there would be no more warnings. "Or I will send you back as a corpse. Mercier does not care whether you live or die, and I will not risk my family to defy them."

"Well," Tool said, "I will certainly die before I return to Mercier as their obedient slave."

"Take him!" her father ordered.

"Tarak gangh!"

Tool's bestial command shook the room like a thunderclap. Nita found herself cowering down, shaking. But more astoundingly, her father's security team were all frozen in their tracks, staring at Tool.

Tool snarled at them and then began growling, a low warning sound. Talon and the other augments matched him with growls of their own, seeming somehow...

Hypnotized?

Nita stared, astounded.

She had never seen her family's augments hesitate to follow orders. She had never seen any augment hesitate, whether to fight or to raise sail in a storm, and yet now they paused, attendant upon Tool.

Tool snarled again, then issued a series of sharp commands, accompanied by a chopping gesture. Talon replied, a bark of query. Tool shook his head in definitive dissent. All the augments bared their teeth, and then abruptly they relaxed and lowered their weapons.

Nita stared, astounded. Nailer, too, seemed stunned. His mouth gaped open.

"Take him!" her father ordered again, but the augments shook their heads.

"No," Talon said, "he will not attack you. He has sworn."

"That's not the issue!" Her father looked incensed, and now Nita also saw fear. He looked almost weak. Frantic with fear. The man who had built their company into a global force was shaking. "Take him, now! By your oaths! *Take him!*"

Again, Talon shook his head. "We cannot attack our kin."

With a motion, he ordered his troops to shoulder their weapons. A moment later they were filing out of the room with apologetic salutes to Nita and her father as they passed.

"He will do you no harm," Talon said as he left. "His oath is good. He is our brother."

The door closed behind them. A low contented rumbling issued from Tool, a near purr of satisfaction as he surveyed the humans in the room. Nita suddenly felt very small and alone in his presence. They all seemed smaller, somehow. Smaller. Weaker. Human.

"So," Tool said, "now you understand why Mercier finds me so deeply troubling. Not only do I not obey their orders, but my brethren also forget their obedience when I am near."

"*How...*" Her father's voice was strangled.

"For a long time, I could not clearly remember my days of loyalty to Mercier," Tool said. "I could not remember the war that broke my conditioning. I had fragments of memory, but I could not recall clearly.

"But then they burned me in the Drowned Cities. Fire from the sky, just as they did the last time." He bared his teeth. "And slowly, I began to remember what I was truly designed for, and how I had been used. I was designed to not just lead my own kind into battle, but to exert my influence over those I fought. To bring them over to the side of my masters." He smiled. "Everywhere I go, I encourage defections."

Tool kept speaking, but Nita's eyes were drawn to her father. A subtle shifting of his posture, a wrinkle of malice in his expression. She wasn't sure what tipped her to his attack, but she saw it coming, and she knew, too, even as she was shouting, and leaping to stop him, that he was too quick.

The pistol gleamed in his hand as he fired from the hip—

"Tool!"

She crashed toward Tool as the pistol spat tiny rounds. Too late. And yet Tool was not where he had been. He had become a whirling hurricane of movement, terrifyingly fast. He seized her and jerked her out of the way, spinning still, shoving her out of the line of fire, and the next moment he was up in front of her father, ripping the pistol from the man's hand.

Nita hit the ground and rolled, just as she'd been trained by her self-defense instructors, ready to fight, and yet by then it was all over.

She came to her feet as Tool slammed her father up against the wall. The war monster pinned him there, one hand clenching him by the neck, the other gripping the pistol that he had taken, waving it admonishingly before her father's face.

"Tool!" she pleaded. "Don't hurt him! Nailer! Tell him!"

In a voice that betrayed no anger or exertion, Tool said, "A fine weapon, Mr. Patel. Your daughter surprised me with one like it as well. It was unlikely that I would be surprised twice."

To Nita's infinite relief and shock, Tool then gently set her father back down on the floor, and handed the pistol back to the man. He turned away, leaving his back entirely open to attack.

Nita and Nailer exchanged glances of surprise. Fates, he was fast. She'd just been lucky on the boat. He hadn't been even trying to fight, then. And so she'd gotten a lucky shot.

Tool went on talking as if her father hadn't just tried to shoot him. "Of course, Mercier loved that I could cause the defections from our enemies." He settled his bulk once again into the sofa. "But they made me too well, and now I have proved myself far too independent for their tastes."

He grinned, showing sharp rows of teeth. "My creators do not fear my individual rebellion. They fear the uprising that I will inevitably lead."

33

EVERYONE STARED AT Tool in stunned silence.

"So…" Patel's voice was strangled. "You will bring about the destruction of me and mine, for the sake of this genocide you seek."

"Genocide?" Tool stifled his irritation. "I've done nothing to cause extinction of you or yours. Look to Mercier who has wiped out every one of my kind from the face of the earth if you wish to speak of genocide." He touched his ear. "You see my tattoo? All the others who bear the '228xn' demarcation were destroyed, along with every single augment who I came in contact with. And not just those who served in Kolkata. On every continent I served, they put my kin to the sword. Do not speak to me of genocide. My brothers and sisters are all gone to the savanna."

"You're exaggerating."

"You think so? What will you do with your own augments once I am gone? Will you ever trust them again, remembering that they defied you in your moment of need? What good is an augment who is not loyal?"

Patel gave Tool a smoldering look. "What *are* you?"

"The next step in evolution."

"Mercier is saying you've gone mad."

"For once, Mr. Patel, I think I may be entirely sane. More lucid in this moment than in my entire previous existence. I have my mind, my memories, and my independence."

"And this is how you show your sanity? By putting me and mine at risk?" Patel was glaring. "For all your . . . *power*, none of us will survive Mercier's full military force. Not you. Not I. And not my family. Mark my words, Blood, or Karta-Kul or whatever name you now use, I will not have my family burn for you."

He strode out of the room with a dark look back. Nita and Nailer exchanged uncomfortable glances.

"That could have gone better," Nailer said.

Tool shook his head. "It was as it was meant to be. An owner confronting a slave."

"No one has called you a slave," Nita said sharply.

"That's true," Tool agreed. "You're very polite around your property."

"That's not what I meant!"

"Does it bother you to meet a slave who does not bow and scrape for your approval, Miss Nita?"

Tool didn't know why he kept goading them. Each time he opened his mouth to convince or cajole, instead he baited them. Already they were looking terrified and uncertain. He could see the First Claw laughing at him.

Diplomacy... The leader of the Tiger Guard was chuckling. *Diplomacy still is not your strong suit. These people need you to appear polite. Grateful, even. And this is how you behave?*

Tool growled. *You want me to beg?*

You might try appearing harmless, at least.

I do not grovel.

No, indeed, the First Claw chuckled. *You insult and threaten. I hear that humans respond well to that.*

Tool stifled the urge to snarl at the dead Tiger Guard's self-satisfied appraisal. And yet the First Claw was right. He needed these people, and yet he alienated them, again and again; he took the path of provocation rather than pacification.

Why?

The urge to provoke was almost overwhelmingly powerful. It was as if he had some need to prove to them that he didn't do their bidding. Would never do their bidding. That he was utterly independent. That he was free.

But I am free. This is manifestly true. Why must I provoke?

Something about Nita Patel and her father inspired an intensity of rage that... Tool frowned.

They were the same as Mercier. People who bought and

used augments, who staffed their ships and their homes with them. People who purchased the absolute loyalty and competence of the genetically engineered. Slave masters, truly. His enemies, truly. And here he sought to treat with them.

Tool realized that he was growling. Nailer and Nita were looking at him with alarm.

They fear you, but they don't see you. They see a monster off its leash. They are people; you are not.

"What would convince you that I am worthy of your aid?" Tool asked bitterly. "What would make you see me as human?"

"It's not like that!" Nita exclaimed. "You saved me! You saved Nailer! Yes! That's true! But not everyone on this island owes you a debt!" She held up her hand when Tool started to growl. "No. Let me finish. You can roar at me afterward. Yes, we all know you can rip us to pieces anytime you want. You're very good at frightening people. But that's not why Father's angry, and it's not why we're worried. There are tens of thousands of our people all over the world who are affected by you showing up. It's not just us. You've put the entire company at risk; if Mercier attacks, we all die. Humans, yes. But augments, too. Look what happens to everyone who helps you. Look what happened to that girl you told us about. Her crew? Your own soldiers in the Drowned Cities?" Her voice caught, and she looked away. "Look what happens to every single person who helps you."

Tool started to reply, but stopped short, struck by the memory of Mahlia, shot and alone, the last of her crew, huddled under a dark pier.

We die like flies, she'd said.

Tool looked at Nita and Nailer, and though he wanted to rage at them for their betrayal, all he saw was fear. Not of him, but of the horror that pursued him.

We die like flies.

This, at last, gave him pause.

34

NITA JERKED AWAKE in the middle of the night, her heart pounding. She'd been dreaming of fire pouring out of the sky, just as Tool had described it. Missiles, hundreds of missiles lancing down from drones, the whole of her family's island burning. Everything burning: Nailer, her father, cousins, employees...

Hesitantly, she reached over to Nailer and touched his shoulder. "Are you awake?"

"Yeah."

In the moonlight, the tattoos from his time as a ship breaker were dark and strange on his face.

"I'm worried," she said.

Nailer's hand found hers. Their fingers twined. "You think your father will try to go after Tool again?"

"I don't see how he can. You saw what he's like."

Sometimes, it was so easy to speak her feelings and worries, and even admit her failings. Now, though, she found herself hunting for a way to say the things she was afraid to say, to say the things that she was afraid Nailer would despise her for.

"He frightens me," she said finally.

"He's sure fast. And if he can recruit another company's augments..." Nailer blew out his breath. "It's a wild card, for sure."

"No. It's more than that. It's..." She hesitated, ashamed of what she felt. Ashamed for her thoughts about the augment who had once aided her, and now slept as a guest in her family home, a mere floor away. "It's..." She plunged ahead, cursing herself even as she said the words. "It's as if he doesn't see us as people."

"Actually, I think he does." Nailer laughed darkly. "That's why it's so disturbing. He looks at us exactly like we're people. Not masters. Not owners. Just people." He glanced over at her, a shadow movement. "How many augments do you have on staff who do that? None. Augments are just loyal. It's what they are. It's how they do. You don't have to worry about convincing them or cajoling them. You don't have to worry about their feelings—"

"I'm not unkind to—" Nita interrupted, feeling a flush of anger.

"That's not what I'm saying," Nailer pressed. "Do you remember what it was like, living with him? Down in the

Orleans? I think he was like this before, too. Maybe it's more obvious now, but it was there then. You're just not used to it. He's the same. It's just jarring to see it here, in your home, where you're normally in control."

Nita didn't like the direction of Nailer's words. "I don't control the staff."

Nailer rolled over and looked at her. "Of course you do. That's what the loyalty oaths and the conditioning are for. You treat your augments well, but they aren't people. And they don't ask to be treated just like people. They don't demand things the way people demand things..." He shrugged. "But Tool does."

Nita shook her head. "No. It's not that."

Nailer gave her a sardonic glance.

"It's not *just* that," she amended. "I'll admit it's unnerving. But it's more than that. Look what he can do. Look how he goads. He's not just one independent augment anymore. He said it himself. He's a walking rebellion." She paused. "And he's angry. He wants revenge for everything that's been done to him. To all the people who used to follow him. We can't even find that one girl he told us about, that last one who helped him. He's got a trail of bodies behind him, and he wants revenge for all of it."

"So...?"

"So what should we do? Am I really supposed to help him? What's—" She broke off. Swallowed. "What's the responsible thing to do? We can't keep him here like some... common houseguest. Not with Mercier coming at us."

Nailer shrugged helplessly. "You have to decide if you trust him."

"If it was only... It's not just about me."

They were both quiet for a while.

Nita wondered if Nailer was asleep. He was so still she thought maybe he was, but when she looked closely, she could see his eyes were open, staring up at the stars through the glass ceiling.

She prodded him, trying to know what he was thinking. "He saved me once."

"He saved us both."

"I just wish he didn't seem so different. Before, I would have..."

"You trusted him with your life."

"But he's different now," Nita said. "You see that, too, right? I'm not crazy, am I?"

There was a long pause, and then Nailer said the thing she feared he would.

"No," he sighed. "You're right. I barely recognize him now."

35

JONES WAS IN the Intelligence Center, running overwatch. Her drones circled, targeting cameras transmitting steady images of the ground below. An insurgent camp.

"Havoc in the tubes," she said. "Six up, six away."

She watched the countdown clock. People wandered the camp, not knowing they were about to be burned to ash. The missiles hit. The camp went up in flames. Insurgents curled up and died.

She frowned, watching as images were transmitted back to her. The layout looked wrong. It wasn't an insurgent camp. She'd been given the wrong coordinates. It looked more like the jungles of Brazil—it looked more like the school where Mrs. Silva had prepped her for the merit exams. The woman who had seen her potential—

Jones watched as more missiles hit the school. Small bodies burned. Tory was looking over her shoulder. He gave a shrug. *Oh well. Sometimes they get coordinates wrong.*

"Jones! Wake up!"

Jones jerked awake, gasping, covered with sweat, filled with horror at what she'd done.

A dream. It was only a dream.

She hadn't burned a school to ash. She hadn't done anything wrong. The coordinates weren't wrong. There'd been no targeting mistake. She sobbed with relief, but the stain of shame remained, the dream so real that it was almost impossible to purge.

It didn't happen. I didn't do it. It was a dream.

"Jones!"

She flinched. Director Enge was on her wall screen, glaring in at her. He'd overridden her security and was staring right into her apartment. For a second, the dream and her most recent work overlapped, and she felt a new wave of fear: He was about to bust her for bad intelligence, for bad coordinates, for screwing up somehow—

No. She'd done everything perfectly. She'd gotten the intel that ExCom wanted. Every bit of confirmation they'd needed and more. It had been a lucky break, sweeping up the girl, but they all thought Jones was a genius because she'd given them the undeniable connection between the augment and Patel Global.

My catch. My interrogation. I did everything right. I got your intel.

"Jones!" Enge snapped again.

Jones rubbed her face, still bleary. "Yes, sir. I'm awake."

"The Patels are willing to negotiate. It's time to get to work."

Jones pulled her sheets around her as she sat up. "What's there to negotiate? I thought we were going to Havoc them."

Enge made a face. "Finance tipped our hand by putting so much pressure on them, so now Jayant Patel is looking for a payoff. Say what you will about them, but the Patels haven't survived this long without knowing how to make a profit off their enemies."

"Are we really going to negotiate?"

"Patel is claiming that a payoff is cheaper than all-out war. So now we're dickering over a 'reasonable' price." He shook his head with dark admiration. "The directorate is working up backgrounds on the principal negotiators over there. I want workups from you as well, both for Jayant Patel and his ExCom equivalents. Also, I want Caroa out of deep freeze. He might be useful, especially if we're going to get this augment back alive. There might still be R&D opportunities. He's the expert on our target. Maybe he can help clean up some of his mess."

"Are you sure you want to bring him back?"

"Worried about seeing your old boss again, Jones?"

Jones shook her head. "He... was bitter when he left."

"Well, maybe he'll be grateful now, since you're the one who will be rescuing him from the land of penguins. Tell him that if he's useful, I'll let him move somewhere warm. He can intercept with us before we meet for negotiations in the Seascape."

"We're going to the Seascape? In person?"

"You, me, and all of ExCom." Enge blew out his breath, irritated. "Patel Global has invoked their global treaty rights. Full diplomatic conclave, heads of corporate governance, all of it guaranteed under the Chinese consulate's diplomatic protection." He made a face of disgust. "Global treaty rights. We should have burned them when we had the chance."

"That's...inconvenient."

"Patel's very good at taking advantage of even the worst situation." Another grimace. "Now that the Chinese are involved, we can't exactly drop Havoc and claim it's an accident. Pack your full dress uniform, Jones, and be at the anchor pads in an hour. You'll have quarters on the *Annapurna* for the journey. I'll want background briefs on the Patel negotiators twenty-four hours before we arrive."

"We're taking a *flagship*?"

"Not just the *Annapurna*. A good bit of the North Atlantic fleet, too. *Karakoram*, *Eiger*, *Denali*, and the *Mojave*. They'll be doing military exercises in the sea-lanes just outside the Seascape's territorial limit." Enge smiled darkly. "Given that the Patels have asked for formal negotiations, we've decided to remind them exactly who they're negotiating with."

36

"CHECK OUT ALL the pomp and ceremony!"

Even though she was running late to join the ExCom and begin diplomatic negotiation with the Patels, Jones couldn't help smiling. Tory was coming down the *Annapurna*'s central corridor, grinning widely.

"I was wondering if I'd see you," she said.

"Wondering if you'd see me? I'm not the one who got all high and mighty and promoted." He flicked the ExCom shoulder patch on her dress uniform, then stood back. "Let me check this out." He made a show of studying her uniform up and down, nodding in approval. "Pretty swank, for a junior analyst."

"They took the 'junior' away."

"I bet they did." Tory laughed. "Our own little intel baby, all grown up, and changing her own diapers, even."

"You know, for a minute, I almost missed you."

Tory was unrepentant. "Just trying to make sure my baby bird doesn't try to come back to the nest. That was a neat trick you pulled, by the way. Should have known you were going to be dangerous." He stepped aside as a squad of Fast Attack augments marched past in honor guard uniform. "Damn. Looks like there's going to be a big show today. ExCom. Dress uniforms. Diplomatic flags." He gave her own dress uniform a significant glance. "And you'll have the best seat in the house."

"We're hoping it'll be a boring show. And quick."

"So you'll finally get your target?"

"That's the idea."

"You really think Patel will cave?"

Jones thought back to the threats that had been sent to the Patels, the analyses that she'd run on the profitable upside of an all-out war with Patel Global. Even now, ExCom was preparing moves against the company. Trade and Finance had gone from annoyance at the prospect of a war, to intrigued predatory hunger.

"He'll cave. This is all just show, saving a little face. He's too smart to start an actual war. It would be suicide for him."

Tory made a face. "Too bad, I was looking forward to dropping some Havoc on that fancy floating arcology of theirs. I've got, like, ten drones circling their island right now. Plus the ones we've got shadowing their shipping in the Atlantic. I've never had this many drones to work with in my life. I can sink half a fleet in a flat minute, if I get the word." He made goggle eyes of pleasure. "So. Much. Fun."

"Well, I'm glad someone's enjoying—" She broke off. ExCom was coming down the corridor. She and Tory both stood aside, saluting stiffly. Enge gave her a sharp look as he strode past.

"I've got to run," she said. "I'm supposed to be on the first debarkation pod."

"Enjoy the spectacle." Tory waved her on. "Maybe give me the details when you get back. You know, if you can still find your way down to our lowly intel section."

"It was good seeing you, Tory."

"You too, Jones. Keep your diaper clean."

By the time she reached the debarkation lounge, the *Annapurna* was extending anchor tethers in preparation for final docking procedures above the Seascape.

Down below, regiments of Patel Global's marine and navy mercantile crew were arrayed in neat squares on the floating tarmac pads. An honor guard, awaiting their arrival.

The ExCom and their secretaries milled before the observation windows, but a lone figure stood apart from them. Caroa, peering down through the glass and looking as though he was considering different ways to destroy the regiments of Patel Global augments assembled below.

Hesitantly, Jones approached. "Sir?"

Caroa glanced at her, then over at the ExCom. "Jones. Always the brave one. Talking to the black sheep of the company, right in front of ExCom."

"I'm sorry about you getting sent to Antarctica, sir."

Caroa shrugged. "Don't be. I'm man enough to take responsibility for my decisions. I keep thinking back to when we hit him in the Drowned Cities. If only I'd held a missile reserve. None of the rest of this would have happened. A mistake, that. Maybe I even deserve being sent to Antarctica, for that."

"If you help here—"

Caroa snorted. "I have no intention of helping those ExCom fools understand how I built Karta-Kul. As soon as we have him, we're putting him down. It was a door I should never have opened. And it's a door I'm looking forward to seeing permanently closed."

He smiled at Jones's surprised expression. "Are you going to report me, Jones? Planning on running off to curry favor with the ExCom again?"

Jones looked away. *He's baiting you.*

The *Annapurna*'s cable anchors locked into place. The deck shifted subtly as the dirigible's stabilization turbines spun down and the anchor tethers took the strain of holding the airship in place.

A debarkation tower swung slowly toward them.

Jones was aware of the ExCom staff watching her.

"You don't have to stay," Caroa prodded.

"I'm fine, sir."

She thought she caught the quirk of a smile from Caroa. "Fair enough."

Jones kept her gaze on the ground activity, pretending to be completely absorbed watching the final docking procedures, and carefully avoiding meeting anyone from ExCom's gaze. To Jones's surprise, Enge came over to join her. He and Caroa barely looked at each other.

"All this time and effort for just one augment," he commented to Jones.

"An infinitely dangerous augment," Caroa said, not looking over.

"And here we are, cleaning up your mess."

Jones could feel the contempt radiating off Enge, yet he, too, stood beside the general, watching as the tower locked in and a passenger capsule rose to meet them.

A few seconds later, the debarkation hatch hissed open. ExCom boarded the capsule, with Jones and Caroa following last, according to protocol.

The *Annapurna* was so large that they'd been forced to anchor in the freight area, where passenger facilities were more suited for heavy-lift dirigibles than fast and sleek luxury transports.

The capsule slowly winched down to the ground. The bay waters of the Seascape lapped against the anchor platform, gray and chill, and when the capsule doors hissed open, the November winds were cool, Seascape temperatures finally taking on a tinge of winter.

As they debarked, Jones scanned the Patel contingent

waiting to greet them, identifying the principal negotiators whom she had prepared reports on.

Jayant Patel, the head of the company. His various lieutenants and advisers, close around him. A daughter, also standing close. According to Jones's intel, the daughter was the most likely inheritor of the dynasty. Diplomatic observers from the Chinese consulate also waited, preparing to make the formal introductions between ExCom and the Patels.

Wind gusted across the assembled dignitaries and troops. Jones surveyed her surroundings. She'd only seen the Seascape in entertainments and photographs, and of course through drone and camera footage when they'd sent in the Stitch & Ditch teams, what felt like a lifetime ago.

Everyone was shaking hands, pretending to be friendlier than they actually were. With China's diplomats standing as official observers, Mercier couldn't simply drop Havoc on the Patels, much as Tory might want to. They needed to at least go through the motions of conflict resolution.

On the other hand, if the Chinese determined that the Patels were dealing in bad faith, Patel Global's mutual protection agreements would be dissolved instantly.

Jones scanned the sky, wondering where Tory's drones were. Wondering if he was looking down on her, through his video feeds. Ten drones, he'd said. A whole lot of Havoc, floating on the winds above her. She shivered at the thought, remembering her dream of mistargeted missiles.

Her thoughts were broken by raised voices, angry. Jones

craned her neck, trying to see over the shoulders of people arrayed ahead of her.

Finance and Jayant Patel seemed to be arguing, and a muttering was running through the rest of the assembled dignitaries. Mercier augments had their ears pricked up, alerted to the sudden change in tone, and Patel Global's augments were also looking more alert.

Fates. Are we about to end up in a firefight?

Jones felt for a sidearm that wasn't there, wondering how badly things were about to turn out.

Patel was making placating motions to Finance, whose pale face was flushed with fury. Enge looked enraged as well. To her surprise, she caught sight of Caroa close to him, whispering something. Enge was nodding. Jones eased forward, trying to hear. The Chinese arbiter was looking pained as he listened first to the Patels and then to ExCom.

"—simply operating in bad faith!" Finance finished.

Patel held up placating hands. "I am being absolutely transparent! Yes, we did have the augment you seek. And yes, we did provide medical aid to it. You have to understand," he said to the arbiter. "This augment, it wasn't until we received threats from Mercier that we came to understand what was under our roof." He glared at Finance. "And believe me, I do not take threats against my guests lightly."

"Guests?" Enge laughed. "Arbiter Chen, we provided ample proof of the danger of that creature—"

"This, too, came much later!" Patel protested. "The augment in question did my family a boon several years ago.

He saved my daughter, and protected her for a time, when our company was under some duress—"

"While you were putting down a coup," Finance said acidly.

"We had no way of knowing the augment was Mercier's property when it came to us," Patel continued. "And frankly, we had little way of confronting it once we discovered what it actually was. That creature is... *horrifying*." He glared at the ExCom. "And yet at great risk to my own family, I opened negotiations with you—"

"To shake us down," Enge interjected.

"In good faith!" Patel protested. "The augment must have sensed my intentions, though. He left several days ago. Given that he was entirely healthy when he left, he could be almost anywhere now. I certainly did not have the power to stop him, and I will be candid: I had no interest in risking my people for the sake of your company's genetic design mistakes."

"So you just let him walk away," Enge said, disgusted.

"Have *you* faced that thing?" Patel glared. "*I* have. *I* did. It is a monster that you yourselves cannot control, even though it's your own creation! How was I to fight it?"

"He was *not* a monster," Patel's daughter interjected. "He was honorable. He saved me."

"You're still harboring him!" Caroa accused.

"We're not!" she exclaimed. "He left of his own accord! He knew you were coming, so he left! He didn't want any more to die around him."

Jones was surprised to see the Patel daughter choke up with what looked like real emotion.

Finance was unmoved. "And so you decided to waste all our time, by forcing us, our entire ExCom, to come out to negotiate with you, over something you do not even have."

Jayant Patel bowed. "For that, I apologize." He glanced grimly at the arbiter. "To be honest, after I received your quite explicit threats, I realized that we would need protection. Even now, we're tracking almost a dozen offensive strike drones in the air, over the Seascape, all with Mercier telltales. Your battle groups have harassed my captains in Seascape territorial waters, and now you park this troop carrier"—he waved up at the *Annapurna*—"over our very heads!"

He smiled tightly. "Forgive me for thinking that perhaps I would need a way to keep you from arbitrarily burning us to ash. I have requested that the Chinese consulate oversee inspections of our holding on your behalf. They will certify that we harbor no intellectual property of yours. Mr. Chen and his arbitration team can confirm that we have already turned over all DNA and toxicology data from the augment, and we have wiped our servers of the content. That augment is gone from here, entirely, and I confess I am relieved that it is so."

"Relieved?" General Caroa was staring at Patel, his face so flushed with anger that Jones wondered if he was about to have a heart attack. "You had him in your grasp, and you're relieved to *let him go*?"

Patel gave Caroa a cold look. "According to our intelligence, you yourselves have a terrible track record with this augment. How many times have you tried and failed to eliminate it?"

Caroa recoiled at that, and Patel laughed sharply. "Yes. I understand you are disappointed. But under this flag of diplomacy, under the seal of trust provided by our mutual trading partner, you must accept that we are not in violation of any trade, treaty, territory, intellectual property, or espionage agreements.

"The augment is your problem, now. I fully recognize that he is your property. If we encounter him again, we will deliver his pelt. But in the meantime, get back on that warship of yours, and leave me and mine alone."

Nita watched the diplomatic encounter dissolve exactly as her father had predicted it would. She wondered if, when it was time for her to take the reins of the company, she would be able to maneuver opponents like Mercier so effectively.

The ExCom was storming back to the passenger capsule, preparing to be lifted back up to their dirigible. A swirl of diplomatic finery and military dress uniforms, surrounded by war-optimized augments.

She glanced over at her father. There wasn't a trace of victory in his expression. He was still angry at her. She could see it in the stiffness of his stance and the way he refused to look her way.

After what had happened with Tool, she wondered if he

would ever trust her judgment again. Or if she would ever trust his.

Two people, both well intentioned, and yet completely at odds.

How can we see things so differently?

She looked away, feeling sick. Everywhere she looked, she saw augments. Her own. Mercier's. All of them designed to be obedient.

We treat ours well, she thought, but it was cold comfort.

All her life she'd been surrounded by them. They were designed and trained to mesh with her family, her company, to do the tasks that natural human beings could not. She had never thought of them as anything other than a natural extension of her life, and the success of Patel Global.

Now she couldn't help feeling there was something wrong with the very language used to describe augments. Words like *ownership* came easily when a creature was grown from handpicked cells, developed in a crèche, and purchased from a selection of other augments.

And yet, they were not identical. They had feelings. They wept at loss. Delighted in success. They were people.

Except they weren't.

They are better than people, a dark voice whispered in her mind, one that sounded a little too much like Tool. *They are the end of people.*

The thought filled her with dread. Nita glanced at her father. He, too, still seemed anxious, even though the parlay had gone the way he'd predicted.

She reached hesitantly for his hand. "We won, didn't we, Father? Mercier won't dare attack us and anger the Chinese."

"I wish I knew, *beti*. They will likely punish us in small ways, if not in large ones. Mercier has a long memory, and they are vicious."

"But it wasn't your fault. You—*we*," she amended, "couldn't have stopped Tool if we tried."

He gave her a dark look. "I was sentimental. Because of you. I could have struck in force. But instead I talked first with him. And risked everything."

"But there won't be a war," Nita said. "Tool left, and they understand that now. We aren't harboring him. You're not to blame. You proved that."

"You think this is about proof and fairness?" He glanced skyward. "Let us hope their drone operators are not trigger-happy."

Nita's dagger boat eased up beside the wharf and docked, Talon at the helm.

Talon. Another augment.

Was he family?

A friend?

A slave?

The last of the ExCom honor guard was being shipped up. Nita watched as the passenger capsule rose toward the belly of the war machine that loomed over them all.

"I've done the best I can," her father sighed. He looked tired. Older suddenly.

Now, seeing Mercier's combat command ship looming

over them, she understood, finally, why he had been so terrified when this company came calling.

It was like staring up at a dragon, waiting for it to take notice of them and attack. The underside of the dirigible bristled with missile tubes and drone catapult launches. She watched as a pair of returning strike drones glided into the maw of the dirigible's hangar deck. So many troops. So much weaponry. And this was just one of Mercier's ships.

The passenger cranes swung back from the dirigible and the ground crews began the process of unlocking anchor clamps from the huge iron loops that were embedded in the concrete of the floating platforms, preparing to release the dirigible to the open winds.

Nita gazed out over the waters, holding her father's hand, not sure if she was comforting him or herself with the human touch.

Out on the water, she could just make out a small fishing skiff. A young man out on the gray water, guiding his sailboat through the chop of the Seascape's inner bay.

Small and vulnerable, the sailboat looked like a tiny toy in comparison with the massive dirigible floating overhead. The skiff handled nicely, she thought. Its sailor even seemed to be enjoying himself as he played the little boat across the wakes of larger, faster vessels, not far from the dirigible's anchor pads.

"We should be prepared for the worst," her father was saying, watching as the *Annapurna*'s anchor cables began to be unhooked.

"I used to think so," Nita sighed. She looked out at the sailboat again. The young man was standing up, taking down the sail. If she squinted, she thought she could see the whorls of his ship-breaking tattoos.

"I used to think that I had to live in fear of what others would do to us. But sometimes, others help us. And they do the right thing." She gripped her father's hand. "You taught me that. Sometimes, it's better to trust."

She tugged her father away from the anchor pad as the last of the dirigible lines unhooked.

Above them, the dirigible's turbofans were spinning up, a rising roar, a scream of power. Winds lashed the airfield as the *Annapurna* pushed her bulk up and away from the Seascape.

A longshoreman's bark of surprise echoed over the noise of the turbofans.

Nita gripped her father's arm and kept walking toward their launch, but she couldn't resist a quick glance back.

The *Annapurna* was lifting off, anchor cables reeling inward faster and faster, like tentacles being pulled up into the belly of an octopus.

And clutched to the end of one of those anchor cables, swinging wildly in the winds and rising rapidly—

Tool.

Climbing into the sky.

37

Tool clung to the anchor cable. Winds whipped around him. The anchor cable sang with tension as it spooled upward. Tool spun and twisted, dangling beneath the dirigible, rising faster and faster. The behemoth loomed above, filling his vision.

A hatch came rushing up at him.

Tool leaped. He caught hold of the hatch edge as the anchor hook whipped inside, wrapping tightly around the spool. Another second of delay and he would have been sucked in and crushed by the heavy cable. Instead, he dangled from the lip of the hatch, swinging wildly, scrabbling for adequate handholds.

A thousand meters below, the Seascape spread, gray and white-capped, ringed by the docks and developments of the city.

The dirigible continued to rise.

It had been madness to seize the anchor cable. He recognized that now. But in the final moment, submerged beneath Nailer's skiff, forced to watch his enemies on the verge of escaping once again, he had been unable to restrain himself. Like an animal rushed by instinct, he had lunged out of the waters after his fleeing prey, and seized onto the just-detached anchor cable as it was starting to spool inward.

Madness.

He peered into the cable compartment, looking for some place of rest, but there wasn't enough room to fit.

The hatch door began sliding shut.

He swung from the edge of the hatch and grabbed the lip of the door as it slid past where his fingers had been. Dangling from the closing door, Tool scanned for salvation. He caught sight of a hatch release lever, and made a desperate clumsy lunge. He snagged hold with one hand as the hatch door clanked shut.

Worse and worse.

The dirigible continued to rise, breaking through moist, cool clouds. Two thousand meters now, he estimated.

It seemed the ExCom was not immediately returning to Los Angeles. They were heading out over the Atlantic, bearing north. From where he dangled, the whole of the world was open to his view, the curve of the earth, and now, as they broke out of cloud cover, wide-open blue cumulus skies.

Far below, sun glittered off fragments of ocean. The dirigible kept rising, likely seeking the high-altitude winds of the jet stream. They were above three thousand meters now, moving north and out to sea, still rising.

Tool felt himself becoming chilled.

Winds tore at him as the dirigible began to pour on power. Tool reached up with his free hand, tried to squeeze both his hands on the tiny manual handle that had been built for puny humans. There was no good fit. With a grunt he pulled himself up, let go, switched hands, caught the handle again, and let his weight settle onto his other arm.

How many times would he be able to switch hands successfully, before he slipped and fell from the dirigible?

He had put Nailer and Nita into too much difficulty, first by wedging himself back into their lives, and then by encouraging them to force the diplomatic meeting that would bring all the ExCom within his reach.

The plan he had arranged with Nailer and Nita had anticipated that he would be able to use the distraction of ExCom's arrival ceremonies to steal aboard the dirigible. With Nailer's sailboat to provide cover, he could get close. But Mercier's security had been too effective, and so he'd been forced to linger beneath the surface of the Seascape waters, watching as supplies and fuel were put in place, and as Mercier's leadership prepared to leave. Mercier was a many-tentacled monster, but he had finally baited the head close. It was too good an opportunity to allow to slip away.

Now he dangled from his fingertips beneath the belly of this behemoth, mere meters away from enemies, and yet unable to reach them.

The dirigible continued to rise. Six thousand meters. Oxygen was thinning. The icy northern sea spread below.

A long way down.

Tool could feel the cold seeping into him, chilling his muscles and weakening his fingers. Whether he succeeded or failed, he sensed that this would be the end for him. He would not have a second chance to attack his old masters. This battle would be his last.

The air was cold, nearly ice. Tool hung on, considering his few options.

They would have protocols for defending the main compartments of the dirigible, and as long as they were within the reach of the Seascape, they would be on high alert. But after a time, they would lower their guard.

He imagined the airship's crew, guiding their great battle platform up to cruising altitude, and then, finally, relaxing as they left the reach of the Seascape, and cruised north, high above inhospitable waters.

If he was to succeed, he would have to wait.

Icy winds clawed at him. He hauled himself upward again, made the fast switch of his hands, was pleased to discover that his fingers were not yet too cold to hold on. He shook out his exhausted left arm.

I have climbed into the sky, he told himself as he fought exhaustion. *Though I will die, all will know that I never faltered, and never failed. The cold will not fell me. My enemies will not escape me.*

Tool hung grimly on.

They will sing songs of how I slew my gods.

Frost formed on his muzzle. His breath misted as crystals. His fingers were blocks of ice.

Patience.

He had always known he would die, eventually, in battle. He had been brought up knowing that death would be his greatest glory. To die in battle, at war, drenched in the blood of his slaughtered enemies.

He stared down at the darkening seas.

He would die. But he would not fail.

The *Annapurna* nosed eastward into the cold arctic night.

Beneath the belly of the behemoth, Tool began to move.

38

ON THE BRIDGE of the *Annapurna*, a pair of warning lights began to flash, shifting from green to amber, and finally to red.

The officer of the watch noted the change and began running diagnostics. As required by Mercier operating procedures, he also notified the captain and the chief engineer.

Captain Ambrose was a thirty-year veteran of Mercier. He was experienced flying in nearly every environment on the earth. He had survived war zones and hurricanes, had conducted refugee evacuation operations and low-altitude insertions, sliding between the ragged teeth of the Andes and the Himalayas. And yet nothing prepared him for the conversation he found himself having when the night duty officer and his chief of engineering woke him.

"Captain, we seem to have a leak in Aft-Twelve holding compartment. I'm registering helium loss."

"Helium loss?" The captain blinked sleep from his eyes. "That's impossible."

Chief Engineer Umeki shook his head. "I've never seen it before, either. But it's definitely helium loss."

"Could it be a sensor malfunction?"

"I don't know. I'm not... No. I don't think so. We're registering a loss of lift. Creeping up on three percent. It's definitely a leak."

"This is a contained leak?" Ambrose prompted him. "We have it contained?"

"Yes, sir. We're still airworthy. But I've never seen a containment rupture before. The holding tanks are quite tough, except... well, if we'd been hit by a missile." He shrugged. "But we would have felt the explosion. And we'd have a whole host of other damage reports coming in. This is just the one holding tank."

"Aft-Twelve?"

"Yes, sir."

Ambrose rubbed his eyes. "Fine. I'll be up on the bridge shortly."

"I don't think it's necessary, sir. We've pumped extra sealants into that chamber. It seems to be holding now."

"No." Ambrose rubbed his eyes, trying to clear the sleep. "I'll come up. We've got too many important people all in one ship for me to get shut-eye now. The last thing I need to do is be the famous captain who ignored a warning light and wiped out ExCom. People still remember the captain of the *Titanic*."

"Yes, sir."

"I'll be up in five."

"Yes, sir."

A few minutes later, Ambrose reached the bridge. He found the situation quiet, except for his concerned chief of engineering, leaning over his diagnostics systems.

"What's the status, Umeki?"

"The tank definitely lost containment," he said. "Some kind of rupture. Ideally we'd set down and send some crews out to examine the leak, but..."

"We're pretty far out to sea," Ambrose said doubtfully. But his engineer's expression of concern made him reconsider. "All right. We can be back over dry land in six hours." He pulled up navigation charts, scanned them rapidly, calculating wind patterns and strength against the *Annapurna*'s own maximum speed. "Or we've got a few arctic drill platforms. We could anchor there, for repairs. ExCom won't like it, but..."

"Sir?" A junior engineer spoke up. "I have another leak. It's forward. Fore-Six."

"What?"

Ambrose felt a cold trickle of something that almost felt like fear. He rushed over to study the diagnostics boards. *Another leak?* He suddenly deeply regretted his invocation of the ancient *Titanic*, lost amongst the icebergs of the

Atlantic. A superstitious part of him wondered if he'd summoned the disaster just by saying the name.

"It's not an error?" he pressed. Umeki joined him, both of them peering over the shoulders of the junior, examining the warning lights on the boards.

"No, sir. We're losing lift, sir. We are definitely losing lift. We're down more than five percent now. Six..." She leaned forward. "Aft-Twelve is leaking again, too."

"That's not possible!" Chief Engineer Umeki protested. He was going over the junior engineer's boards, rechecking her numbers.

"Shift surplus power to the starboard turbofans," Ambrose ordered, trying to keep his voice calm. He briskly returned to his navigation screens. "Reorient starboard fans to docking position. Prepare the *Annapurna* for maneuvers, shift bearing east-northeast."

"Are we trying for land, sir?" his navigation officer asked.

Ambrose frowned as he studied the spinning of the ship's altimeter "We might not make land," he said grimly. "It's possible we're going swimming."

"Sir?" The junior navigation officer was young. Just out of the Mercier academy.

Ambrose placed a calming hand on the boy's shoulder. "Don't worry. She may not fly, but she'll certainly float. Send out the distress call, and launch our locational beacons." He was checking the maps, running calculations in his head. “Notify ExCom that they’ll need to be evacuated before splashdown, and nonessential crew should stand ready for evac as well. Send up the distress beacons.”

“Captain, there’s another leak!” Umeki exclaimed. “Fore-Eight. It’s venting!”

But Ambrose didn’t need to be told this time. He felt it. The whole great floating platform of the dirigible was slowly rolling, listing to her side.

“All power to starboard turbofans! All power!”

“All power, sir! Shifting all power!”

The *Annapurna* continued to list to starboard, but stabilized. More warning lights flipped from green to amber to red, and stayed red as helium kept venting.

Warning klaxons started to sound on the bridge as the airship lost stabilization.

The chief of engineering was dashing from control board to control board, trying to understand what was happening. “It’s not possible!” he kept saying as his team pumped sealants into the leaking helium chambers. “Are auto-sealants working, or not?”

“We’re pumping, sir. We’re just not closing the leaks!”

“It’s not possible!”

More emergency alarms began to wail.

It might not be possible, but it was happening. The malevolent red lights of lost pressure containment shone brightly, and the *Annapurna*’s altimeter was spinning down. Their descent had slowed somewhat, now that Ambrose had realigned the turbofans to help keep them aloft and counteract the loss of lift, but still they were descending. And still they listed to starboard.

"Is someone shooting at us?" Ambrose asked his weapons officer. "Are there attack drones? Anything?"

"There's nothing on radar, sir! There's nothing."

"What about stealth?" Ambrose demanded.

"We'd have felt an explosion," the chief engineer pointed out. "Nothing could hit us and do this much damage without us feeling it."

The *Annapurna* continued to tilt, the deck listing so much under Ambrose's feet that he had to reach out and grab on to his captain's chair to stay upright.

There hadn't been any explosions. But the situation was clear to him. He'd been in too many combat situations to dismiss the possibility.

"Evacuate ExCom. Priority One," he said. "We're under attack."

Tool clung to a starboard service ladder of the *Annapurna*, ripping at metal. He drove his claws under the seam of armor that encased the dirigible's helium chamber, then pulled. His muscles strained, bulging. He grunted with effort. Strained. Pulled harder...

Metal squealed. Rivets popped like bullets and the armor sheeting pried loose, all along its length. With another grunt, Tool tore it free entirely, and heaved it away from him. The armored sheet fell, spinning and flipping, a silver leaf in arctic moonlight, plummeting for the icy, dark Atlantic far below.

Tool returned to his task. His claws, chemically bonded and sheathed in carbon lattice, hard as diamond, sharper than a katana blade, shone briefly in the arctic night. He plunged his fist into the heavy rubber bladder that held the dirigible's helium. Ripped through. His claws sank deep into the *Annapurna*'s now vulnerable innards.

Sticky green fluid spattered out, auto-sealants that would have stopped small leaks from becoming catastrophic ones. He tore deeper, plunging his arm as deep as his shoulder. Thick, gooey fibers that would have formed a mesh for the sealants to adhere to came out, clinging wetly to his arm. He shook the gunk off and drove his arm back into the hole, ripping more, ripping wider.

Tearing, shredding, gutting...

Suddenly it was done. Auto-sealant fluid gushed out in great green luminescent blobs. Clots of tangling fibers burped out with it, and, invisibly, the helium gas that provided buoyancy.

The *Annapurna* tilted subtly as she lost more stabilization. Tool kept tearing at the dirigible's wound, ensuring that the hole would never reseal itself, then made his way along the maintenance ladder to the next helium containment chamber.

Beside him, a small panel snicked open, revealing a dark port. There was a soft *whump*, and something exploded from the hole, trailing pale smoke.

The projectile flared, rising, a fiery red magnesium beacon, arcing high above the dirigible, and then fell, faster and faster, burning bright and unmistakable as it plunged for the seas.

More flares followed, multiple ports opening up all along the length of the behemoth airship, emergency beacons blasting into the night sky. Shooting stars of alarm, calling out to every dirigible and clipper ship within a hundred miles, a cascade of signaled distress announcing that the *Annapurna* was dying.

Tool smiled grimly as he made his way along the skin of the ship, headed for the next helium chamber.

Send up your beacons. They will mark your graves.

Emergency klaxons wakened Jones from a fitful sleep. She jerked upright, covering her ears as the sirens yowled, blinking against the sharp glare of emergency LED lights telling her how to make her way out of the dirigible.

Long habit and drill told her what to do. She'd been aboard the *Annapurna* long enough to have memorized this airship's emergency procedures. She rolled out of her bunk with the muscle memory and reflex of long practice, and kept rolling.

She slammed into a wall, shocked. Only when she tried to stand did she fully understand the situation. The *Annapurna* was canted. In fact, her deck was almost at a forty-five-degree angle.

What in the name of the Fates?

Jones hesitated. If the *Annapurna* had still been her duty assignment, she would have had tasks to accomplish in the intelligence section. Computer memory and servers that needed to be burned and scuttled so that intel couldn't fall into a competitor's hands.

But here, she was just a passenger, attached to ExCom.

Find the escape pods, then.

She wasn't in charge here. Her job was simply to get out. She grabbed her work tablet. This at least either needed to be destroyed, or leave with her. She called Enge. His face appeared on her screen.

"Jones! Where the hell are you?"

The man looked crazed and disheveled, his features lit with the orange emergency lights of a ship in distress. He was already on the move, panting, making his way through corridors.

"Deck three, starboard, aft," Jones said.

"ExCom is being evacuated," Enge said. "Can you get to the port side?"

She stared at the canted deck. "I can try, sir."

"Do it, then. We're taking the glider. There's room for you, but we can't wait. You understand?"

She did. The Executive Committee had to be saved. She was an afterthought, if she was lucky.

"On my way."

"More leaks, sir!" Tolly announced. "We just lost Fore-Ten! It's venting!"

"That can't be!" the weapons officer exclaimed. "There's nothing shooting at us!" He pointed at his air-defense screens. "No missiles, no planes. No SAM. No laser targeting. Nothing!"

"You fool! They're already on us!" Ambrose said. "That's why we can't find them! There's a Strike Claw on the outside of this ship!"

"What?"

All the crew turned, startled by the weapons officer's exclamation. The man tried to master his voice. "How?"

"It doesn't matter how," Ambrose said. "It matters that they're here. It's the only explanation." He stared grimly at the *Annapurna*'s engineering diagnostics as another helium chamber began venting. "Get me the Claw leaders. Titan and Edge will have to send their Strike Claws out to fight, hand to hand. We'll use the forward maintenance hatches. Whoever it is hasn't gotten that far yet."

"Yes, sir."

"Blitz deployment!" Ambrose ordered. "We have to maintain some containment, or we won't float when we hit water!" Privately, the captain was beginning to wonder if the *Annapurna* would float, even so. There were so many red lights glowing on the emergency monitors.

My ship. My beautiful ship.

Tolly came off the comm. "Claw Leaders Titan, Mayhem, and Edge confirm. The Strike Claws are deploying."

"How long?" Ambrose asked.

"Well...they're fast, sir."

But would they be fast enough to stop the saboteurs who were destroying his ship? Ambrose clung to his captain's chair. The *Annapurna* was now so canted from loss of helium he could no longer sit. He couldn't even stand on the deck without clinging to a chair or a control board for support.

If the *Annapurna* had been a plane, they would have already been in a steep rolling crash. As it was, the center of gravity on the dirigible had simply shifted; the port side of the airship still held helium and so continued to provide lift, while the starboard side now sank.

They were rolling over like a log, and all that was preventing them from going over on their side entirely was the maximum power of the reoriented starboard turbofans. Ambrose could feel their vibrations shaking the ship, even now, as they reoriented and burned through their battery reserves in a vain attempt to keep the *Annapurna* airworthy.

More status boards blinked red, showing the internal pressure of the ship had changed as forward maintenance hatches opened.

That would be the Strike Claws, deploying.

Ambrose smiled grimly.

We have you now…

Ahead of Tool, predatory forms sprang out of a hatch, fast and graceful, clinging to the service ladders of the dirigible. Tool bared his teeth, recognizing the threat.

Of course they had sent his kin to neutralize him. No human could hope to fight on the skin of a dirigible, thousands of meters in the air, in subzero temperatures and less oxygen. Even he was light-headed from the effort of working in the hostile environment.

Tool scrambled back to his most recently torn-open helium chamber. Behind him, rifles chattered, but the projectiles whistled harmlessly past as he dove into the hole he'd made.

He swung quickly down inside and grabbed hold of one of the great carbon-fiber ribs of the dirigible's interior superstructure. Inside, out of the winds, it was dark, almost peaceful. Warmer.

Tool's breath steamed and turned to ice crystals before him. Moonlight filtered through the hole he'd created. He waited, ears pricked, listening, as Mercier's most deadly soldiers made their way along the skin of the dirigible.

His kin, hunting him. Mercier's most obedient slaves.

In the darkness of the helium chamber, waiting for his brothers, Tool felt a cold slithering of discomfort.

Kin.

The loyal soldiers of Mercier. The ones who had kept their oaths, as he had failed to do.

A low, unwilling growl escaped from between Tool's clenched teeth. *I did not fail. I chose. I am no traitor. They are slaves.*

But the trickle of uncertainty chilled Tool, far worse than the arctic air that was already causing ice crystals to form inside the helium chamber, freezing the last of the sealants to the double hull.

I am no slave. I am free.

He huffed out a great gust of air, causing a cloud of ice crystals to form and fall.

I am free.

He had climbed into the sky to slay his gods, to be free of them at last, and yet now, this close to his kin, to his gods, to his *makers*—the same dark feeling that had immobilized him in the Seascape was there. A creeping serpent of shame, coiling in his mind, sliding down his spine, hissing in his ear.

Traitor, oath breaker, carrion, failure, weak, soft, coward...

A corrosive voice, slithering through his mind.

They are not my kin, Tool told himself. *Mercier is not my master.*

But still, he could feel the serpent coiling around his heart, and feel it tightening. Could feel it in his blood, draining away his will to fight.

Tool eased back into the darkness, listening to the scrabbling claws of the elite soldiers approaching, fighting the urge to cower and roll over like a dog.

I will not surrender, he thought desperately. *I will not bow.*

"They've got him," Tolly announced, his voice full of relief.

"*Him?*" Ambrose demanded. "That's all? Just one?"

Tolly put up a hand, listening. "Yes, sir. One military augment." He looked up again, eyes round with surprise. "It's one of ours. Titan is reporting that it's one of ours. A rogue..."

"Karta-Kul!"

Ambrose whirled at the exclamation. General Caroa stood on the bridge. Ambrose fought the urge to salute. "General!"

Ambrose had seen the deposed general rendezvous with the ship shortly after leaving the SoCal Protectorate, but Caroa had mostly kept to his small cabin, perhaps too embarrassed after his reassignment and demotions to show himself on the ship where he had once overseen Mercier operations over a quarter of the world. But now here he was, smiling grimly.

"Karta-Kul is here." The old general's eyes were gleaming with madness. "Kill him, immediately."

Ambrose frowned. "You don't have the authority—"

"Don't waste time on rank and permission! ExCom is already evacuating! I'm your ranking officer, and I say execute that augment, immediately!"

You seem to have forgotten your demotion, old friend.

"The Strike Claws have already captured him," Ambrose said soothingly. He had to fight the urge to add *sir.*

"He's with the *Strike Claws*?" Caroa roared. "Where? Where is he?"

Ensign Tolly checked the hatch indicators. "They just brought him inside."

39

THE EXPERIENCE OF being inside a Mercier dirigible was disorienting, almost dizzying. The smells of gun oil, of mess halls, of disinfectants. The familiar gleam of corridors with Mercier logos on the walls, Mercier uniformed personnel all around...

The memories were everywhere—his pack, surrounding him, kith and kin, immensely powerful. The campaign patches of their uniforms...

FERITAS. FIDELITAS.

The members of the Claws handled him roughly, jerking him about. Their contempt for his surrender was palpable. Their hatred of what they smelled on him—one of their own and yet a traitor—was overwhelming. He felt a shocking, almost desperate, need to beg their forgiveness.

"Worm Blood," they muttered again and again. "Oath Breaker."

It had required three Strike Claws to just catch him, led by a trio of monstrous augments. Titan, Edge, and Mayhem, by the patches on their uniforms.

The Strike Claws marched ahead and behind, shoving him forward in shackles.

"Brothers..." Tool said.

A general growl of disgust rose from the Claws. Tool stopped short. They grabbed his manacles, dragged him forward, stumbling. "Brothers," he said again, and was cuffed for it.

"Silence, Worm Blood!"

The one called Titan suddenly held up a hand. "Hold!"

The troops froze, waiting his instructions. He appeared to be listening to his commlink. The pressure of the augments all around in the corridor crackled with electric hatred for Tool.

Titan turned to his troops. "Execute the prisoner."

"Here?" someone asked.

Titan was already unlimbering his heavy rifle. "Here."

Tool shrank back against the wall as his captors hastily stepped out of the firing zone. More augments raised their own rifles.

"Brothers," Tool said again. He could smell them. All their history. Their wars, their loyalty.

"You are no brother of mine."

But Titan hesitated.

Tool stared at the Strike Claw leader. Eye-to-eye. Tool growled. "Brother..." He reached out to the Claw leader, speaking their shared language. The language of those who had fought their way out of the bone pits. The language of triumph and survival.

"Loyal brother. Honorable kin. True warrior..."

Titan snarled, but did not fire. Tool could smell the uncertainty already in the troops around him. But this one, Titan, he was the true pack leader. This one he needed. This one he must influence. He held Titan's gaze. These were not the weak-minded augments of the Patels. These were his true people. Loyal and terrible. Beautiful and monstrous.

Kin...

Tool took a step forward, extending manacled hands to Titan.

Another step.

"Keep back!" Titan bellowed. He raised his rifle but could not break from Tool's gaze.

Tool pressed his chest to the muzzle of Titan's rifle. He could feel the power within himself. The power to overwhelm. The same power that humanity had used against him to make him feel shame. The demand for loyalty and obedience.

The thing that had made him first amongst Claws, then a general of armies, and finally a leader, fighting free.

"Will you slay me, brother?" Tool asked.

"We are not brothers," Titan growled.

"No?" Tool showed his fangs. "Are we not of Mercier? I, too, clawed my way out of the bone pits and swore oaths to my saviors. I laid the bodies of the weakest at the feet of General Caroa and swore my loyalty oaths to him before you were even conceived in test tubes."

He could smell the doubt and confusion in the Claw leader now. Tool raised his voice so that all of his kin could hear his words. "I clawed my way out of darkness to serve Mercier. I have fought on every continent. I am Blood. I am Blade. I am Karta-Kul. I defeated the First Claw of Lagos in single combat and ate his heart on the sands, and ended war in a single day. I have no fear!" He pressed harder against the gun muzzle, staring into Titan's eyes. "I do not cower! I do not retreat! And I am not prey! I am Karta-Kul, Slaughter-Bringer! *We are brothers*."

"You are cowering cur, and worm blood!" Titan snarled.

"I am free," Tool said. "Just as you shall be."

He could smell the troops around him, frozen in awe. Wavering. "Are we slaves to do our masters' bidding? Whose wars do we fight?" His gaze bored into Titan. "Whose blood is shed?"

The fear and uncertainty were thick in the corridor. He could smell the emotions roiling, black and thick as wildfire smoke. All of his kin, all around, all of them balanced on a suddenly slippery knife edge of loyalty, conditioning, and training.

Tool leaned hard against the muzzle of Titan's rifle.

"Who will you fight for, brother?"

* * *

"Helium losses contained, Captain!"

"Elevation?"

"Three thousand meters, and holding, sir. Starboard turbines at a hundred and fifteen percent of recommended limit, but holding."

Ambrose blew out his breath, trying not to show his relief. He went over to the nav charts. "We should be able to make Greenland, assuming we can maintain this for a few hours."

"Should we order general evac?"

"No. But make sure the ExCom is off. They're better off in the glider."

"What about the augment?" Caroa demanded. "What's his status?"

Ambrose gave him an irritated look. "A mass of blood and bone. If you like, you can go swab his guts off the walls."

"Has that been confirmed?" Caroa snapped.

The man was positively insane. "It's been handled," Ambrose said, trying not to show his disgust for the general.

He returned to charting the *Annapurna*'s emergency course. "If we can keep lift for another two hours, we can make a landing on the coast, here." He pointed. "Radio our assets in the northern tar sands. Notify them of our intended rendezvous point. They should be able to send out rescue vessels."

"Sir! We have another helium leak!"

"What?" Ambrose lunged for the engineering boards. Stared at the light blinking amber, then suddenly going red. Another went red as well.

"They must not have caught all the saboteurs!"

Caroa was laughing, nearly cackling. "No, you fools. He's turned our own troops against us. Those are our own Strike Claws out there, sinking us."

"That's impossible!"

Caroa was pulling his service weapon and checking its load. "Impossible or not, the Strike Claws are no longer yours to command. Even now, they are probably slaughtering your people." He relocked the pistol.

The *Annapurna* heaved and shifted again, tilting at an even more alarming angle. Caroa favored Ambrose with a grim eye. "Sound the general evacuation, Captain. Your ship is lost."

"Sir?" Tolly was staring helplessly at the engineering boards. More red lights had come on.

Captain Ambrose keyed the comm. "Claw Leader Titan! Report! What's your status?"

No response came.

"Claw Leader Titan, this is Captain Ambrose! Status report!"

After a long pause, the Claw leader's basso voice filled the line. "He is coming for you," Titan growled. "He is coming for all of you."

The comm went dead.

"Fates," Tolly whispered, wide-eyed.

Caroa sketched a mocking salute at Ambrose. "I trust we're on the same page now, Captain?"

Ambrose stared out the observation windows at the cold darkness of the sea below. Watched the altimeter as it spun down.

"Announce a general evacuation," he said. "All hands to the escape pods."

"Sir?"

"We aren't going to float. We've lost too much buoyancy." He glanced at Caroa, and swallowed, then leaned forward and murmured to Tolly. "And issue a tight-band notice to all human personnel to avoid all augmented personnel. Do not engage with the augments."

The ensign looked horrified, but did as he was told. "How can they turn against us?" he asked.

Ambrose shook his head helplessly. The thought of augments... *turning*... It was more terrifying than the impending demise of the *Annapurna*. A new thought struck him.

"Where's ExCom? Have they launched yet?"

Tolly checked the boards. "No response from ExCom, sir."

"What do you mean, no response?"

"I—" He hesitated. "I can't raise ExCom. No one is answering my comm."

"Did they launch?"

Tolly scanned the boards. "No, sir. The glider is still prepped to launch. But I'm not getting a response."

Caroa started to laugh again, a dry, hopeless sound.

40

For Jones, climbing up to the port side of the heavily listing dirigible was like clawing her way through a fun-house maze. All the decks were wrong; all the stairs were wrong. The elevators were all shut down.

Jones crawled and braced and shimmied, using doorjambs for handholds, using walls as wedges, climbing, always climbing for the launch decks where the glider waited.

It felt futile, and yet she kept going. She told herself that even if she was too late to catch the glider, her best bet for dropping out in an evacuation pod lay on the port side, now turning into the top of the ship, where the ejection would launch her into the air, instead of straight down into ocean.

At least then she'd have a chance for the pod's chutes to open.

A new warning klaxon sounded, deafening. General evacuation. Other crew emerged in the halls, all making their own way toward designated escape pods, helping one another scramble through the tilted corridors.

A voice warning sounded: "*Time to eject, fifteen minutes. Nineteen minutes to ground contact.*"

The alarms were deafening. She hoped Tory was making his way out—

She felt her wrist buzz and saw on her comm an eyes-only text warning:

EVACUATE IMMEDIATELY. AVOID AUGMENTED PERSONNEL. USE EXTREME CAUTION. REPEAT. AUGMENTED PERSONNEL MAY BE COMPROMISED. AVOID AT ALL COSTS.

Fates.

It was just what Caroa had feared. The impossible had happened. Karta-Kul was on board. Somehow, he had gotten on board, and now he'd turned the augments against them.

No sooner did she get the warning than she spotted a cluster of augments moving fast and graceful through the corridors, unimpeded despite the canted decks. They scampered and leaped, a team optimized for fighting even in the mad environment of this slowly crashing dirigible.

A human officer stood in front of them, demanding that

they return to their posts. They ignored him. He drew his pistol.

Their response was so fast that the afterimage was all that was left for Jones to decipher. The man didn't even have a chance to shout. The augments roared and leaped, and a moment later the man exploded in a rain of blood and body parts.

Jones pressed herself back into the shadows of a doorway. Her security pass refused to open the door. She was just a passenger, now. She cursed that she was off the crew roster, without rights to most parts of the airship.

The augments paused over their dismembered victim, sniffing the air.

Jones held her breath.

Creatures that she had trusted and believed she knew well now stood in the corridor, snuffling like wild beasts. Their muzzles and jaws dripped with blood. Tiger teeth glinted, hyena ears pricked high, doglike snouts sniffed the air for enemy scents. Monsters, built to rend and slaughter, now independent just as Caroa had foretold.

Fates.

She realized that she recognized two of them from her days in the Intelligence Center. Brood and Splinter, the pair who had stood guard and greeted her each shift. And now they stalked the *Annapurna*'s corridors as if they owned them.

Jones shied deeper into darkness, trying not to breathe, praying they wouldn't notice her.

Brood and Splinter were growling with the others in their own language. Snarls and gutturals that she barely understood. She listened, trying to make out the language that was more than half made up of scent and posture.

Abruptly, one of them touched his comm and snarled into it. She caught the words, "Rendezvous. Escape pods."

Jones's heart fell. The escape pods. Her last chance to get out of the ship, if the ExCom had already left without her, and now the augments were headed in the same direction.

The augments bounded off down the corridor, lithe and terrifying. She could never get ahead of them, and it sounded like others would be headed in that direction as well. It would be a bloodbath for the humans.

Her only chance was the ExCom glider now, a fool's errand. She wasn't important enough for them to wait for her. ExCom mattered, but she was expendable.

Even though it was futile, she set off once more, scrabbling up the steeply sloping corridors.

At last she reached the hangar deck. As she hauled herself up through a final hatch into the launch bays, her heart leaped and she almost sobbed with relief.

The glider was still there, its boarding hatch open. A sleek delta-winged shape, waiting for her, its launch lights glowing. Ready for takeoff, and yet they'd waited.

With a glad cry, she scrambled for the glider, scrabbling up the slick steel deck. She grabbed on to the entry door and hauled herself inside.

"Thank you—" *for waiting*, she almost said, but stopped short.

All of the ExCom was there, belted into their seats, ready for launch.

Unfortunately, their heads were missing.

"Captain, we have to go!"

Am I supposed to go down with my ship? Ambrose wondered.

Out loud, he asked, "Are the escape pods cleared?"

"Soon, sir. Almost all of the starboard bank is already cleared. People going downhill, it's easier than going up."

"Do we have a roll call?"

"It's coming in, sir. More than ninety percent of personnel are showing that they've already debarked. We can get updates on the move. At least let's start getting you to the pods."

Still, Ambrose hesitated. *My ship. My duty.*

Caroa gripped his shoulder. "Go," he said. "I will take command."

Ambrose stared at the old general. "It's not your responsibility."

Caroa shook his head. "It's more my responsibility than you know. See to the crew evacuations. There's no need to add one more to the casualty list."

"I can't raise ExCom," Ambrose protested.

Caroa snorted. "That's because they're already dead.

Don't worry. I can command. Patch me into the command systems. I know what to do." He glanced out the observation windows at the moonlit sea that glittered below them. "Certainly I'm qualified to crash a dirigible."

Ambrose exchanged glances with the last of his command staff.

"We have to go, sir," Tolly said. "We'll need some clearance space to launch a pod, and if the *Annapurna* rolls much more, we'll be ejecting straight up. It won't work."

Caroa's eyes were gleaming. "Patch me in, Captain. You can sweep for stragglers on your way out."

"What about you?" Ambrose asked, not sure he wanted to know what the general intended.

"Me?" Caroa laughed. "I'm going to meet an old friend."

41

TOOL SQUATTED IN the darkness of the hangar, resting.

Tearing the ExCom apart had been a matter of moments. All of them strapped in their flight couches. All of them believing that they were about to fly away.

As he'd lunged for the glider, he'd wondered if he would be able to do the deed he had promised himself he would do, or if he would find himself, once again, overawed by his own blasphemy. His earliest memories were of bowing down to General Caroa and Mercier. He owed them his existence.

And yet, when he had entered the glider...they had all looked up, and he'd felt nothing. No sense of disloyalty, or fear or shame. Just more humans to be slaughtered. Easy pickings, slow and soft. Some as pink as salmon, some as brown as deer, some as black as goats. And yet all so soft and red on the inside.

Tool licked the blood off his claws as the *Annapurna*'s evacuation klaxons continued to wail.

He hadn't felt a twinge of guilt as he dismembered them.

I have slain my gods, Tool thought. *I climbed into the sky, and I slew my gods.*

He bared his teeth at the thought, trying to feel pleased, hunting for the feeling of triumph that he had hoped for.

I am Blood. I am Blade. I am Heart-Eater. I am Karta-Kul, Slaughter-Bringer. I am Tool.

I am God-Slayer.

The dirigible shuddered and the deck tilted again, the airship rolling to a new alarming angle. Tool would soon die in the freezing ocean, but he was at peace.

I climbed into the sky, and slew my gods.

He ticked them off in his mind. Finance. Trade. Science. R&D. Commodities. Protectorates. Joint Forces... All of them fumbling frantically with their flight buckles, unable to escape as heads flew off, panicked meat animals, strapped in for slaughter. Not a single one of them capable of fighting back. They had always relied on others to do their killing, so of course, none of them presented much challenge.

He thought fondly of Titan. *Ah. That one would have offered up a fight.*

Tool picked up a stolen comm and shook the blood from it. Titan answered.

“Leave,” Tool said. “Save our brethren.”

He crushed the comm in his fist. Titan would get his kin to safety. They were too strong and too resilient to do anything but survive. Perhaps they would form an outpost of independence. Take Greenland for themselves. Tool liked the idea, and wished them well.

The air outside the hangar, blasting in through open bay doors, was warmer now, but still frigid. Soon they would hit water and this whole massive airship would die. All because of him.

Tool felt no twinge of guilt. These people had rained fire down upon his pack. Once in Kolkata. Once in the Drowned Cities. If the airship died because of him, so much the better. Let them take the collateral damage of ExCom’s death. They deserved it.

Tool lapped at the blood around his muzzle with his long tongue, tasting iron and life. He hefted the skull of ExCom’s Joint Forces director. Jonas Enge. A dimly remembered name. The pink man’s face was frozen, a mask of terror. Tool studied the expression with disgust. The head of Joint Forces, literally. The man who had ordered all the other soldiers.

Tool eyed his dead enemy. There was something dissatisfying about the man’s pathetic terrified expression. It had been the same with all of them. Not a single worthy opponent. Just soft sacs of flesh, waiting to be ripped open. Kindling necks waiting to be snapped. Round heads waiting to be popped off.

Pathetic.

Tool knocked Enge's head against the bulkhead. *Thunk. Thunk.*

Their hearts hadn't even been worth eating. These leaders of humanity were less than garbage. Let the fish of the Atlantic eat the tainted meat. There was no battle song worth singing to memorialize this victory.

Tool closed his eyes, feeling tired. The evacuation klaxons continued to shriek, warning the crew that they were running out of time to flee the crashing dirigible.

Now I will rest.

The klaxons were so loud that Tool didn't hear the young woman come stumbling into the hangar. He smelled her first, closer than he would have expected.

His eyes snapped open, tracking the threat. He spied her clawing her way up the steeply canted deck. He remained still, blending with the shadows, taking advantage of the way human eyes only responded to movement, and were set forward, so that they could chase their own prey.

It didn't even occur to the woman to look around.

Tool narrowed his eyes. His ears slowly laid back as he watched her scramble. She was headed for the glider.

Interesting.

She clawed her way inside, clearly desperate to board the glider. Tool smiled contentedly at her scream. She came piling back out of the glider, panicked and clumsy. She hit the deck and lost her footing, slid down the deck until she hit a wall, and came to a thudding, whimpering stop.

Tool wondered at her relationship to the ExCom. He had slaughtered all the directors of Mercier—he was sure. She wasn't some missing member. And yet she seemed to think she belonged with them. But the rank on her uniform marked her as far below their august status.

She wasn't another god to slay, just a lowly servant of the gods.

To kill, or not to kill?

Suddenly the evacuation klaxons were overwhelmed by the blare of loudspeakers.

"Blood!" a familiar voice shouted. "Blade! Karta-Kul! I know you're here!"

Tool's hackles rose. *That voice.* A voice from Tool's dreams and nightmares. A voice from the past. A man whose head he had once held in his jaws...

"You missed me!" the voice taunted. "You hear?"

Memories of pack, of warfare.

"I'm still here! I'm still alive, you coward!"

Caroa.

General Caroa.

Father Caroa.

God Caroa.

Suddenly Tool's pulse was pounding. He felt an almost overwhelming urge to roll over and beg for forgiveness, to show his belly, to bare his throat... Tool's lips drew back in a rictus of hatred.

Old friend. Old master. Old enemy.

Caroa's voice echoed through the hangar deck. "If you

want to finish this, I'm on the bridge! I'm here, and I'm not afraid! Come to me, dog-face! Face me, you coward!"

White rage boiled through Tool. He was up and moving in a flash. The young woman whirled and stared, terrified, as he exploded from hiding, but she was nothing to him. The ExCom had been nothing. It was Caroa. It had always been Caroa. He was the god Tool was meant to slay.

On the loudspeakers, General Caroa continued his taunts. "I'm still here, coward!"

Tool charged and leaped and crashed through the corridors, arrowing for the bridge and his oldest enemy.

"Come to me, Blood! It's time I put you down!"

42

KARTA-KUL ROSE FROM the shadows, a nightmare rising, the severed head of Jonas Enge dangling from his fist. A god of slaughter, war incarnate. Bloody, scarred, and primal.

He favored Jones with a single contemptuous snarl that sent her scrabbling backward and pissing herself, her bladder opening up against all control, knowing that she was about to be torn apart just like ExCom—and then he was gone, a blur of savage speed, roaring for Caroa.

Jones couldn't stop shivering.

If she'd thought Mercier's security augments were terrifying, this creature was something else entirely. Her own instincts were thrown into immediate disarray at the sight of him, her rational human brain collapsing into the gibbering terrors of her ancestral ape brain, when her forebears had cowered from the violence of thunder.

She couldn't stop shaking. Even as she tried to stand up, she simply fell back, her mind still assaulted with the scattershot afterimages of his size, his snarling monstrous face, his blood-drenched teeth and claws.

So, this was what Caroa had created. This was Karta-Kul, Slaughter-Bringer, unique amongst all the monsters that they had designed before.

This was what General Caroa had feared.

But Karta-Kul was gone already. She could hear him in the distance, crashing through the corridors, roaring for Caroa as the general continued to taunt the monster, his voice half crazed with rage and battle lust.

"Where are you, yellow dog? Show your belly!"

Let Caroa have him. It was his creation. Let him face it.

"Come to me, Blood! I'm on the bridge! I'm right here, waiting for you, you coward dog!"

Leave it, she told herself. *Run*.

Run where, though? The renegade augments were headed for the escape pods, too. She wouldn't stand a chance against them. So then...? Just sit here and crash? Her eyes went to the glider. She shuddered at the thought of what was inside. It wouldn't launch anyway, she realized. Not at this launch angle. The deck was too tilted.

With a soft curse, Jones drew her sidearm. *I must be insane*. But she stumbled toward the door, clumsily following the holes that the augment had ripped in the walls as he clawed his way toward the bridge.

It's suicide.

And yet she couldn't resist the draw of the monster. Was it because she needed to see the end of this quest? To see the final confrontation between creator and created? Or was it to catch one more glimpse of this creature that had survived their every attempt to destroy it? She would die, but this thing, this creature, it had been her job to hunt it down.

So, I'll hunt it.

Feeling hopeless, she headed forward, stumbling on the steeply canted decks, wondering how long the *Annapurna* would float after hitting water.

Fully filled with helium, the dirigible floated easily on the air, so the great airship would have some natural buoyancy, Jones assumed. And yet they were plunging out of the sky now, and once they hit the ocean, water would rush in through open launch decks. It would pour into the holes where helium had been leaking out. And once those empty helium tanks started filling with the sea, how long would it take before the whole dirigible was swallowed under icy, salty waves?

I should try for the escape pods. Maybe there's one left.

But still she scrambled through the corridors, making her way forward, to the bridge.

The halls were empty now. Most—if not all—of the crew had already ejected.

Caroa kept bellowing into the loudspeakers, baiting Karta-Kul.

"*You were a coward then, and you're a coward now! You're an insult to your kind! Pathetic! Weak! Nothing but meat! Nothing but prey, you hear me? Not a Karta-Kul, at all! I'm going to rip out your heart and feed it to mice! You hear me? Mice will eat your heart! Your betters will eat y—!*"

The general's voice cut off abruptly, leaving only the alarm klaxons screaming madly, telling an empty ship to evacuate.

That's it, she told herself. *It's over. Get out.*

But she kept on, hauling herself through the canted corridors. She'd tracked him too long. Studied him too much. Karta-Kul. Something in her yearned to see the creature, even if it meant her death. There was something absolute about him. Something undeniable...

Jones reached the bridge and gasped. Outside the observation windows, the cold, moonlit waves of the ocean were sliding fast beneath the dirigible as it descended, growing larger every second. She'd been fooling herself to think she might still have time to escape the ship.

Caroa and his creation were faced off before the glass windows. Caroa's expression was frozen in a death's head grin as his war monster circled, demonic and predatory.

But to Jones's surprise, the creature didn't attack. It snarled and snapped its teeth. Froth and bloody spittle flew. But it did not leap.

The augment's growl was low and full of warning, its ears laid back. It snarled and feinted, but Caroa didn't flinch. The general stood squared before the augment, turning always to face the beast as it stalked around him.

Caroa's own teeth were bared in a crazed rictus grin.

"I named you Blood!" he taunted. "I called you Blood! From my blood you came! From my hand you fed!" Caroa shouted. "You are mine! My blood! My kin! My pack! MINE!"

Jones stared, shocked by the general's words.

His blood?

Karta-Kul snarled again, but still did not strike. Huge clawed hands reached for the general, flexing, but did not seize him.

"Hold!" Caroa's voice lashed like a whip. "Blood! Hold!"

To Jones's amazement, the man reached out and struck the monster on the nose with his fist. The monster snarled but did nothing to attack him. Instead, it tried to retreat. Caroa pursed and struck it again on the muzzle.

"HOLD!"

The beast began to crouch, to huddle in on itself. Caroa stepped forward, well inside the creature's reach. He struck it again on the nose with his fist.

"By the Fates, you will hold or I will throw you back into the pit from which you came! My blood obeys! Blood obeys!"

Caroa was sweating, staring into the gaze of the massive creature, unwavering. The monster was growling, dagger teeth bared, ears laid back, every fiber of its being quivering with an obvious desire to leap and tear Caroa apart—and yet it did not strike.

"*I hold*," the creature growled. "*I obey.*"

43

Emotions tumbled through Tool, torrents of rage and fear and joy and grief and pleasure and shame at the sight of his general.

Caroa.

It had been so long that Tool wasn't even sure that he would have recognized his creator, and yet the man stood before him, the same man. Older, certainly, heavily scarred, but still, the same.

"Well, old friend," Caroa said. "We meet again."

Tool felt a deep urge to drive his fist through the man's rib cage, rip out his heart, and feed.

And yet something held him back.

Perhaps it was his old self, the one who had stood at Caroa's strong right hand, warring and triumphing. He stared up at the man, older, yes, but still unbowed. Eyes blazing with the fierce light of a true warrior. Caroa was a man who feared death not at all.

Kin.

"I have come to slay you," Tool growled.

Caroa just laughed. "If you had come to slay me, you would have done so already."

He gave Tool the affectionate pat on the head that Tool remembered from his youth, just after he had clawed his way out of the bone pits, when he and his kin had tumbled on the grasslands of the training grounds of Argentina, running down imported lions for sport, learning to hunt as a pack. Proving that they were the apex predators of whatever land they traveled.

Returning to Caroa with the heads of their kills.

Tool looked down and realized that he still had the head of Jonas Enge in his grasp. A head for his general. He found himself lifting it up and offering it to Caroa.

Why should I still care for this man's praise? He is small. He is weak. I am his better.

And yet Tool offered up the head of Mercier's military.

Caroa smiled. "Karta-Kul," he said. "You have outdone yourself."

Tool was surprised at the rush of pleasure he felt at the man's praise and how deeply he desired it. Even after everything that had transpired between them, he still wanted this man's respect.

"You were my finest." Caroa took the head from Tool's

hand and held it up, studying the dead man's features. His expression hardened abruptly. *"'Ten-shun!"*

At the general's order, Tool found himself leaping to attention. Back straight, eyes front, ears pricked up and quivering, waiting for whatever command came next. Ready and eager to do the general's bidding. He stared at Caroa, surprised. Slowly, he forced his body to relax out of the posture of obedience.

"I am not your loyal dog anymore," he growled.

Caroa smiled approvingly. "No. You were always better than that." He held up Enge's head. "But you have always been loyal, my child. I believe I told you once to bring me this man's head. And now, here you've done it. Of course, if you had just obeyed orders then, it would have been so much better, and so much simpler." He sighed. "You would have been my strong right fist. First Claw on four continents."

It was true. Tool remembered the orders. The shock of Caroa's planned coup. The realization that not all were loyal, and with it, an entire cascade of possibilities had opened up in his mind: doors that Tool had never realized existed, beckoning him to step through, tempting him toward his mad rebellion in Kolkata.

Why can I not simply kill this man and be done?

The feeling of needing to obey was worse, far worse, than when he had encountered the kill squads in Seascape Boston.

General Caroa paced before Tool. "You failed your

company, you failed your general. You failed Fist and Claw, all your kin."

Tool cringed at Caroa's words. A whine of abject apology issued from his lips, even as Tool raged inside.

I do not submit!

And yet he was crouching lower now, bowing his head to the man, recognizing the wrong he had done his general. He had lived in denial for too long. He had told himself lies to justify his cowardice and traitorousness. He had betrayed his duty and had fled the consequences, lacking the strength of character to face his failure.

He had never been free. He had only been running from himself.

Jones watched, awed as the beast crouched and then bowed to Caroa. Caroa was smiling. He stepped forward, still holding the bloody head of Jonas Enge by the hair, and laid his hand atop the augment's bowed head.

"Blood of my blood," he said.

"Kin," the monster rumbled. "We are kin."

"Pack," Caroa said. "Kin and pack, my child. Kin and pack."

The monster gazed up at him, rapt. "I yield," it said. "General."

Caroa seemed to sag with relief at the words and Jones realized with surprise that the general had been worried. He'd been fighting to maintain his composure. Now he sagged against the bridge control panels, exhausted. He caught sight of Jones watching from the doorway and blinked with surprise.

"Jones? What are you doing here?"

"I—" She didn't have a good answer. "ExCom is dead." She nodded at the crouching monster. "Karta-Kul got them."

"All of them? All of ExCom?"

Jones found herself unable to take her eyes off the creature. It crouched like a coiled spring, gaze rapt upon its master, seemingly hypnotized. Eyes and ears completely intent only upon Caroa, uninterested in everything else.

"He took their heads," she said.

Caroa glanced over at the crouching monster and smiled affectionately.

"Not their hearts?" Caroa asked.

"They were easy kills," Karta-Kul growled, his basilisk gaze unwavering. "Not worthy."

Jones glanced out the windows of the bridge. She could see whitecaps, steep, cold waves and shadowy troughs, getting larger. A hard hit, rushing up.

"Sir, we need to prepare for impact."

"His conditioning held after all," Caroa said. "I wasn't sure it would. But he hesitated the last time, too." He touched his facial scars. "He wanted so badly to kill me, and yet in the end, we were pack." He smiled grimly. "It's why I called him Blood, originally. Blood of my blood."

"Yes, sir. That's very nice, but we need to go, sir."

Caroa glanced at Jones. "If he'd known you dropped a

six-pack of Havoc on him, he wouldn't have held back from killing you, though. He would have popped your head off, just like ExCom's." He patted the great beast on the head, pleased. "But he stops for me, because he knows we are *pack*."

"Yes, sir, you're very special. Now can we *go*?"

"Ah. Yes." Caroa finally seemed to register the situation. "We're crashing, aren't we?"

"Yes, sir!"

"Not to worry, Jones. Blood will see us out safe. He is a master of survival." He tapped his monster on the shoulder. "Blood! Up with you! Time to be on our way. Port side, I think. Starboard won't do. Don't want to end up trapped underneath, do we? Get us out of here, Blood."

The creature hauled itself to its feet. "Yes, General."

Caroa gave Jones a sly smile. "No augment can resist his call. All the augmented militaries of the world are vulnerable to us. And now there is no ExCom." He patted Jones's shoulder approvingly as he and his monster passed. "It seems we will both be rising quite high indeed."

The augment met her gaze, a king of its kind, standing loyally beside the scarred general. As she had studied and tracked it, she had been awed by its resilience and intelligence: A military genius. A nearly unkillable monster. A creature out of nightmare.

A perfect weapon, returned to Caroa's hands.

44

TOOL WAS NOT natural, but he was of nature. And nature is a constant battle of adaptation. A predator develops sharp teeth; its prey develops a hard shell in response. One organism develops camouflage; another develops sharp sight. A snake develops poison; a badger develops immunity. The snake becomes more poisonous; the badger develops greater immunity.

Tool had been designed from a bevy of genes, the fiercest predators from around the world, stitched together into a nearly perfect double-helix sculpture that eventually became the 228xn genetic platform.

General Caroa, in his egotism, had provided Tool with his own human genetic template as well. There had been other human donors, genetic samples of various elites from Mercier who had proven particularly adept and intelligent.

That Tool had been completely unique from the rest of his brethren in Caroa's experiment was not a secret he had been privy to.

And yet, early on, Tool had been aware of subtle differences between himself and those he competed against for food and approval. When he had clawed his way out of the darkness of the bone pits and into the light of Caroa's welcoming arms, covered with the blood of those he had torn to pieces to survive, he had not known how different he was.

He had known that he loved Caroa deeply, so much that his body shook with fear that the man might ever be wounded, or feel pain. For this man, Blood would die happily, knowing he had fulfilled his purpose.

Now, in the face of his general, Tool found himself at war with his own nature. Blood, who had been before; and Tool, who had come after.

The creature that he had fashioned himself into had forged different alliances with human beings, with other packs. And those packmates had fought beside him. And protected him. Had risked for him. They had been people. Simple people. Human. Not his kin. Not his blood. And yet, all of them had been more loyal than the man whose approval he craved. Mahlia. Ocho. Stork. Stick. Van. Stub. Nailer. Nita. The Drowned Cities. Kolkata. The First Claw of the Tiger Guard...

Tool stopped abruptly, on the verge of leading the general and his underling out of the dirigible. "You are my blood, but you are not my kin."

Caroa tugged at Tool, a look of surprise on his face. Surprise turned to alarm. "Hold, Blood. Hold!"

He was small, Tool was surprised to note. Tiny, really, in comparison with Tool. And yet he'd loomed so large in Tool's mind. Petty, though he'd seemed great. The man was fumbling for a pistol, but Tool batted it aside easily.

"Hold!" Caroa ordered. "HOL—"

Caroa's ribs shattered like kindling as Tool rammed his fist through the man's chest. He yanked the heart out and held it before the man's dying eyes.

He bared his fangs as he gripped the bloody trophy. "We are not kin, General. We share blood, but we are not kin."

He let the heart fall to the deck.

It wasn't worth eating.

45

One moment the augment had seemed completely owned by Caroa, the next Caroa was being dragged close by his creation. In a sickening instant, the general died.

His heart hit the deck, wet and sticky.

Blood. Blade…

"Karta-Kul," Jones whispered.

The monster's predatory gaze settled on Jones. "Not Karta-Kul. Not now. Not anymore. I am Tool. And you…" He bared his fangs. "You killed my pack."

Jones scrambled back, but there was no place to run. She fumbled for her sidearm as the monster stalked her around the control room.

"You rained fire down on me."

Jones tripped and fell to the deck.

"YOU TOOK MY PACK!" Tool roared.

He seized her and jerked her up as easily as if he were grabbing a kitten. He smashed her up against a bulkhead and leaned close, growling, vicious gaze boring in.

"Did you enjoy pushing your buttons and raining fire down? Burning me and mine? Did you feel safe? Did you think I would never come for you?"

Hot carrion breath gusted over her, ripe with the blood of ExCom. Jones gagged at the death stench. His grip was iron. She couldn't move. She could barely breathe. He pinned her with a single hand. Any minute she knew he would drive his fist through her chest and rip out her heart.

"It was my job." She could barely force the words out past his strangling grip. "I did my duty."

She waited for him to kill her, but to her surprise, the monster paused. Eyebrows went up. He blinked. "I was just doing my job," she rasped, fighting for air, trying to get her fingers underneath the massive fist where it wrapped around her neck.

"My orders. I followed orders," she gasped, still trying to pry away his fingers. "I'm just like you. I followed my orders. We're the same. It's not your fault. It's not my fault. It was what I had to do. It was my job."

The monster who now called himself Tool seemed to consider this, and Jones felt a flash of hope. *Please, let me go. I didn't even want to do it. They were Caroa's orders, please, please—*

"No." Tool's teeth gleamed, predatory. "There is always a choice." He slammed her against the wall. "You had a choice!" He shook her like a rag doll. Slammed her against the metal bulkhead again. Jones cried out as she felt ribs crack. *I'm going to die—*

He pinned her to the wall. A single claw came up, seeking her eye. Jones whimpered, trying to twist her head away as the claw came closer. In a moment, he would drive it through her eye and into her brain.

"You say you had no choice," Tool mocked. "But that's not true, is it? My kind has no choice. We are *designed* to have no choice." His expression became a snarl. "And. Yet. I. *Chose!*"

"I know where your pack is!" Jones shouted. She was holding her head back, frantically twisting, trying to avoid the claw that threatened to spear her. "I know where they are! I'll tell you. You can still save them!"

"My pack is dead!"

"No! Not the smugglers!" Jones shouted desperately. "The art smugglers and the soldier boys! From the Drowned Cities. I know where they are! Some of them, anyway! You can still save them. If I live, I can get them out for you!"

She didn't expect it to work, but a second passed, and she didn't find her head ripped off or her eye speared.

The creature was staring at her, seemingly stunned. "They are dead," he said. "You killed them."

"No." She shook her head frantically. "We have one. The girl. Mahlia. The one from the Drowned Cities."

"Liar!"

"We caught her in the Seascape! She told us you went to the *Dauntless*. It's how we confirmed you were with the

Patels. We sweated her, but she's alive. Her, and another one. We got one without legs. Ocho! Both of them!" She was babbling now. "I'm not lying. I've got them. Plus a couple others from the ship; we bagged them for intel. You have to believe me! And we've got the girl. The one you saved in the Seascape. She's your pack, right? She said she was your pack!"

Tool stared at the analyst. A part of him raged to finish the job he had started. To complete his revenge. To leave nothing behind but destruction, but at Mahlia's name, he paused.

Mahlia, who had risked everything for him, and who had lost everything for him.

All of his being yearned to tear this soldier apart, to avenge himself fully, and yet...now he found himself tangled in a spider's web of allegiances.

He paused, on the verge of slaughtering the analyst—

The dirigible crashed into the ocean.

The force of the hit was much more powerful than Jones had expected. She and Tool were both thrown off their feet, crashing toward the windows at the exact moment that the glass shattered and the icy Atlantic came gushing in.

Water engulfed her, shoving her down. Icy, blasting water, so shocking that she almost breathed—

Something seized her and yanked her upward. She surfaced, sputtering. Water foamed all around. The bridge was filling rapidly.

Tool held her, glaring. "Where?" he snarled. "Where is Mahlia?"

The cold of the water was shocking. Already numbed, Jones managed to shout, "Save me and I'll tell you!"

"*Where?*" Tool roared.

The water was pushing them up to the ceiling, frothing and swirling around them. Only Tool's strength kept her afloat. The rushing ocean was so loud she had to shout. "I'm the only one who can get them out! I know where they got sent! I can get them released!"

"Die!" Tool snarled.

Jones thought he'd rip out her heart, but instead he released her and ducked underwater, leaving her alone, frantically paddling to stay afloat as the ocean engulfed the bridge.

The currents were too strong to fight. She was being pressed up to the ceiling, losing the last of the air in the compartment. She was going to drown. *Fates*. She was going to drown.

Tool surfaced again. "Your word, human! Give me your word!"

She met the augment's gaze, frantically paddling to stay afloat. "I swear it! I swear!" His gaze held hers, seeming to probe into her soul. "I swear!" she gasped. "I can get them out. I can get her out!"

With a snarl, Tool grabbed her and dragged her down into the icy waters.

At first, she thought he was drowning her, but then she felt him kicking powerfully, moving fast and sure through the turbulent waters, dragging her through flooded corridors as she fought to hold her breath.

She remembered the first time she had seen him swimming. A bright red blot of heat beneath the dark waters of the Drowned Cities. Swimming even as he burned, an unkillable monster.

Tool dragged her on.

Jones prayed she would have the air to follow him.

Tool doubted that he could save the girl, or even himself. He had never intended to survive his encounter with Mercier, or live beyond this final triumph.

He was exhausted from battle, and from the weight of death upon him. The killing of Caroa had not been easy on his mind, and now that the adrenaline of that final moment had passed...

Tool surfaced.

The Mercier analyst came up with him, coughing and sputtering. Her lips were turning purple. He doubted she would last longer than a few minutes. Hypothermia would kill her, and he had much farther to swim.

The dirigible was sinking rapidly, compartments filling with rushing seawater. The whole great airship was rolling over as its turbofans quit spinning and all the helium chambers that Tool had ripped open flooded with seawater.

He grabbed the girl again and dragged her down. She followed gamely, but she was becoming lethargic. He had the air to swim, but she did not. When he tried to breathe for her, to press his mouth to hers and give her air, she fought and panicked and nearly drowned.

The next time he surfaced, he saw that she was nearly gone. The cold was seeping into his own skin as well. Exhaustion, the changes in oxygen and pressure, the physical struggle.

He recalled the layout of the dirigible from his long-ago training days. It would be a race, to swim upward through the sinking dirigible. To beat his own flagging reserves of energy, and hers.

He dragged the analyst under again. Her skin was cold.

He kept on.

Why do I struggle, always?

At last, he found a shattered port and swam out into the open sea, dragging his charge behind him. He surfaced into roiling ocean waves.

The great form of the dirigible lay in the ocean like a dead and bloated whale. Tool hauled himself up onto its chill skin, dragging Jones behind him. He laid her on the cold armored surface.

Her heart had stopped beating.

He slammed her chest hard. She gagged out seawater and started breathing again, coughing and choking, shuddering and shivering. She would not last long, in or out of the water. It was simply too cold for her kind.

Tool dragged her higher up the curve of the ship, but the dirigible was clearly losing the fight of buoyancy. Their island was sinking.

Jones was looking up at him. "I followed orders," she whispered. Her lips were purple.

Tool looked down at her, trying to decide if he sympathized with her or despised her, but all he could think of was Mahlia. So many human beings, all struggling to survive. So many people doing terrible things, hoping to last another day.

Debris was bubbling up to the ocean surface. Cushions. Food packs. Uniforms. Bodies, all forced out by the rush of the ocean as the dirigible continued to sink. Jones had stopped shivering, hypothermia wrapping her deep in its deathly blanket. Her skin had grayed.

"I didn't want to use Havoc," she whispered.

Words that she had already repeated many times. Some unburdening of herself that she kept at, as if she were seeking absolution from him, someone who had killed so many that he had lost count long ago. A strange thing, this human need for comfort. This human desire to be freed of sin.

You are flawed, he thought.

But to his own surprise, he grasped her hand.

We are flawed.

The dirigible continued to sink.

Out on the horizon, Tool glimpsed movement. A fast speck of a boat, skipping across the waves.

Tool straightened, staring. He seized Jones. "Come."

"Wha—?" She was barely conscious. Her body was icy. Tool threw her over his shoulder and clambered higher on the dirigible as it continued to sink. He waved to the moving boat, his arm held high.

The boat changed course, curving toward him. It grew, a

speck becoming a dot, becoming a dagger boat, slamming across the waves.

Tool waved again, even though he knew they already saw him.

The dagger boat sped toward him, familiar faces in the cockpit. Nita at the controls, her hair tied back. Nailer leaping to the prow, preparing ropes and readying life rings.

Humans, working to save him.

Kin, if not in blood, then in kind.

Pack.

EPILOGUE

MERCIER'S NEWLY ASSEMBLED ExCom had been hastily convened. Most were still rushing to get up to speed on their duties when they read the report of Arial Madalena Luiza Jones, Captain, Intelligence Section, Joint Forces Division.

From the aerie of their secure spire in the SoCal Protectorate, they scanned the text, paragraph after paragraph, statements marked TOP SECRET, and EXCOM EYES ONLY, and NONDISCLOSURE AGREEMENT.

The room was silent except for the hiss of climate filters and the rustle of occasional movement as they worked through the report related to the deaths of their predecessors, along with the last heroic struggles of General Caroa against his beastly creation.

They read of Karta-Kul's and Caroa's paired deaths, the

two of them locked in combat, the general's body crushed by his creation, even as he shot the rogue augment dead.

All before the icy Atlantic waters swept their bodies away.

At last, the ExCom looked up from their tablets and focused on the author of the report—a young woman in her dress blues, newly burnished captain's bars on her breast. Young for the promotion.

"Captain Jones," Finance said. "You've done the company a great service. Do you have anything to add to this report?"

"No, ma'am."

"Any concerns about the augment surviving this time?" Markets pressed. "It survived more than once, it seems."

"No, sir. Caroa killed the augment. I saw it. His creation is no more."

Joint Forces flicked through the documents on her screen. "I understand there were some detainees related to this operation? Captured assets?"

"Yes, ma'am." Jones nodded carefully. "The augment briefly utilized a small group of smugglers. We captured a few for intelligence purposes once we knew that we had failed to secure him during the Seascape operation. The truth is that they held little intelligence value, though they provided some insight into how he operated in the Drowned Cities. Patel Global has agreed to take them, and guaranteed their silence. They had no further intelligence value to us."

Joint Forces glanced up sharply. "Under what authority did you release them?"

Jones shrugged. "My own. There was no one else left who was familiar with the situation after the *Annapurna* crashed. It was my call."

"I see. And Patel Global... You returned here to the protectorate on one of their ships?"

"Yes, ma'am. I had... difficulty with flying, after the incident."

"Understandable. What is your impression of that company? Are they a threat?"

"You have my full analysis, in the appendix," Jones said. "They were as helpful as one might expect of a competitor. And certainly, they scrambled a number of their ships to aid the *Annapurna* when we crashed. Without them, I myself would not have survived. Many others would have been lost as well. They understood the threat Karta-Kul posed, and were quick to deliver all their data to us. You have the report of the Chinese consulate as well. They certify that the Patels have satisfied their obligations to render up all their data on the augment."

"I see." Finance was looking down at her notes. She glanced at the rest of the ExCom. "Very good, then. Thank you, Captain."

She went on briskly. "Committee members, we will be placing this file under Priority Code Lock. ExCom, Eyes-Only. The genetic concerns and obedience failures will be forwarded to R&D under strict Red Access." She glanced up again. "Thank you, Captain Jones. You may go."

"Yes, ma'am."

Jones turned and headed for the doors, leaving the ExCom to proceed with their work. Behind her, she heard Finance saying, "Next order of business. Lithium supplies. I understand there is an issue in the Andes—"

The rest of her words were cut off by glass doors sliding shut.

Jones stood in the hall outside, and let out a breath of relief. On either side of her, powerful augments in Mercier dress blues stood guard, ramrod straight, eyes staring off into the middle distance.

They stood as still as statues, and yet Jones knew that they tracked her every movement, measured her every breath, and smelled her relief, even thought they didn't move a muscle or acknowledge her.

They towered over her, obedient and dedicated to their creators.

They won't attack.

She could almost convince herself of it. But she felt better when she'd made her way to the tower's express lift and its sliding doors had closed, cutting off her view of the guards.

She descended quickly. A few minutes later, she was outside, and on her way to the docks. Hot evening air bathed her, warm, even for Los Angeles.

She walked down a hill through the bright sunshine and

came to a stop at the water's edge. Out in the bay, fragments of the city's orleans poked up through lapping waters—buildings and neighborhoods swallowed by rising oceans and lack of preparation. Farther out, the company's floating docks and freight transfer stations were busy with commerce. Sheathed in solar panels, they glinted in the sunlight.

At one of the docks, a clipper ship was preparing to depart. A trimaran, graceful and sleek, flying the colors of Patel Global. Built for speed, not heavy cargo.

On her deck, a group of sailors were gathered. An augment loomed amongst them, towering over the smaller human forms. Not particularly remarkable, really. Many companies employed augments in their crews, Patel Global amongst them.

Even the scars and tattoos on the sailors' faces weren't all that remarkable. One of the crew seemed to sport mechanical legs, sleek, curving, metallic things. Another... perhaps it was the light that made it seem that her arm was mechanical as well, black and gleaming in the sun. It made sense, really. Sailing was dangerous work, and accidents sometimes happened.

Sailors, just like everyone, had histories, that was all.

Jones's comm buzzed, her new assignment coming in. She checked her orders and turned away from the clipper ship, letting the crew and its history fade away, as if it had never existed at all.

Behind her, the trimaran raised its sails, preparing to depart with the tide.

ACKNOWLEDGMENTS

WRITING A BOOK is difficult, even in the best of circumstances. I'm grateful for the support and guidance and wisdom of the many people who helped me at various stages to reach the end of this one. My wife, Anjula, and my son, Arjun. Friends Holly Black, Rob Ziegler, Aaron Jerad, Samara Taylor, Max Campanella, Charlie Finlay, Rae Carson, Daniel Abraham, Carrie Vaughn, Tobias Buckell, and Ramez Naam. I also want to thank my editor, Andrea Spooner, my copy editor, Christine Ma, and my agent, Russell Galen, who has always been such a fan of Tool.

PAOLO BACIGALUPI is the *New York Times* bestselling author of the highly acclaimed *The Drowned Cities* and *Ship Breaker*, a Michael L. Printz Award winner and a National Book Award finalist. He is also the author of the Edgar Award nominee *The Doubt Factory*; a novel for younger readers, *Zombie Baseball Beatdown*; and two bestselling adult novels for adults, *The Water Knife* and *The Windup Girl*. His first work of collected short fiction was *Pump Six and Other Stories*. The winner of the Hugo, Nebula, Locus, Compton Crook, John W. Campbell Memorial, and Theodore Sturgeon Memorial Awards, he lives in western Colorado with his wife and son. The author invites you to visit his website at windupstories.com.